Wildest Dreams

MERIDITH CLAIRE

ISBN: 979-8-218-56932-7

Book Cover and Illustrations by Ben Goldman

Edited By M.E. O'Connor, Tenyia Lee and Megan Morine

Dedication

To My Sister Moira O'Connor

My soul twin, my insides, my biggest cheerleader

Thank you for a lifetime of dropping everything to celebrate my happiest moments as well as running fearlessly into my darkness to hold my hand every time I needed to find my way out.

Thank you for always taking care of me, protecting me and being my person.

Thank you for being My Bianca...

Acknowledgements

Sally Goldman- For unwittingly facilitating this novel's creation

My Beta Readers – Nicole Wolf, Mary Goldman and Moira O'Connor. Truly, I could not have finished this without you.

Justin Murry- For inspiring and reminding me to channel my creativity

My Editors- M.E. Tenyia Lee and Megan Morine Thank you for being patient with this dyslexic basket case with way too many ideas and thoughts.

My Squad of Believers- Michael Hatcher, Kayla Chauvin, Susan Kamaiopili, Gabrielle Burke, John Mellis, Cai Trevillion and Jason Hunter.

My Extraordinary Cousins- Eileen, Rachel, Aileen and Romina. It has been an honor to watch you grow up and become role models to Filipina Girls everywhere. You four are the sum of all of Mackenzie's parts. Hopefully your *Até* did you justice.

Ben- For all the things. So many things, you know the rest.

Wyatt and Shaela- You two are all my reasons

Finally, Uncle Narding – For seeing and loving me when it felt like no one else did.

"the free soul is rare, but you know it when you see it - basically because you feel good, very good, when you are near or with them."
— Charles Bukowski, Tales of Ordinary Madness

Chapter 1

MACKENZIE

"I swear on my prized pink Hermes pumps, if you don't get that dopey look off your face, I will throw this piece of focaccia at your head."

Mackenzie snapped out of her near-rapturous state at her partner in crime for the last seven years and best friend, Bianca Jones, threatening her. Mackenzie—often called Mac—blinked a few times, dramatically thumping her hand over her heart.

"Jesus, it can't be that bad?" she laughed, knowing the reverence Bianca had for her five-hundred-dollar pink suede pumps and all forms of bread.

"You seriously look dazed, like that chick in that movie you force me to watch when you get depressed," Bianca replied, shaking her head in mock disgust.

"Her name is Joan Fontaine, and the movie is Rebecca. It's a cinematic masterpiece!" Mackenzie sat back in her seat, pouting when Bianca rolled her eyes.

"I will give you a pass just this once because I haven't seen you this happy in a while. But seriously, get yourself together," Bianca commanded, winking at Mac to let her know she was just giving her a hard time.

The two best friends were at Sweetgreen, a restaurant at the Platform, a shopping and dining area in the heart of the Culver City art district. There were casual places like Sweetgreen and upscale dining at Margot on the Roof and Roberta's. All the restaurants had outdoor seating, so you could sit, eat, and soak up the California sunshine.

"It's been a while since we've been here. I miss this place," Mackenzie commented, knowing how much Bianca loved the Platform—it catered to two of her greatest passions: fashion and food.

Bianca and Mackenzie often met for lunch here when Mac's office was in Culver City. The accounting firm Mackenzie worked for had since relocated to downtown LA. The commute was brutal, but the upside was that her office was now only a block away from the investment firm where Bianca and Mac's fiancée worked.

Earlier that day, they had visited The Inn of the Seventh Ray to look at wedding packages and sample a few appetizer choices. The Inn of the Seventh Ray, nestled deep in the hills of Topanga Canyon, was romantic and secluded, yet still only a stone's throw from Venice Beach, where Mackenzie was born and raised.

"So, you think Stuffy Sam is going to sign off on the venue?" Bianca asked, thumbing through one of the brochures they had been given.

"I'm positive. It's where the wedding needs to happen. It's the perfect compromise, bohemian yet elegant. And it's so close to home that I could get ready there. I think Uncle Deano would have liked that," Mackenzie said softly as she watched the cars whizz down Washington Boulevard. She swallowed, trying not to get choked up.

"It's okay to miss him, you know? Especially now," Bianca said, reaching over and squeezing her hand. Mackenzie nodded, trying to smile away from her momentary sadness.

"I know. That's why I love the idea of getting ready at home. I think it will make me feel like he's there."

Mac had spent the entirety of her twenty-five years in a small, two-room bungalow three blocks from the beach, near the boardwalk. It was, also, just down the street and around the corner from where her uncle's record shop used to be. Unlike most first-generation Filipinos, she didn't have a mother commanding her to get straight A's or a father who wanted their little girl to play an instrument. She only had her Uncle Deano. He'd come over from Cebu and broken the mold—and he'd raised Mackenzie to do the same.

Venice Beach was her home, and she doubted she would ever leave. All her best memories were associated with Venice Beach. It was where she met her fiancé, Sam. Like herself, Sam had grown up in their beloved beach city. Mac struggled to remember a time in her life when Sam hadn't been there. They used to be kids, running up and down the street or through the boardwalk, aggravating tourists. Moody teenagers experimented with their limits in ways that would make most parents shriek. Even at UCLA, they were tied at the hip, always trying to find ways to get back from campus without meeting traffic that would cut into their study time.

Mackenzie hadn't dealt with the commute as long as Sam had; she had to drop out midway through her second year. Their life paths had forked in two different directions, yet they stayed dedicated to each other. It was no shock to anyone that they were now engaged and planning their wedding.

"If he doesn't agree, I'll get Ezra to pry the stick out of his ass," Bianca muttered.

Mackenzie gave her best friend a playful glare. She knew Bianca loved Sam like a brother. However, she'd often frowned at how much he'd changed since they met in college. The three of them—along with their friend Ezra—were a small, fiercely loyal pack. They were sometimes way too painfully honest with each other, which was why Bianca had no trouble telling Sam to his face that she thought he was becoming way too uptight.

Sam had long since given up his beach bum style and was now more Hugo Boss than Vans Off the Wall. While he'd never shared the same laissez-faire attitude to life that Mac had, he'd been less intense and ambitious growing up than he was now.

Still, they worked. Obviously, they would butt heads when it came to personal style, which is why The Inn of the Seventh Ray was the perfect compromise. They had decided to trek up the hill and to the local treasure after Bianca had an epiphany about the location. It also helped that Bianca was good friends with the manager, Avery. Mac suspected Avery had a thing for Bianca, which might be why she was convinced that Avery had dropped everything. She told her to bring Mac up the canyon when Bianca called.

Mac couldn't fault Avery for having a crush on Bianca—her best friend was gorgeous. Bianca's skin was a warm, caramel melanin-rich tone. Bianca's eyes were striking, and her face was perfect. Currently, her hair was a huge, picked-out afro.

Bianca, like Mac and Sam, was a LA native who grew up in South City, or what locals once called, South Central. She'd fought her way out of the stereotypes and got a full ride to UCLA. She wasn't opinionated; however, she did speak her mind. She was an avid advocate when it came to Mac.

Bianca took a sip of her kombucha. Their agreement was if Bianca took the day off to look at venues then Mac would have to be the designated driver. Bianca hated driving around Los Angeles. Mac didn't mind, she was just glad Bianca was there to hold her hand.

"B, thank you," she said, squeezing her best friend's hand. "I know you and Sam haven't been as close as you used to be. He truly does appreciate all the time you've put into helping me with the wedding plan."

"I know the doofus loves me, and more importantly, he adores you. That's all that matters to me, so I am happy to help," Bianca muttered.

"Is it also because I said you could have carte blanche when it came to planning my bachelorette party?" Mac teased.

"That too. I swear, I am going to have to make it a destination trip. It's the only way I can make sure Sam doesn't crash the thing," Bianca huffed.

"Sam gets a little overprotective," Mac said unapologetically, shrugging her shoulders.

"All right, enough with the sappy love-bird defense. Hurry up and finish eating. We can give Ezra a call, then find that fiancé of yours to let him know today was a success."

As they were finishing their meal, Bianca announced that she wanted to get Blue Bottle coffee. They were avid coffee connoisseurs, and Blue Bottle was in a class of its own.

They walked through the small corridor between Sweetgreen and Roberta's, an upscale Italian restaurant known for its wood-fired pizzas. It was a sought-after spot, nearly impossible to get into for dinner without a reservation. Even at lunchtime, it was packed. The smell of fresh pizza and snippets of conversations drifted toward them as they came up on the crowded outdoor dining patio.

Suddenly, Mac bumped into Bianca as she stopped short in front of her. Mackenzie opened her mouth to playfully protest that she'd nearly fallen, but the look of shock and surprise on Bianca's face stopped her. Bianca turned to look at her with wide eyes and muttered,

"What is Sam doing at Roberta's?"

Chapter 2

MACKENZIE

Mackenzie blinked a few times and peered around Bianca to see Sam sitting with a few people at a table. She reached for her phone in her back pocket, scrolling through the few texts she had sent to Sam. Making sure she remembered telling him they were coming to Sweetgreen. Confirming that she had, she realized he hadn't replied.

"I texted him earlier, telling him we'd be here. Maybe that's why he's here," Mackenzie replied, trying to not sound as unconvinced as she felt.

"Come on, we could tell him the search is over," Bianca said cheerily.

Mackenzie shook off her momentary confusion, chuckling as Bianca dragged her over. Suddenly, she felt eager to share the good news with Sam, anxious to hear what he thought of their would-be wedding location.

She watched as Sam laughed while talking to the people at the table with him. It wasn't his usual laugh. Normally, when Sam laughed, it was nearly silent. He held in a chuckle, even when it was something he found hilarious. He would hold in his laughter to the point where he doubled over, still trying not to let it out. This laugh was loud and disingenuous, and even the smile on his face looked plastic. Her Uncle Deano always told her that she had the strongest sense of intuition he had ever seen. If there was a moment that she wished he was wrong, it would be this one.

For some reason, she felt dread bubble up in the pit of her stomach.

Mackenzie took a deep breath, exhaling as Bianca continued to pull her toward the small gate right by Sam's table. There were two people she didn't know; she assumed they were from the C-suite in his firm's UK branch. Mac knew they had arrived a day or so ago to assist Sam in trying to land a deal with his clients from Japan. Sitting there with them was another manager, Clarissa, from Sam's department. Clarissa and Sam had been working on this huge deal for nearly a year. She worked at the same international investment firm as Bianca, although Bianca and Sam were in two different departments. It was Sam's biggest deal to date; closing it came with a guaranteed change in job title and salary.

Mackenzie watched as Sam spotted them. He stood up awkwardly, scooting his chair back so far that it bumped into the patrons sitting at the next table. Sam apologized to them before redirecting his attention back to Bianca and Mac. Mac lifted her head as he looked at her. Sam didn't tower over Mac completely, mostly because she was tall as well; she still had to look up in order to meet his eyes. He was the epitome of what a California golden boy should look like, yet he still had some uniqueness due to the Ashkenazi Jewish traits inherited from his mother.

He was tall at 6' 3", with chestnut brown hair that would lighten a little when he was in the sun, jade-green eyes, lean yet muscular. His physique was the typical come-on she had heard from people. Mac had to restrain herself from laughing or rolling her eyes every time she heard, "Do you work out?" Every time she went to visit him at work, she would see at least one girl swoon as he walked past them. Sam never seemed to notice, though. It was one of the many things she loved about him.

When she teased him about it all he would do was shake his head, give her a small shy smile, and kiss her temple. Then he would give her a look of adoration. Everyone always commented on the warmth between them. Nothing like what she was seeing now. He looked at Mac, blinking in shock and nervousness.

"Gentlemen, Clarissa—what a coincidence running into you here!" Bianca exclaimed, laying it on a bit thick.

"Hi," Sam said, clearing his throat. "We were just leaving. You all know Bianca; this is Mackenzie. These two are attached at the hip," Sam explained, sounding more like he was giving a presentation than introducing his fiancée. There was a lack of any warmth.

The rest of Sam's party rose and began walking out of the small outdoor seating section, a foot or two away from where the two best friends stood.

Mackenzie nodded in their direction. She kept a smile plastered on her face. The fact that he hadn't introduced her as his fiancée was not lost on her.

"Hi, nice to meet you."

"Nice to meet you, too! We asked Sam and Clarissa to take us to one of their local haunts," one of them said, looking over at Sam and Clarissa expectantly.

Mackenzie nodded, still feeling numb. Sam often went out with out-of-town coworkers who were visiting Los Angeles. Like Mackenzie, they would be hard-pressed to find anyone who knew LA, like Sam. It never bothered her before. The difference this time was he hadn't told her. Sam was usually adamant that they text each other anytime they left their downtown high-rise buildings. Mostly because parts of downtown Los Angeles were still dangerous. Sam was better at it than she was. He always shot her a quick text letting her know he was leaving and when he expected to be back. He often checked their phones to make sure location sharing was on. This time, all that was communicated was that he had a daylong meeting about his Japanese clients with people from the UK.

He obviously was not paying attention to his phone. Suddenly, she felt a bit stupid for texting him every little detail and letting him know she was going to lunch with Bianca, thinking that he might worry or want updates.

"We better get going," Clarissa announced.

Bianca glanced over at Mackenzie, who gave her a smile.

"Actually, Mac and I were headed over to Blue Bottle. Why don't you all join us? My treat, of course," Bianca offered. Mackenzie felt Bianca squeeze her forearm gently. She was unsure if it was for reassurance or to snap her out of her silence.

"Sam, Mac has some news to share. I'll order for the both of you," Bianca smiled at Mackenzie again. She watched as Bianca turned, giving Sam a subtle glare.

Mac nodded for the third time.

"Yeah, coffee sounds great," Clarissa said.

Mackenzie lowered her head for a moment to try to center herself as Bianca, the two men, and Clarissa made their way to Blue Bottle.

Mackenzie looked up at Sam; her confusion and hurt must have been evident.

Sam gently nudged her away from the host stand. He stopped them near an empty table. She deduced he was trying to find a place that was out of ear shot.

"Don't overthink, Mac. It's not that big of a deal," Sam sighed, rubbing the back of his neck. Sam did that anytime he was uncomfortable or aggravated. Belatedly, she realized he had been doing that a lot. She assumed it was because he was stressed about this deal. Slowly, it dawned on her that these days, he was doing it most of the time when he was talking to her. Still, Mac gave him a smile, hands locked behind her back, rocking back and forth, trying to calm herself as a foreign feeling of dread crept through her veins. She had felt that particular emotion throughout her life, never once when it came to Sam.

"I guess you didn't read any of my texts. You didn't tell me you'd be here," Mackenzie held up her phone.

She watched as Sam reached to pull out his phone, reading the few texts she had shot off.

"It shouldn't be a big deal, but why do I feel like it is?" Mackenzie asked quietly.

She knew it sounded ridiculous, but it was so unlike him not to tell her. It was something he had drilled into her head and unfalteringly led by example. That, along with the guilty look on his face, made her know he had not texted her on purpose. She was acutely aware of Sam's nervousness.

"It's not like I would have asked to come with you. I get it was for work," Mackenzie explained.

After all, this was just a business lunch, not a dinner or an after-hours event. She'd accompanied him to a few of those in the past. Most of the time, she'd enjoyed herself. She did her best to support him whenever she could. Mac had thought she always left a decent impression with his more prestigious clients and out-of-town executives. At least, she thought she did. Something about him not telling her needled her so much that she could not just let it go.

"Yeah, sorry, I put my phone on silent right before I left the office. I know you took the day off to look at wedding venues, so I didn't want to bother you." She watched as he put his phone back in his pocket and looked down, not looking up for a moment. She wondered if he realized how flimsy his excuse sounded. "I invited Clarissa because she has been working on the deal with me this whole time," Sam explained.

The explanation sounded rational. Yet, she could tell that bothering her wasn't the reason. Most people would think something was going on between Sam and Clarissa. Sam would never cheat on her; it wasn't in his DNA, so she knew it wasn't that.

He stood there looking over his shoulder. Then back at her fidgeting a bit, it was as if he was trying to escape or afraid, they would come over. She watched as Sam looked her up and down, clearing his throat unnecessarily.

That's when it hit her. She blinked a few times, realizing why he had not introduced her as his fiancée. She leaned over Sam's shoulder, looking at the three of them. They were all dressed in attire that would cost her entire paycheck. She, on the other hand, was dressed in a thrift store mini-bohemian tank dress that came down to her knees with a pair of jeans underneath. It screamed boho Venice Beach. She looked down at her outfit and then back up at Sam. That's when a tearing feeling inside of her started to rip slowly. Sam didn't tell her or introduce her as his fiancée because he was afraid she would leave them with a bad impression.

Nothing could quell the feeling of shame that crept up her spine. Mackenzie shouldn't have felt ashamed, but for a moment she did. She felt, irrationally, that somehow, she had disappointed Sam. How? By being who she was? The shame morphed into pain. Not just any pain. Pain that felt like the unthinkable. Sam, the one person she knew who loved her unconditionally, the man that was her touchstone was ripping out her heart.

"I should get back to the office. I don't want to keep them waiting. Listen..."

Mackenzie looked up at him as he spoke. For a moment, she couldn't make out the words coming from his mouth. It was as if everything else had shut off, the world around muted, as she felt her entire existence shifted. Things became clear to her in a massively miserable way. All she could feel was resignation and humiliation.

Sam leaned in, giving her a kiss on the cheek squeezing her shoulder and smiled like he had just closed a deal. The proverbial glass shattered in that moment, so intense that she had to stop herself from physically flinching. She tilted her head while looking at him. Whatever Mackenzie felt must have shown through in her eyes because Sam stood there frozen for a moment.

His eyes widened in what appeared to be fear. No one knew her better than he did. He took a shaky breath, peering down at her. She knew he was trying to figure out what she was thinking. He shuffled again, then turned away from her without a word. She gulped hard, doing the same, starting to walk in the opposite direction. Sam didn't call after her. The man she'd spent the bulk of her life with must have sensed that this was something that couldn't be resolved with a few words.

She gasped a few times, keeping the tears at bay. She felt as if her insides were collapsing with every breath she took. Still, she had to say something, let him know she understood why he did what he did. She turned around, calling his name.

"Sam," she called out.

When he pivoted to face her, she saw the shame in his eyes but didn't stop to acknowledge it.

"Quick question," she spoke, plastering a brave smile on her face.

Sam nodded at her, giving her a weak smile.

"When did I become not good enough for your world?" she asked, trying to mask the pain behind her insincerely bright smile.

He flinched as if she had just slapped him. His hard gulp made Adam's apple more pronounced as it slid down his throat. They had been together since they were kids, so she knew the motion well. He was speechless and petrified. Normally, she would follow up with something that would reassure him that everything would be fine. This time, she couldn't. She gave him a weak smile, not giving him a chance to answer. Then, she mirrored his previous action by turning her back to him and walking down the small corridor toward Sweetgreen. She knew he wouldn't follow her. He would wait until he got home, expecting her to be at his place. She could see him now, standing in front of her as she sat on his leather couch and watched him make his argument while he paced.

He'd expect that she would ask a few questions, challenge him for a bit then either take a few days to cool off or forgive him right away.

But this time was different. Why today? She wasn't exactly sure until the moment he leaned in and kissed her cheek. She wondered if he understood the magnitude of what had just happened. Mournfully confident that he didn't.

Chapter 3

SAM

Samson Madden stood in the elevator of his apartment building, looking down at his phone, rereading the few texts Mac had sent over and over.

"Good morning, Mr. Madden. Starting the search bright and early. Bianca says she has a killer idea; will let you know how it pans out."

"I think we found the perfect spot!! Treating Bianca to lunch at Sweetgreen at Platform. How is your day going? Anything you need while we are out and about?"

"Text when you have a second, Samson."

The last text was to playfully get a rise out of him; Mackenzie knew he preferred to be called Sam. Anytime someone asked him about his name, he'd have to admit that he was indeed named after the biblical figure. His hippie mother loved the idea of his strength being determined by his hairstyle. Sam couldn't fault her; his grandparents were also part of the Flower Power movement. He was thankful that his mother hadn't gone completely out there with his name. Her own name was Clover, after all.

Growing up, Mac used to joke about his name all the time, reminding him that he could have been named Spruce or Cedar. While Mac had disliked people shortening her name when they were younger, Sam insisted that they did. He'd even, at times, immaturely ignored anyone who called him Samson. That's how he and Mac were—completely in sync or polar opposites. Still, he couldn't help but think about the look in Mackenzie's eyes when he did not introduce her as his fiancée. He knew that what he did was catastrophic and was still stunned by his actions.

Mackenzie had been at Sam's side since she was eight and he was ten. He could still remember the day they met; she was on her skateboard trying to do tricks outside of her Uncle Deano's record shop, her various scrapes and bruises revealing that she was failing miserably with her quest.

He'd slowed his pace down to see what she was trying to accomplish. From what it looked like, she was attempting a hospital flip—a trick that began by popping the tail down with the back foot and flicking the front foot forward. If done correctly, she'd land back in her original stance.

"Your footing's wrong," he said as he stopped in front of her.

He had reached out toward her, conveying that he wanted her skateboard. Mac handed him the cause of her frustration, taking a step back to watch him. Sam proceeded to show her how the trick was supposed to look. It took most of the afternoon, but Mac finally did it. Her determination melted his adolescent heart. Sam didn't know at what point they introduced themselves to each other. Clearly, they had. He recalled looking down at the tiny, tan Filipino girl in braided pigtails sitting on the ground, leaning against the side of her uncle's shop, and feeling as if something had shifted inside of him.

It wasn't a matter of seeing her again; he was sure that was going to happen. It was as if he knew she was going to be so significant to him. At the time, he didn't realize how important she would become, but from that moment on, the bulk of his childhood revolved around Mac. After that day, she stopped trying to learn tricks. Her Uncle Deano thanked him later, admitting to Sam that watching her fall and land on the pavement was the closest thing to a heart attack he had ever felt.

Mac became content with standing behind him on his board while he zoomed them down the street, yelling "excuse us" to people who had to jump out of their way. He would have to occasionally bark at her to stop wobbling. Knowing every time she let go of his waist she had her arms stretched out teetering as she see-sawed them from side to side, trusting he would never let them wipe out.

Being with Mac sometimes felt like he was in the middle of this crazy whirlpool. Yet, Sam never felt unsteady. In fact, he'd never felt more grounded than when she was around. Her energy and personality were unlike anyone else he'd ever known. She was loving, charming, and the kindest person he had ever met. Her empathy for others was humbling. Brilliantly hilarious, there was an aura around her. All eyes went to Mackenzie anytime she walked into a room. It wasn't just because she was beautiful. It was because she lit up the space with her presence. In one of his sappy, drunken moments, he told his friend Ezra that Mac was like both the Sun and the Moon.

He felt the cold steel against his back as he leaned against the side of the elevator, his head tilted up, eyes closed, praying he would smell the scent of peaches and see Mac sitting on his sofa. Every time he closed his eyes, he could see Mac standing in front of him as he introduced her. Not recognizing her as his fiancée. The look in her nearly black irises was one that he had never seen. He couldn't quite describe it. If he was being honest, he didn't want to try to figure it out. When he shut his eyes, he would see himself introducing Mackenzie as if she were an acquaintance, seeing the look in her eyes again and again. It felt like he was being emotionally disemboweled. Sam knew he had intentionally kept the lunch outing from her. He had very few non-negotiables when it came to Mac. Knowing where she was had been one of them. It wasn't because he was controlling. She only had him, his mother, and their two best friends. He always made it a point to return the request in kind. This time, he didn't. On top of that, she texted him. He hadn't bothered to check. He was too focused on working on the deal that he had spent the last eight months living and breathing. Focused on the people who could help him close it.

The ding of the elevator announcing his floor pulled him out of his thoughts. Sam walked down the long hallway and stood in front of his door, taking a deep breath and exhaling.

He pulled out his key and slid it into the lock, hearing the tumbler slide open. He gripped the doorknob, twisting it, gulping hard, knowing he had really messed up this time. She hadn't answered any of his texts or picked up the phone, and her parting question had stabbed him through the heart. Mostly because there was a truth to it. She sacrificed so much. Helped him finish grad school. Encouraged him to take night classes to get his Master's in Finance when everyone else told him he was insane because he already had his MBA. He had still wanted the extra accolade.

She was his biggest cheerleader. There were times when he had nothing to offer; Mackenzie hadn't cared. She had stood by him and believed in him even when he didn't believe in himself. Stayed up with him sketching every time he had to pull an all-nighter. She even dropped assignments when he was sick or in an important seminar.

How had he repaid that? He was an asshole; he knew it. He opened the door slowly, scanning the room, trying not to feel dejected that he didn't smell peaches. He walked over to his vacant leather sofa and dropped his suit jacket and messenger bag onto it. He felt his shoulders slump as he yanked his tie down, making his way to his bedroom, stopping short at the doorway.

The shock of what was on his bed paralyzed him. Sitting on his mattress was the key to his apartment, a small box with what looked like all the things he had kept at her place, and the bright green with a hint of blue colored Tiffany's box her engagement ring had come in.

He stumbled into the bathroom, pulling his tie over his head, heart beating out of his chest. His blood ran cold as he looked around the small room and saw none of Mac's things there. He took a step backward, opening his closet door. He heard a soft sob of disbelief, belatedly realizing it was coming from him as he looked at the empty space that once held some of Mac's outfits.

He told himself this couldn't be real. It wasn't that bad, was it? Sam turned around and raced to the key rack, looking for the keys to her place. He had to make things right. He staggered to a stop, seeing that the keyring with the tiny wooden surfboard with "Venice Beach" written across it with her keys no longer hung there.

Mac wasn't one to be very emotional or dramatic when it came to their relationship. Her tolerance level had always humbled him. What terrified him was that he knew once Mac made a choice, she stuck by it.

He reached into his pocket pulling out his cell phone, dialing her number immediately, but then getting not her normal cheery voicemail but an automated message saying the caller was unavailable. She had blocked him.

He took a deep breath, trying to calm himself, repeating to himself over and over again that this was fixable. He tried to tamper down the rising fear that she would not give him a chance to repair the damage he had caused. He was downtown, and she was all the way in Venice Beach. It would take at least two hours to get to her because it was rush hour, and the famous LA Gridlock was in full effect. Normally, he'd wait it out and go later, but he knew he couldn't this time. He was going to lose her—if he hadn't already.

Chapter 4

MACKENZIE

Mackenzie sat on a weathered wooden bench facing the street vendor stalls of the Venice Boardwalk. The area was known for its mass tourism, which brought street performers, people taking pictures at Muscle Beach and the famous Venice Beach Skate Park, and trendier parts like Abbot Kinney with upscale restaurants and various small boutiques. And last but certainly not least the infamous Venice Boardwalk.

Being here always made her feel close to her uncle. On the weekends, he would open the shop a bit later, at 11 a.m., so he and Mackenzie could sit there and eat brunch. Uncle Deano would tell her about the Venice Art Walls between Muscle Beach and the skate park. His favorites were the one of Jim Morrison, a recreation of Van Gogh's Starry Night, and a piece called Venice Kinesis that riffed on Sandro Botticelli's Venus. Or he would ask her about her week. Sometimes, the conversations were just silly; other times, they were more somber, especially after he was diagnosed with cancer.

Like clockwork, Sam would roll up at 10:45 a.m. on his skate-board, bike, or just on foot. Uncle Deano took it as his cue to walk to his shop, sometimes Mac and Sam would follow, other times, they would take off to get into trouble elsewhere.

It had only been three hours since her life had suddenly stopped making sense.

She thought back to the aftermath. Mac vaguely remembered turning toward Bianca when she called out to her. Whatever look she gave Bianca made her best friend put the coffee on the ledge next to them. Mac recalled nearly stumbling because her feet couldn't seem to move. Bianca had dragged Mac behind the small building, away from curious eyes. She pulled Mac into her arms, hugging her tightly. Mac wasn't sure when she'd started crying, only that she'd soaked the fabric of Bianca's top. She wondered for a moment if her legs had given out and if Bianca was holding her up. Mac wasn't sure. All she knew was that nothing in her world would ever be the same.

They'd gotten into Mac's Prius and made it downtown. Bianca didn't ask where they were going, didn't ask any other questions, and didn't try to make small talk. This was unchartered territory for both. Mackenzie was grateful Bianca had just followed her lead. Before they knew it, they were parked in one of the visitor stalls of Sam's apartment complex.

Bianca followed Mac into Sam's apartment, standing in the doorway, waiting to see what Mac's intentions were. Once she realized what Mackenzie was doing, Bianca sprang into action. Appearing next to Mac, she started stuffing the items Mac was gathering into trash bags. Mac calmly started pulling her belong-ings out of the closet and bathroom. She was on autopilot and did not try to stop it.

The scene reminded her of the time Bianca came to her house armed with unbuilt cardboard boxes and packing tape. Uncle

Deano had been gone for eight months, and Mackenzie hadn't gotten rid of any of his things. Everyone around her hinted at her to make the change, but Mackenzie could not bring herself to do it. Bianca took it upon herself and made the call. They worked in silence, knowing talking would only lead to tears. About an hour later, Ezra and Sam showed up to finish the job, bringing Uncle Deano's stuff to Goodwill.

There would be no Ezra and Sam this time. She hoped battle lines wouldn't be drawn when it came to Ezra. Battle lines were imminent when it came to Bianca. Mac knew she would die on the 'You're a fucker for humiliating Mac' hill.

It didn't take too much time for them to finish gathering all of Mac's things. She just wanted to get out of there. Sam was subletting the place from an associate in his firm's UK branch for the next year, so she'd always been nervous about breaking his glass coffee table or leaving rings on his bedside nightstand. She had never been comfortable there.

Soon enough, they had piled her stuff into Mackenzie's car and were back at Venice Beach, gathering all of Sam's things. Mac noticed the lack of his belongings at her place. There were a few items but nothing substantial, not like when they were in college or after her uncle died when Sam had basically lived there with her. Now, there was only a small footprint of his presence. Mostly clothes that he only wore when he would forget to pack a bag for his weekend stays.

Just as they were about to load everything into Bianca's car, Mac looked down at her engagement ring. It was a pre-owned Tiffany's ring that Sam found on an estate sale site. Bianca had pointed out to him that Mac would want something that she didn't have to worry about someone chopping off her hand to steal. Sam told her he noticed Mac always looking at the Tiffany store in Beverly Hills whenever they were there. He had decided long before he actually proposed it had to be a ring from Tiffany's. She hadn't taken it off since he put it on her finger three years ago. She looked down at it, now wondering if the COVID-19 outbreak and trying to save up money to have the wedding were the real reasons for their long engagement. Slowly, she slid it off her finger. She tried to calm herself, holding back the tears. Mac took a deep breath and then placed it in the Tiffany's box. She felt Bianca hugging her from behind as the box snapped shut in her hand.

"Let me drop this stuff off in case you run into him," Bianca offered. It made sense since Bianca lived in Koreatown, just west of downtown LA. Mac gave her a smile and nodded.

As they finished packing up Bianca's SUV, her best friend looked her in the eyes, putting her hands on Mac's shoulders.

"You sure about this, Mackenzie?" she asked.

It was rare for Bianca to ask questions when it came to Mackenzie needing her help. She was sure that Bianca would show up with bleach and tarps if Mac called and told her she needed to move a body. Mac nodded again, giving Bianca a brave smile and hugged her.

"I'm sure," Mac whispered.

"Text me if you want me to come back down, okay?" Bianca pleaded.

"You know, I am not going to ask you to navigate LA for the third time today. I will give you a call tomorrow, though," Mac promised.

With that, Bianca pulled out and left with Sam's things and the key to his apartment.

Mackenzie looked down at her ring finger and saw the tan line there.

She didn't think the way she chose to handle the breakup would be accepted. It wouldn't be that simple. She expected to see him tonight. Especially since she blocked him on her phone and all social media sites. She wasn't being purposely hurtful. She just needed to digest everything that happened without being swayed, and she knew Sam would try. But him being embarrassed by her cut too deep. She had no idea how to deal with it.

There were certain times in her life where she ached for her uncle to still be there and this topped everything on the previous list. She knew her uncle wouldn't question her decision but rather ask her how he could help her get through the day to day. She could be wrong. Uncle Deano was the president of the Sam Madden Fan Club.

She would give anything to feel a hug from her uncle. Hear him say, "it's ok, *anak*." He always called her *anak*, when she was scared or hurt. It was a term of endearment in Cebuano that parents used for their children. She'd hoped that sitting on their bench would somehow soothe her heartbreak.

The distant sound of feedback from the speaker of a busker startled Mackenzie, pulling her out of her thoughts. She listened as they strummed the first few chords of Joni Mitchell's "Both Sides Now". She shook her head, chucklingly mirthlessly. The song could not be any more perfect for how she felt. Mackenzie took a deep breath, unable to not smell the pot smoke and incense in the air. She looked up at the sky; she didn't need answers; she just needed her world to stop shaking all around her.

"Mind if I sit here?" Mac heard a slightly accented voice say, breaking her from her reverie. Looking up, she saw a guy standing in front of her in a gray hoodie and a pair of jeans. She deduced he was of Chinese descent, close to her age, and, like her, taller than the average person of their ethnicities. Mackenzie also noticed that while his clothes were casual, they were high-end brands. He stood there smiling down at her, pointing to the space next to her.

She scooted over, making room for him and returning his smile. "Sure," she replied. "But you have to excuse me If I'm not very talkative," Mac confessed. Mac had a good sense of awareness when it came to guys wanting to hit on her. She also had the ability to be completely icy when she felt it was necessary. The guy sitting next to her didn't make her feel apprehensive.

As he sat down Mac noticed he had a buzz cut. She immediately wondered if he was in the military.

The man held out his hand. "My name's Chaoxiang Zhou. Or Hunter."

Mackenzie took the hand he offered, shaking it. "Mackenzie Almazan," she replied. "Do you prefer Chaoxiang or Hunter?"

"Hunter is good mostly because people abbreviate Chaoxiang. I don't think anyone wants to be called Chow. Also, listening to them, in vain, trying to pronounce my name correctly takes way too much time."

Mackenzie chuckled, turning her head to look at him. "I can sort of relate. Most people called me Mac when I was a kid. I hated it, but now I am used to it, so I get it somewhat." She swung her head back toward the boardwalk, watching the tourists go by, her mind flashing to the memory of that afternoon and how Sam had treated her. Mackenzie shook her head as if trying to rattle the memory out of her mind. Hunter witnessed her strange behavior.

"Sorry not to sound dramatic, but the life I was so sure of completely changed today," Mac laughed, looking up and rolling her eyes. "Wow, I guess that's pretty dramatic. Believe it or not, I don't make that statement lightly. "

Mackenzie watched him squirm nervously as he cleared his throat. She spied the blush that started to creep up his neck and spread across his face. "So, this is going to sound creepy and stalkerish. And trust me, if you jump up running, I wouldn't blame you," he admitted.

"Go on, but I'll warn you, my voice carries, and letting out ear-piercing sounds is my specialty," Mac replied, bracing herself for whatever he was about to say.

"I, umm, I saw you at the Platform earlier."

Chapter 5

MACKENZIE

Mackenzie shrank back a little, blinking a few times as she wondered if she needed to bolt.

"Well, first I heard you, then saw what was going on," Hunter explained, holding up his hands as if he was surrendering. "I swear, as nuts as this sounds, it's purely coincidence. My assistant Ollie and I were having lunch at Roberta's. I was just as shocked as you seem to be right now when I looked over and saw you sitting here." He pulled out a key card for a hotel room, holding it up for her to see. "I'm staying at Hotel Erwin down here. I have been there for three weeks. You can call and ask the concierge desk if you want to confirm."

When Mackenzie didn't say anything, he continued, "Anyhow, I hadn't been to Roberta's in a while, so we went there for lunch. That's where I saw you."

Mackenzie's body tensed for a moment. Growing up in Los Angeles, wariness was part of her native survival instinct. Bianca always said Mackenzie had "spidey senses" when it came to sniffing out if someone was bullshitting her. Something about Hunter disarmed her. She could see he was truly nervous and afraid that Mac wouldn't believe him. Relaxing, she blinked a few more times, letting out a low whistle. "Hotel Erwin... pretty snazzy. Not a cheap place to stay. Why Venice and not Santa Monica?"

Hunter smiled, visibly relieved that she hadn't thought he was a maniac. "It feels more real here. Sure, the tourists swarm during the day, but there are a few hours in the morning when it's just the locals. Less pretentious, I guess," he laughed.

"I completely get it. I have lived down the street from here my whole life," she replied, pressing her hands down on the bench.

"Are you here on business?" she asked.

Hunter shook his head. "I live here in Los Angeles," he answered.

"So why the hotel? Are you renovating your place or something?" Mac asked curiously.

"I did recently sell the place I lived in. There's nothing wrong with my current property. I just wanted to see the city from a different perspective."

"You in the industry?" she asked, meaning the entertainment business—anyone who lived in Los Angeles knew that. His statement about owning more than one property let her know he had money, maybe movie money.

Hunter chuckled, shaking his head. "I'm in the tech industry. I know it's completely cliché, right?" he chuckled, pointing at himself, referring to the fact he was Chinese.

"Believe it or not, I didn't become a nurse," Mackenzie quipped. It was widely known that Filipino women were pushed into the nursing profession by their parents.

Hunter jerked back a bit in mock shock, both laughing. "How did you escape that?" he asked.

"I was raised by my uncle. He was an engineer; I know again, shocking, right? He stopped working at Northrup and opened a record store here. Down the street, actually, so going against the norm was the norm in our household."

Hunter turned his head. "Does he still run it? I have an extensive vinyl collection."

Mackenzie gave him a small smile, shaking her head before looking down for a beat. "No, he passed away a while ago."

Hunter groaned, tilting his head back and burying his face in his hands. "Sorry, remembering that is probably not what you need right now," he said, his hands muffling his voice.

Mackenzie shook her head, patting him on the back. "Actually, I was already thinking about him, so it's okay."

Hunter turned his body toward her, hanging his arm off the back of the bench. He crossed his legs, one over the other. "So, from the sound of it, things aren't going well with your boyfriend. Don't worry. No one else besides Ollie and me seemed to notice. Ollie barely admits he knows me, so there is nothing to be concerned about there. I feel like it's dumb to ask if you are okay."

Mackenzie released a big breath, truly hoping no one else heard the most degrading moment of her life. "That's relieving, all things considered. Fiancé. By the way." Mackenzie gulped hard. "Well, ex-fiancé, to be precise," she said, correcting herself. "As for if I am okay, how could one be, right? I can't say I didn't exactly see it coming. I think I was just hoping I was wrong. I kinda pulled an asshole move and just dropped all his stuff off, as well as my ring, at his apartment. Harsh, right?"

"From what I heard, I feel like it's understandable. You think you made a mistake?" he asked.

She shook her head. "Honestly, right now it feels like it's the right move. We'll see how I feel tomorrow," she joked, then sighed again, looking toward the boardwalk once more. "We're just so different now. I don't fit in his world. I'm not even sure I want to."

Mackenzie pressed her hands down harder on the seat of the bench, this time raising herself for a moment, hovering over the bench before plopping back down. The bench was hard, and parts of her body were going numb because she had been sitting there too long.

"So, how old were you when you came over?" she asked, changing the subject.

Hunter laughed, "Is it my accent?"

Mackenzie shook her head, pointing at his legs.

"It's the way you cross your legs. Stereotypically, most American-born guys don't cross their legs one over the other. The archaic reason is really stupid."

She crossed her legs in a figure four position, one ankle propped on the opposite shin, giving him an example of how most men sat.

Hunter mimicked her stance, groaning as he did.

"That feels like it would be incredibly uncomfortable after a while. I can't help but wonder why it's different."

Mackenzie shrugged her shoulders. "Maybe our forefathers thought you guys needed ventilation down there or something," Mac muttered loud enough for Hunter to hear. She gasped, covering her mouth, realizing how crass her comment was.

Hunter looked at her, stunned for a moment, then doubled over in laughter, hands holding his stomach.

"I have this habit of saying inappropriate things." Mac felt her cheeks get warm.

Hunter leaned back on the bench, taking a deep breath.

"Interesting observation, though," he said, still catching his breath. "I was ten when we first came over for my sister. I went back and stayed with a family friend during high school. Well, what you would call high school. It made it easier for me to get into university in China."

"Tsinghua University?" she asked.

"Yeah, how did you know?"

"I didn't. I just threw it out there. It's one of the best colleges in the world. Did you do the whole abroad thing?"

It was common in China for college students to leave the country to further their education.

"Yeah, Oxford," he smiled.

"Holy crap," she muttered. Hunter laughed, turning his head toward the ocean. "It sounds impressive, but at the end of the day, it was a goal, not a dream."

Mackenzie noticed his shoulders hunch slightly and saw a far-off look in his eyes as he continued to stare at the waves crashing against the shore. His statement obviously brought back memories. Mackenzie knew better than to press on the matter. He hadn't supplied more information. She respected that. After all, what lunatic shares their woes with someone they just met sitting on a bench at the beach, right?

"So, this is going to sound psycho as hell, but my assistant Ollie is about to pick me up in a bit. I'm going to Dockweiler to have a bonfire. Would you like to come?"

Mackenzie fidgeted in her seat. "I don't think it's a good idea."

Hunter pulled out his phone and took out what looked to be his driver's license from the small compartment on the side of his case.

"Take a picture of it. Then, when Ollie comes, take a picture of the license plate and his license. Send all the pics to someone you trust. Maybe turn on your location services for them," he suggested.

Mackenzie tilted her head, looking at him, impressed.

"I had a sister. I get it. You can't be too careful," he explained.

Mackenzie caught the past tense—had instead of have—and tried not to react.

"Besides, you want to avoid your ex, right? Something tells me he's going to try to come around tonight. I won't plead or push; I'm just offering you an option. If it makes you feel better, I only plan on being there until sundown."

Mackenzie leaned back, studying Hunter. He looked back at her, waiting for her response. He didn't come off as anxious or aggressive. His invitation was sincere. He had watched her go through something fairly humiliating. Also, Ezra lived right there in Playa Del Rey. He could be there in five minutes if things got sketchy. She shrugged her shoulders, giving him a smile.

"Sure, I'll come along. If I die, it would make for an awesome murder podcast segment."

Chapter 6

MACKENZIE

Mac sat on a nylon folding chair next to Hunter, staring into the small fire Ollie had made. When they got to the pit, Hunter admitted he had no clue how to make a fire. Both of them laughed as they tried to figure out how to lay the wood in the pit. Luckily, Ollie was well-versed in camping. He got the fire started easily and situated their seats where the smoke from the bonfire wouldn't choke them out.

It was dusk now. Mackenzie wondered if Sam had shown up at her house. She knew he probably did and most likely left. He had a meeting early in the morning. This deal, his job, was more important than anything else, including her. She suspected that was the case. Mac just never wanted to admit it until now.

"You thinking about calling him?" Hunter asked.

Mackenzie twisted her lips a bit, then shook her head.

"No, it would be too easy to let go of what happened today. Believe it or not, I don't blame him. I thought he could change, and it would be okay if I didn't. I know my taking off with a stranger and running from him for a night doesn't reflect what I am about to say, but somewhere inside, I always felt like without Sam, I would lose myself, so I stayed at his side. I think part of me wants to test if that's actually true," Mac confessed, shrugging her shoulders contritely.

There was a lull of silence between them. It wasn't uncomfortable, both lost in their own thoughts.

"Did you go to college?" Hunter asked, breaking the silence.

"I did for about a year and a half, but I didn't finish. My uncle got sick, so I needed to run the record shop and be there with him," she explained.

Hunter nodded. "Ever think of going back?"

Mac shook her head and shifted her body to the side, toward him.

"After he died, I realized a lot of things. Sure, I could try to get a degree at something I don't love. What I do love doesn't pay the bills. But I don't want to go into debt studying something when my heart isn't in it, only to end up buried in student loans. My uncle wouldn't want that either."

"What does pay the bills?" Hunter inquired.

"Being an assistant to an Executive Project Manager at Synergy Financial Group Downtown," she revealed. "It does help that I own my place. My uncle left it to me. The property tax kills me, though. Luckily, he did everything he could to make sure I would be okay financially."

"So, what do you love doing that doesn't pay the bills?" Hunter asked.

"Being a painter. I can't really say I am good at it, but it's where my heart is and what I am passionate about," Mackenzie explained.

"So, yeah, that's why I never went back. Even if I did, I think I would have dropped out eventually. Honestly, I don't think I had the stamina to try at that time. Watching the person you love the most in the world laying in a hospital bed changes your perspective on things."

She noticed Hunter tapping a finger against the arm of the chair. She looked up and immediately recognized the look on his face. His uncomfortable squirming verified it.

"Cirrhosis of the liver that led to pancreatic cancer. Before I came to live with him, he was a heavy drinker," she answered without him having to ask the question.

"Sorry, blame my culture; we are nearly offensively curious," Hunter joked, slightly elbowing her.

"Oh? Filipinos are just plain old nosey," she quipped back. The two of them laughed for a minute.

Hunter cleared his throat, then turned to Mac, crossing his legs. "Pancreatic cancer—that's rough. Actually, I can relate somewhat. Not that we need to swap our sorrows, but I know how you feel. My parents passed away in a car accident in China. And my sister died of Leukemia four years ago. I took care of her until the end."

Mackenzie reached out to him, laying her hand over his. She didn't say she was sorry because she remembered how that made her feel. It was an automatic response. Most of the time, it was sincere, but after a while, it just started making her feel uncomfortable. Like she was saying something that would bring people down.

"It's hard, right?" Mackenzie uttered, gazing at the fire for a beat before refocusing on Hunter.

"First, you put all you have into the belief that they will get better. Then, watch them go through treatment. Doing your best to be their cheerleader when secretly inside, you're terrified."

"The looks on the doctor's face when there is nothing else they could do," Hunter interjected, shaking his head. "I still remember getting the news. Phrases like 'quality of life' and 'making things comfortable' are being thrown around."

Mackenzie nodded. "I didn't cry in front of him for a long time," Mac muttered.

She remembered waiting for her Uncle Deano to go to sleep for the night before leaving the hospital. She'd driven over to Sam's house and stood at the doorway for a few long moments, afraid to take another step in. Some irrational part of her thought that if she had not said Uncle Deano was dying out loud, then maybe it wouldn't be true. The second she stepped into Sam's house and told him there would be no going back, no denying the reality of it all.

She'd watched Sam come out of the kitchen. He must have known by the look on her face because the next thing she knew, he was running over to her. He picked her up, princess-style, plopping them down on the couch. He held her, saying to her over and over, "I'm here, Mackenzie, I'm here." She sat in his lap for what felt like hours, just staring out at nothing. Mac knew she had cried a little because she remembered Sam wiping her tears away as he continued to just sit there holding her. She knew he was crying as well. Uncle Deano was like a father to him.

"Not me," Hunter chuckled. "I broke down crying in her lap and told her she couldn't leave me. I know, pretty wimpy of me, right?"

Mackenzie shook her head.

"She would have wanted you to be honest. I wasn't at first, I tried to stay sunny and happy. Then Uncle Deano called me out on it. I still censored things, though," Mac confessed.

"I didn't want to make things harder for him. The absolute worst thing is watching them in pain."

Hunter looked up and groaned. "All you can do is sit there holding their hand. Feeling like your heart is being torn out piece by piece."

"Still, we had some really good moments during that time. Really honest talks and a lot of dark humor. I cherish those," Mac smiled, looking up at the sky. "In the end, I think he left knowing I would be all right."

"My sister worried until the end," he whispered. "I get it, though she understood I would be all alone. I was a late-life baby. She was seven years older than me. In a lot of ways, she was more my mom than my sister," Hunter professed reverently. "She did ask me to do one thing, which I have been able to do for the most part."

"What's that?" Mackenzie asked.

"She always said her biggest regret was all the time she spent lying in the bed when she got the news. There were so many things she wanted to do. One night, she took the back of one of the hospital's little postcards and told me to write seven of my wildest dreams. Asked me to promise to finish the list no matter what."

"How many have you got through?" Mac asked.

"Three. I was hoping to do the fourth soon."

"Why seven?" she asked.

"Eight is a lucky number in China. She told me writing down seven means you have time to figure out your eighth dream. It would be your biggest because you would have done seven already."

"Have you figured out your eighth dream?" Mac asked.

Hunter shook his head.

"I still have to get through the rest of the things on my list."

"It has to feel amazing to be able to do that," Mackenzie replied.

"It's not that hard. Here," Hunter said, opening his small messenger bag and pulling out a pen and what looked like a postcard.

Mackenzie took it, flipping it over to see it was an ad for one of the tattoo parlors on the boardwalk.

"List seven of your wildest dreams," Hunter instructed, turning his back to her before lowering himself to give her a somewhat hard surface to write on.

Mackenzie shook her head in protest.

"Just do it," Hunter urged, turning his head toward her, continuing to hunch over.

Mackenzie closed her eyes for a moment, then smiled. She wrote down the first four with relative ease, then tapped the pen against her mouth, thinking about what else to put down. Once she figured out the last three, she tapped Hunter's shoulder, letting him know she was done.

Hunter turned toward her and took the list from her hands to read it.

Hunter smiled. "Great list," he said, giving it back to her. He stood up, motioning over to Ollie, who had been leaning against the Lincoln Nautilus they had driven here in, messing with his phone. "We're done!" Hunter yelled, then looked down at Mackenzie.

"Head to the car. Ollie and I will pack things up."

"Oh, we're leaving?" Mac said, standing, brushing the sand off her jeans. It had gotten dark, true to his word, Hunter's intent was to stay until now. "Thanks, this took me out of my head for a while. I really appreciate it."

"Thank me later. We have one more stop."

Mackenzie knitted her brows, looking over at him in confusion as Hunter looked back at her, smiling.

"We're going to knock number six off your list."

Chapter 7

MACKENZIE

After an embarrassingly short amount of time, Hunter coaxed Mackenzie into going to Echo Park with him. Hunter was right—staying out guaranteed she could hide in her avoidance a bit longer. Before she knew it, she was sitting next to Hunter in a swan-shaped boat floating around Echo Park Lake.

For a long time, Echo Park was considered a dangerous part of town. The area around Echo Park Lake had been restored and was now a date or family outing venue. It had lotus flowers and a central fountain that shot up high in the sky, with palm trees surrounding most of the lake. Most people who grew up in the city considered it slightly cheesy, something for the tourists and little kids to do. So, it was treated as if it was almost a dirty little secret.

After putting on the mandatory life vest and comically figuring out how to paddle in sync, she and Hunter were sitting there just floating, looking around, and making jokes about playing bumper swans with couples making out around them.

"This one was an easy one, right?" he chuckled, "Why is it a wildest dream?"

"My friends would rather die than be caught doing something this kitsch unless they were drunk and high. As for Sam, it's just not the kind of thing he'd think to do. And I was always too embarrassed to suggest it," she explained. There was a time when she wasn't. Mackenzie knew all she had to do was ask Sam, to pull on his arm, and they would be off. Thinking about it now, she realized at some point she had become too embarrassed or afraid to ask Sam anything these days.

She looked out toward downtown LA. The skyline on the high rises were visible from where they were. She wondered if Sam was there in his luxury apartment. She remembered how excited he was when his coworker had offered the place. Mackenzie, on the other hand, was terrified. She couldn't look out the window from such a high floor because she had vertigo. Mac had tiptoed around for the first four months, afraid she was going to break something, suggesting as often as possible that they go to her place. She realized now that Sam getting the apartment was the start of not only the physical but the emotional distance that had grown between them.

She saw Hunter turn toward her, paddling slowly, then looking in the same direction she was.

"He works in Finance?" Hunter asked.

"Yeah, at Heritage Holdings. My best friend Bianca works there too. Both of them are in senior positions in their departments. They probably take home twice what I make. I guess that's the benefit of not wanting to be a starving artist."

"This is going to sound nuts coming from someone like me. Success and money really aren't everything in the world. I would give up everything I have for another five minutes with my sister," Hunter whispered.

Mackenzie nodded in full agreement. "Same here, I would give anything to feel a hug from my uncle. Although, I wonder if he would be disappointed in the way I am handling all of this." Mackenzie sighed, shaking her head. "I get this looks extreme, but I know myself too well. I would make it alright for Sam to discount how I feel. Or worse, I would have to watch him be stressed out every time I had to meet someone that he needed to impress."

"If it makes you feel better, in China, women are trained since they are children to be docile and graceful. Not that I agree with that philosophy at all. Just saying, knowing how to navigate elite circles isn't something that comes easy," Hunter offered.

"Thanks. I am going to have to eventually face him. Probably as soon as tomorrow since we both work downtown. But right now, I just feel like there are these pieces of me kinda floating around. I guess I need to figure out how to make them all fit again. Does that make sense?" Mackenzie asked.

Hunter nodded. "It does. As selfish as this sounds, I'm happy to be here to put a line through one of the dreams on your list."

Mackenzie smiled over at him. "The first one at that. Most likely the only one. So, I feel like I owe you one. Let me treat you to a late dinner," Mackenzie offered.

Hunter laughed, raising his hand up and giving her the 'OK' symbol

"Sounds like a plan."

It was close to midnight by the time they arrived at LA's Famous Urban Lights. The large-scale installation was located at Wilshire Boulevard in the same space as the Los Angeles County Museum

of Art, or LACMA as locals called it. They were sitting there in the middle of the structure, eating take-out chicken noodle soup from Canter's Deli. Mackenzie swore Canter's was the best deli in all of LA, even though her statement was widely contested.

Mackenzie explained that the 202 lights around them were restored street lamps from the 1920s and 1930s, most of them from all parts of streets in Southern California.

"You ever thought about being an LA tour guide?" Hunter asked, putting his empty container in the plastic bag next to him. "Seriously, is there a part of LA that you don't know?"

"Uncle Deano used to take me on what he called *pasyál-pasyál* which means to roam around in Tagalog or he call it *suroy -suroy*, I guess it's a slang term for *pagsuroy-suroy*, which means sightseeing in Cebuano.. He would find some new spot or attraction that wasn't widely known, and we would head there," Mac explained.

"Find any place particularly interesting?" Hunter asked.

"Graystone Mansion in the Hollywood Hills. It's my favorite place in all of Los Angeles. Even though I have never been inside. They only open it for filming and really exclusive events," Mac answered.

"Would you hate me if I said I have actually been inside? My sister was a widely admired international interior designer. She was invited to the Design Showcase event there every year, and I went with her a couple of times. It's a nice place. She always loved it, too." Hunter drew his knees up to his chest, smiling sadly.

"Hate? No. Jealous? Absolutely. Do you mind me asking what her name was? You haven't volunteered it, so I didn't want to pry," Mac said softly.

"Her name was Xiāng. It means fragrance. Our last name, Zhou, means surrounding or whole. So, it translates into 'fragrance all around'. She never took on an American name. Unlike me, she was tenacious when it came to people pronouncing her name right." Hunter chuckled.

Mackenzie looked down, biting her bottom lip, debating if she should ask the question in her mind.

"Acute myeloid leukemia," Hunter supplied the answer as if he instinctively knew what she wanted to ask. "Most forms of leukemia can be managed. Acute myeloid leukemia isn't one of them. The life expectancy is five years. My sister fought it for three."

Mackenzie crossed her legs, leaning forward and listening intently.

"The last year of her life was a series of experimental treatments and hospital stays. She always said she regretted spending time doing that instead of being out in the world with me. Hence why she made me make the list," Hunter shared, looking over at Mackenzie.

"I guess you should get cracking on the last four on your list then, right? You don't want to let her down," Mackenzie offered.

Hunter chuckled mirthlessly. "We will see."

Mackenzie noticed the change in his demeanor. She opened her mouth to ask him if he was okay.

Hunter spoke up right at that moment. "I feel like I should tell you something. Not that I am banking on you to be around after tonight," Hunter said, shrugging his shoulders.

"I mean, this whole thing is pretty bizarre, right?" Mackenzie teased. "So, I'm bracing for it. Hit me."

"There are so many little but important things I got to share with Xiāng before she died. There is one thing I am relieved that she didn't have to experience with me," Hunter whispered.

Mackenzie felt her heart start to pound. Like earlier today, she hoped her sense of intuition was wrong.

"What's that?" she asked, not entirely sure she wanted to know.

"My diagnosis," he replied. "The rate of a sibling getting AML is really slight, but I guess we rolled snake eyes." Hunter spit out his slight accent, which got a bit thicker with the rise of his emotions.

"Are you in treatment now?" she asked quietly.

Hunter shook his head looking into Mackenzie's eyes. He leaned forward taking Mackenzie's hands in his. He raised his head and smiled weakly then whispered, "I'm dying."

Chapter 8

SAM

Sam looked down at his phone, reading the time. It was only 8 a.m. He had already been in the office for two and a half hours for a conference call with their UK office. Normally, this wouldn't be an issue for him. He was used to working twelve-hour days. Coming in early never affected him. However, today it did. Sam had to get Visine for his bloodshot eyes. He barely slept.

Mac would usually walk into the firm with Bianca around 8:15 a.m., leaving Venice Beach a good hour before she needed to be at work. The morning traffic into downtown was murder. So, she would drive down well before she needed to be there to avoid it. Normally, Sam and Bianca would find Mackenzie sitting in the lobby. She'd accompany them to their office, wait for them to get settled, and then the three of them would go down to the coffee shop next to their building to grab a cup of joe. Lately, Sam had been getting in way earlier. So, it was just her and Bianca these days. He would look up and see Mac stopped in the aisle between cubicles, then pantomime drinking out of a mug to ask if he needed a cup as well. He'd decline, having drank too much coffee already after getting in so early. He glanced down at his phone again, hoping for a text or phone call from Mac. She had gone radio silent since she'd walked away from him at the Platform.

It took forever for him to get down to Venice Beach the night before. Sam took the stairs to Mac's small bungalow two at a time, knocking frantically at her door. When Mac didn't answer he ran over to the boardwalk, expecting to see her sitting in her favorite spot, panicking when he saw she was not there. He felt the vibrating of his phone in his back pocket as Ezra's name appeared on the screen.

"If you're at Mac's, she's not there. B said she was fine. Mac left location services on for her," Ezra said.

Sam bent over, winded. Knowing she was okay did not make him feel better. "She turned them off for me," Sam replied.

"Yeah, she did for me, too," Ezra responded.

The four of them had shared their location since they started living in different parts of the city. Again, something Sam suggested but insisted on when it came to Mackenzie. It was clear Mac was hurting and hiding herself away. He heard Ezra let out a loud breath.

"What the fuck did you do, bro?" Ezra asked.

"B didn't tell you?" Sam questioned, straightening up and looking around to see if he could spot Mac.

"I think I got some of it between the 'pricks,' 'bastards,' and 'fucking assholes.' I haven't seen B this pissed since the time she caught that sorority chick trying to roofie your drink," Ezra declared.

"I fucked up, Ez," Sam admitted.

"I gathered that. Apparently, you made Mac cry?" Ezra uttered into the phone. Sam heard the tinge of disbelief. It was as if Ezra wanted him to deny it.

"Did B say what she was doing?" Sam asked, trying to swallow down the lump in his throat.

"All B said was that she was fine and that if your dumb ass drove down there to go home. Mac will reach out when she's ready," Ezra supplied.

"I don't know what the right move is here, Ez," Sam whispered in distress, still looking around the boardwalk, hoping to catch a glimpse of Mackenzie. He was positive she would be here. It's where she always went when she needed to calm down or think about something. Anytime they fought, he knew she would go there. He would sit next to her, and they would work it out. The fact that she was not here reaffirmed that things were different this time.

"Honestly, I would listen to B on this one. She sounded like she was on the verge of tears as well. Give Mac some space. I know how weird that must feel, but try. Call me when you get home and tell me what the hell happened," Ezra advised.

Sam didn't leave right away. He waited in his car another hour before making his way back to his apartment. He sat on his couch for what felt like the whole night, staring at his phone, hoping to hear from Mac. Even if it was just a text telling him she was okay. The feeling of despair intensified as every hour passed.

Sam jumped to his feet as soon as he heard the elevator ding right outside the open glass doors of the firm. His heart dropped, seeing only Bianca walking to her desk. Sam raced out of his office, making his way to Bianca's workspace. Mackenzie's best friend looked up from her desk, unsurprisingly giving him an icy glare.

He watched as she took a deep breath, rolling her chair back and turning toward him.

"She took two and a half weeks off. After all, she doesn't need to save her PTO anymore," Bianca said venomously. Bianca held her hand up, letting Sam know not to interrupt her.

"Before you ask, no I don't know what she's doing or what she is planning to do next, even if I did, I wouldn't tell you. She said she would call periodically and let me know she was okay," Bianca explained.

"Look, B..." Sam started.

"It's Bianca," she snapped. "Only the people closest to me can call me B."

She turned her chair back around and began to type. Effectively dismissing him. He knew this would be her attitude. Still, it stung. Bianca had got on his case a lot recently about his treatment of her best friend. Ironically, Sam introduced Bianca and Mac to each other. While all four of them had been friends since college, Sam was well aware that, ultimately, Bianca's loyalty would belong to Mac.

He stood there trying to figure out how to get through the wall of flames Bianca had put between them. Bianca had been irritated with him even before the events at the restaurant.

A few weeks ago, Bianca and Sam had to attend a seminar. He had been there when she arrived. Sam was with Clarissa, talking to a few of their coworkers. He was so focused that he did not see her come in.

Bianca and Sam were at one time a unit at things like this. Lately, Sam had been buddied up with Clarissa—something not lost on anyone in their firm.

After a while, Sam noticed Bianca. He shook a few hands as he made his way to her. He remembered Bianca waving her hand in front of him in a zigzag motion.

"What the fuck is all this?" Bianca had whispered to him.

"What do you mean, B?" Sam asked, confused.

"This new air you got all around you. Is this the new you, Sam? Are you even paying attention?" Bianca had said, taking a sip of her water.

"B, I'm just networking."

Sam was genuinely confused.

"With Clarissa attached at the hip," Bianca spat out.

"B, there's no way you think..."

"It's not what I think; it's how everyone is perceiving it," Bianca argued. "Seriously, I know you aren't doing anything, but it doesn't mean people in the firm are not whispering about the two of you," Bianca interrupted. "The Sam I know would rather bleed out of his eyes than let people think that Mac wasn't the most important person in his life."

Bianca walked away from him and went to greet a friend from a different firm.

He didn't try to talk to her again that day. He had been so busy working on this deal that he'd barely seen Bianca in the last few weeks, much less spoken to her about what she'd said. This was more pressing, though.

"Bianca, this isn't like Mac. I'm freaking out here," Sam confessed.

"You should have thought about that before you left her hanging and made Mac feel like she was something to be ashamed of," Bianca responded.

"I told them as soon as we got into the car," Sam argued.

"Right. Was that because you felt guilty about breaking your fiancée's heart or because it was safe to do it since Mac wasn't around to say the wrong thing or act the wrong way?" Bianca said, her voice wobbling a bit.

Sam opened his mouth to argue, then realized he didn't have a rebuttal. The truth of Bianca's accusation hit him hard.

"Bianca, please, I'm begging you, please tell Mac I need to talk to her." That was all he could come up with.

Bianca turned her chair back around, looking up at Sam. "There's no way I am giving her that message. Not because I am pissed, because trust me, I am," Bianca said.

Sam watched as the look on her expression went from anger to hurt.

"It's because of the look on her face after your dick move. I have never seen that look from her. Even when Uncle Deano died, she didn't seem as lost as she did yesterday. It was like the light around Mac had gone out, and she doubted everything, especially herself. So, don't ask me to tell Mac anything for you. She'll reach out when she can think about talking to you again."

Sam felt as if his legs were going to give out. Hearing how hurt Mackenzie was was like a dagger to his heart.

Just then, he heard Clarissa calling his name.

"Sam, daily conference call in five." He heard Clarissa announce from behind him.

Bianca let out a snort and then continued typing.

Sam turned toward Clarissa. "I'll be right there," he called back.

"Your work wife wants you," Bianca muttered, not hiding the snide tone in her voice.

Sam walked away, Bianca's words still ringing in his ears.

Chapter 9

MACKENZIE

Mackenzie stood on her balcony, gazing out toward the ocean. She looked down at her phone, debating her next move.

Earlier, she had called HR and her boss to let them know that she was taking PTO. She explained her reason, hoping they would understand. Luckily, her boss adored her. He was more concerned about Mac's state of mind than her missing work. He also promised to keep things to himself. She knew people in her office would talk.

Yesterday's events still rocked her. From breaking up with Sam to Hunter confessing that he was not long for the world. At the time she didn't know what to say to Hunter. Instead of trying to find the right words she had leaned over and gave him a hug. Hunter accepted it, neither of them spoke for a while. Finally, he broke away and announced he and Ollie would take her home.

"Mind if I have your phone for a sec?" Mackenzie asked as they drove back to Venice Beach.

Hunter tilted his head, looking at Mac for a second before handing it over to her.

Mac saved her number in his phone and titled herself "Crazy Beach Girl." She handed it back to Hunter, who looked down at it and laughed, then sent her a text that said

"Here's my number; put me in as 'Probably Not A Stalker,'" Mackenzie read.

"Call me if you ever feel like venting to someone that isn't going to take it personally," she said to him.

Mac called Bianca as soon as she walked through the door. Knowing her friend was showing an incredible amount of restraint by not calling her right after she sent the pictures over.

After one ring, Bianca answered and screamed, "How in the fuck did you hook up with Chaoxiang Zhou!"

Mac knew that Bianca had gathered an entire dossier on the man within five minutes of her receiving a picture of his driver's license.

"I didn't hook up with him, B. We just hung out. It is such a random story that I think you wouldn't believe it," Mac replied.

"Girl, the man is both hot and loaded. If he didn't sell his company, he would have broken into the Fortune 500 eventually. He's not quite 'Crazy Rich Asian' rich, but he could give them a run for their money. It's pun completely intended," Bianca said.

They talked for a few more minutes. Mackenzie let her know she was going to take some of her PTO.

"Do you, Mac. I'll handle the other stuff." Mac knew she meant fielding Sam.

Now, Mackenzie leaned against the rail of her balcony still holding her phone. Normally, the smell of the ocean and the light breeze coming from the shore comforted her. This time it wasn't working. Her phone vibrated in her hand just as she was debating whether to make a cup of coffee or go down to her favorite cafe.

She held her phone up seeing "Probably Not A Stalker" on her screen.

"Hey, hey," Mac said.

"Hey, just seeing if you need a pep talk. You mentioned that you would probably see your ex today," Hunter explained.

Mackenzie continued to watch the waves crash onto the shore. "Actually, I took some PTO," Mackenzie confessed. "I'm not brave enough to face him yet."

"Don't give yourself a hard time about that. You have to do what works best for you. Since you are home, are you up for some company? I am at the coffee shop you raved about. My treat," He offered.

Mac debated for a beat before she answered.

"Sure, I will be there in five."

Mackenzie walked into the small cafe, smelling the comforting whiff of coffee. Beach Beans had been her go-to spot for a while now. She waved over at the barista, who merely nodded, then proceeded to make Mac's drink. Everyone who worked here knew Mac. Her café au lait' order was always the same. She looked in the far corner, spotting Hunter seated at one of the four small tables that had a row of chairs on one side and a wall bench running down the other. Mackenzie felt her face warm, noticing he was staring at a painting in front of him.

Mac slid into the booth, turning her head to look at the wide canvas. It was an oil piece, the style somewhere between painterly and impressionist, of a popular alleyway along the boardwalk with street vendor stalls nestled between two buildings.

"What do you think of it?" Mac asked.

Hunter continued to look up, examining it. "I think it's great, seriously. How long ago did you paint it?" Hunter asked.

Mac's eyes widened, looking at him in surprise.

Hunter chuckled, pointing at the bottom left-hand corner.

"Your initials are right there. It's interesting; most painters have their initials on the right side," Hunter commented.

Just then, a barista came and dropped off her drink.

"Taking the day off?" they asked.

"Hey, Maggie. Yup, taking a breather," Mac answered.

"Cool, tell Sam to stop being a stranger; we haven't seen him in forever," Maggie said before walking away.

Mac gave her a tight smile, looking back at Hunter.

"I sign everything on the left side of my paintings because my uncle was left-handed. It's my own little tribute to him," Mac explained.

Hunter nodded, then cocked his head toward the barista, "that's going to happen a lot, isn't it?"

Mac sighed, shrugging her shoulders as she rested her arms on the table, framing her drink between them. "I guess I need to get used to it," Mac muttered. "Maybe that's why I took some PTO. Gives me some time to digest it and, well, I'm being a total coward. I don't know if I can see Sam right now." Mac felt a painful hollow sensation in the center of her chest, thinking about what had happened the previous day.

"I can't imagine how that must feel," Hunter said, taking a sip of his drink.

"It feels, like, really minuscule compared to what you are going through," Mac whispered, then looked around.

"Ollie lurking somewhere?" she asked.

Hunter laughed and shook his head. "He's having breakfast with his husband, Parker, at the hotel. I am not a spoiled tyrant; I can walk down to a coffee shop all on my own and stuff," Hunter winked.

"Touché," Mac took another sip and then a bigger gulp since her drink had cooled off.

"I had six weeks in the bank anyway. I needed to take some of it off, or else I would stop accruing it. I haven't taken time off in the three years I have been there. I was saving it for wedding planning and the honeymoon," Mackenzie explained, looking out the window. "Which obviously isn't happening now. I guess I need time to figure out how to rewire my brain and my heart, right?" she asked.

Hunter finished off his drink then cocked his head to the side.

"Then you should do something productive with your time," Hunter said, crossing his arms in front of him.

Mackenzie nodded in agreement, looking out at the street again, trying to figure out how she was going to deal with everything. She turned back toward her painting above them, remembering how confident she felt as she brought her vision, stroke by brushstroke, onto the canvas. She wanted to feel that way again: brave and determined. Mackenzie knew she had it in her to pick herself back up. She just had to figure out how. Straightening her spine, she spun her head around looking over at Hunter.

"You eat an elephant one bite at a time, right?" Mac declared, holding her mug up. "So, what's on Hunter's docket today?" Hunter gave her a smirk, pulling out his phone and typing something in.

"That depends on the next two answers you give me," he said, still looking at something on his phone.

"Okay, I'll bite. Hit me," Mac said confidently.

"Question number one: do you have a passport?" Hunter asked, looking up at her.

Mackenzie nodded slowly. She had gotten it in case she and Sam wanted to drive into Canada while they were on their honeymoon. That was, of course, if she could convince Sam to go to Niagara Falls.

"Awesome!" Hunter exclaimed his accent sounded a little thicker. "Second question: how quick can you pack?" he asked.

"Why?" Mac asked, looking at him dumbfounded.

Hunter just smiled, not looking up from his phone-swiping and, from the looks of it, shooting off a text.

"Why else? We are going to knock number two off your list."

Chapter 10

MACKENZIE

“This is all some weird fever dream I am having, right?” Mackenzie asked Hunter.

Mackenzie still couldn’t believe what she was doing. The whole thing felt unreal. Yet, there she was on a plane, sitting in first class, in a convertible seat that could turn into a bed, looking over at Hunter. She leaned over a bit more to see Ollie sitting on his other side.

“This is crazy,” she said, shaking her head.

Hunter laughed while leaning back in his seat.

“I mean, this whole thing is bizarre, right?” Hunter teased, mimicking her statement from last night.

It took her exactly 11 minutes to pack. Then, she spent an hour debating whether or not she needed to seek professional help. Who in their right mind would get on a plane with zero notice and with someone they barely knew? Yet, there she was, listening to the sound of the whooshing wind against the plane she had boarded a few hours ago. How they got on this flight the same day was beyond her comprehension.

"If I were you, Ms. Almazan, I would just go with it."

Hunter leaned back, closing his eyes for a second before turning to Mackenzie again.

"So, Mackenzie. That's a really unique name," Hunter commented.

Mackenzie nodded, returning his gaze.

"My uncle was afraid that my mother would give me a name that was a derivative of Mary, Rosa, or some other super Filipino name," she laughed, "he told me that when he came to the States, the first thing he saw on TV was this sitcom called One Day At a Time. One of the actresses was named Mackenzie. He said he always liked how it wasn't a common name."

"Your uncle named you?" Hunter asked.

Mackenzie nodded, taking a sip of her water. Ollie had told them they had to keep drinking water the entire time they were up in the air. Mackenzie complied to ensure Hunter would do the same.

"Can I ask how you ended up with your uncle?" Hunter said quietly.

Mackenzie gave Hunter a reassuring smile letting him know it was okay to inquire. She was asked that question a lot, and to most people she responded with a quick and vague answer. She decided to give Hunter an in-depth reason.

"My parents are still alive. They just had other ideas for their lives. My uncle came to the States first, and then my mom followed him after she got her nursing degree. She met my father shortly after. They got married, but you know that song, Papa Was A Rolling Stone?" Mackenzie questioned.

Hunter nodded, taking a sip of his drink.

"That was my father. My mother tried to hold on to him, but he was a heavy gambler and drinker. When I popped out, and I was not of the male persuasion, he bolted and found someone else to give him a son," Mackenzie said.

"Shit, Mackenzie, that's horrible," Hunter said.

"My mom had severe postpartum depression. She had trouble bonding with me. It's funny because usually it goes the other way. Filipino children get sent back to the Philippines if their mom and dad can't take care of them here. Then come back and live with an aunt or uncle when they get older. My mother went back home to the Philippines, and I stayed. There were other factors. To be perfectly honest, I heard she was embarrassed because I had a Morena skin tone.

"Morena?" Hunter asked. Mackenzie held her arm up, pointing at her forearm with her other hand.

"Darker skin. Filipinos typically have Mestiza skin, which is lighter, showing one has some European blood somewhere in their line. Then there's Chinita, which...well, it's in the name, right?" Mackenzie explained, pointing to him.

Hunter looked down at his arm and nodded in confirmation.

"And then Morena," she held up her arm again. I pretty much just have to think about the sun, and I tan quickly," she joked. "My uncle was Moreno, too. Anyway, my mom decided to go back to the Philippines to recover and be with the family, and then never came back. She got a nursing contract in the UK, then got remarried and had a son. When I was growing up, she would occasionally call or write. I haven't heard from her since I was eighteen."

Mackenzie watched Hunter's eyes go wide.

"Fuck, now I feel like an asshole for asking," Hunter muttered.

Mackenzie chuckled, "It's okay; it doesn't bother me. It bothered my uncle, though. He pretty much wrote off our entire family. He told me he had lived through their prejudice his whole life and didn't want me to deal with that. So, it was always just me and him. I didn't know what normal," she held up her fingers, making air quotes," was supposed to look like. Sam grew up in a single-parent household, too. It wasn't like I was peering through windows wishing for a mom and dad."

"The whole skin tone thing I get. Chinese beauty standards are the same. I hate that I get what you're talking about," Hunter sighed in disappointment.

"Like I told you before, I left the US and went back to China for school. Living with family and friends when your parents were overseas wasn't abnormal there. A lot of kids lived with close friends or relatives other than their parents," Hunter said.

Mackenzie looked out the window and then back at Hunter, pulling in her lips and twisting her mouth to the side in indecision. She didn't want him to feel like it was tit for tat every time she talked about an aspect of her life. Hunter smiled over at her.

"I was at graduate school at Oxford when my parents were killed," Hunter said quietly, knowing she was going to ask. "It was harder for my sister than it was for me. I mentioned I was a late-life child, right?" Hunter asked.

Mac nodded in response.

"For as long as I could remember, it was my sister that took care of me. Even before she got sick, they worked all the time, so Xiǎng was the one picking me up from school, helping me with homework, and making sure I was fed. Then she got sick, and we went to the U.S. I got sent back to China when I was thirteen. I didn't spend that much time with them, so I get what you mean about not really having a typical relationship with your parents," Hunter offered.

"Did you decide on Hunter for your English name, or was it your parents?" she asked.

"It was a negotiation between my parents," Hunter chuckled. "My father wanted to name me Hēng tè. It's Mandarin Chinese Pinyin for the name 'Hunter.' My mother put her foot down. She said it sounded too violent. She chose Chaoxiang. It means expecting fortune. I think she chose it because she thought it would be cute to have my sister's name at the end of mine," he explained.

"When we moved to the U.S., my dad insisted that my English name be Hunter."

"Do you guys have ridiculous childhood nicknames like us?" Mackenzie asked, turning to her side and leaning a bit closer.

Hunter gave her a weary look, nodding slowly.

"Shing-Shing," he said quietly, coughing and clearing his throat.

"That isn't a bad one," Mackenzie said.

She watched as Hunter turned to his side, looking at her, holding out his hand, waiting for Mackenzie to return in kind.

"Zie-Zie," she confessed.

Hunter nodded.

"What's up with the repeated one-syllable nicknames?" he asked.

"It's like they thought their kids didn't hear them the first time, so they had to repeat themselves," Mackenzie offered.

"Because what, we would listen better? If anything, I always wanted to ignore it. Even if it meant having a slipper hurled at my head," Hunter confessed.

"That's a thing for you, too?" Mackenzie squealed.

"Yeah, I don't know about you, but it sharpened my reflexes. I crush at ducking for cover," Hunter said proudly, pretending to brush imaginary dust off his shoulder.

They looked at each other for a moment, then laughed hysterically for a good while, so loud and long that Ollie looked over at them. Mackenzie realized her laugh was echoing, then stopped quickly.

Hunter shook his head. "Don't do that, your laugh is great, it's infectious," he said. Mackenzie straightened up, shrugging her shoulders. She was never good at taking compliments.

"Thanks, but seriously, some of the nicknames are really terrible. My Uncle had a friend that called his son Jefrox."

"Jefrox?" Hunter exclaimed. "Was his name Jeff?"

"No, it was Lito," Mackenzie said, trying to hold in her laughter.

"What?" Hunter squeaked, looking over at her. Both resumed their hysterical laughter, uncaring if their fellow passengers stared.

Mackenzie stood next to Oliver Barlowe, or Ollie as his friends called him, in the small lounge area on the plane, the two of them looking over at Hunter sleeping.

Mackenzie turned toward the tall, muscular man with a shaggy, curly brown mop and trim beard. He wasn't what she expected when Hunter said he had an assistant. At first, they were making small talk across the aisle, but then they noticed that Hunter had drifted to sleep. Ollie pointed to the lounge, wanting to continue getting to know each other without disturbing Hunter. Ollie told Mackenzie how he met his husband, Parker.

He even pulled out his phone to show Mackenzie his wallpaper image of the two of them at their wedding. It was a picture of Ollie with a tall, devastatingly handsome, deep ebony-skinned man. Ollie told her Parker was born and raised in Inglewood and graduated from Howard Law. He wanted to be an estate lawyer and was also close to Hunter. "Hunter hired Parker to assist in managing his estate," Ollie said.

"Parker does not have the luxury of just taking off the way we did. He had to stay in LA to take care of a few things for Hunter." They both quieted for a moment. Ollie didn't need to explain the whys.

Mackenzie told him about Sam. Giving him a condensed version of what happened between them. She wasn't sure how much Hunter had shared. She knew he had heard them at the restaurant.

"How long have you been working for Hunter?" Mackenzie asked, still looking over at her sleeping friend.

"Six years. He hired me when his sister got sick. I'm actually an LPN," Ollie explained. "I took care of Xiāng for two years. After she passed away, Hunter offered way more money to be his assistant than most licensed practical nurses were making anywhere. Being an LPN, unfortunately, came in handy when Hunter got sick. He found out almost a year after his sister passed away. She died four months before the Covid lockdown. Hunter found out three months after the lockdown ended," Ollie said, quietly looking at his employer.

Mackenzie could see the sadness in his eyes. She already had guessed that Ollie and Parker were like family to Hunter.

"Did you go with him when he was working on his list?" Mackenzie asked, trying to lighten the mood as best she could.

Ollie nodded and chuckled. "It's a pretty savage list, but it certainly makes for some great adventures. It's fun," Ollie confessed.

Mackenzie looked over at Ollie, suddenly worried that he thought she had ulterior motives.

"Ollie, I want you to know I didn't ask him for any of this. Please know I'm not taking advantage of him," Mackenzie pleaded, seeing Hunter turn in his sleep, his blanket falling to the floor. Ollie quickly left the lounge to pick up Hunter's blanket and cover him again. He bent down, feeling Hunter's forehead, and then made his way back to Mackenzie.

"I know Hunter. He never does anything he doesn't want to. I heard him on the phone with you, convincing you to get on the plane. So, no, I don't think you are taking advantage of him," Ollie said, reassuring her.

Mackenzie let out a breath of relief as they returned their watch. She felt Ollie's arm come around her, pulling her into a sideways hug. Mackenzie accepted it, feeling Ollie stiffen a bit. She looked up at him, seeing him gulp hard with eyes watering up.

"If anything, Mac, I'm grateful to you. More than you know."

Chapter 11

SAM

Sam took a deep breath, got out of his SUV, and made his way up the stairs of his mother's trailer. Sam saw his mom sitting on her white, shabby-chic patio chair, smiling over at him. He smelt the habitual scent of pot smoke coming from her direction.

Clover Madden marched to the beat of her own drum. She had opened one of the first yoga studios in Venice Beach. Jewish, vegan, and a believer in the healing power of crystals (though not to the point where she disregarded modern medicine), she meditated every morning and always made it a point to call her son once a day.

While Clover was a free spirit, she was also the best mother in the world as far as Sam and Mackenzie were concerned. Sam smiled over at her. She was the embodiment of 'mother earth'. Long blonde hair, wearing a bohemian dress with Birkenstocks on her feet as she smoked a joint on a long silver holder.

He saw his mother look at the weekender bag in his hand then look up toward Sam's car.

"Mac busy with wedding stuff?" Clover asked, sitting back down

Once a month, Sam and Mac would come to Clover's place after work on Fridays and spend the night with her in the Malibu retirement community of manufactured homes and trailers.

Clover had long closed her studio and now taught private classes and meditation sessions. Mac and Sam never knew if they would walk into her house and see the dining room table set up for Shabbat or Clover doing tai chi in the living room.

Sam gripped his bag, gulping hard as he sat down. He let out a heavy breath.

"Mom, Mac broke up with me," Sam whispered, closing his eyes and bracing himself for his mother's reaction. As far as Clover Madden was concerned, Mackenzie hung the moon. He waited for hysterics; instead, he was met with silence and an even stronger scent of pot.

He opened his eyes to see the joint in his mother's hand right in front of him.

"You probably need this, then."

Sam took it, taking a hard toke before exhaling and closing his eyes, waiting for the high to kick in. Sam rarely smoked. In fact, he only smoked with his mother. The irony of that not lost to him. Most kids hide smoking from their parents. Clover didn't encourage it; however, she made no secret about it. He handed it back to his mother, watching her put it back in the long silver holder before taking another hit.

"This is not the reaction I was expecting," Sam commented. "Don't tell me you saw it coming."

Clover shook her head, reaching across the small table to squeeze his arm.

"Of course not, son, but at the same time, I am not as shocked as you thought I would be," Clover explained. "Things between the two of you have been different for the last year. In fact, I thought you would drag your feet as far as the wedding was concerned."

"Let me guess, you are going to lay into me about how I have been treating Mac," he groaned, rubbing his face.

Clover chuckled, shaking her head and getting a far-off look in her eyes. "Do you remember when you were fifteen? You came running into the studio, begging me to close up and come back to Uncle Deano's with you. Mackenzie had locked herself in her bathroom crying because she got her period for the first time."

Sam's head snapped to the side, his eyes widening. Clover always referenced events from the past to talk through any difficulties. Still, mentioning this particular memory stunned him.

"Mom, that's a weird thing to bring up, don't you think?" Sam said in surprise.

"You ran out of Uncle Deano's house as soon as we got there, saying you would be right back. I was talking to Mackenzie through the door, trying to get her to open it up when you came back with a grocery bag with maxi pads. Most guys, especially teenage boys, are embarrassed to buy the damn things. Not you; you went as far as buying three different sizes. Mac was scared and needed you. You have always been that way with her. I always knew you cared for her, but that's when I realized just how much. She was everything to you." Clover sighed, smiling wistfully.

"The intensity of your feelings for her makes any sort of disregard concerning. To be honest, you have been acting differently for a while. I can see this is torturing you, so there's no reason to make you feel worse than you already do. "

Sam crossed his arms in front of him.

"I messed up. I made her feel like she wasn't good enough for me in front of some co-workers," Sam explained.

Clover pursed her lips, making a "om" sound."She's hurt."

Sam nodded."She won't even talk to me."

Clover reached over to him, giving his arm another squeeze." You understand why, right?"

Sam nodded, then looked out toward the ocean."I don't know why I did it. Who could be ashamed of Mac? She had to know that wasn't the case. She knows me better than that," Sam argued.

"Does she?" Clover asked.

"Mom, of course, she does."

Clover took another hit from her joint. "Do *you*?" she challenged.

He looked over at Clover, confused for a moment, slowly he realized she was asking if he himself knew who he had become.

Sam blinked a few times, taking in what his mother had just asked. Did he know who he was now?

"She knows Sam, the guy whose world revolved around her. It was like the two of you were in this secret club to which none of us were privy. You told me you went back and got your Master's in Finance to work your way up the corporate ladder faster because you promised Deano you would always take care of her. It was like the two of you were the extension of each other. Maybe that's not who you are anymore."

Clover reached across the table, resting her hand on his cheek. "You were always so serious and responsible growing up. You prided yourself on it. There's nothing wrong with that. For the first time in your life, you are doing something big, and Mac isn't at the center of it," Clover said. "It's okay that you are different from who you were growing up, my dear boy. Right now, you need to figure out where Mac fits in your world. Ask yourself honestly why you acted the way you did. If you don't, and she comes back to you, you will only hurt her again."

Sam reached over and took another hit of his mother's joint.

"Do you think she is doing the same? Trying to figure out all of this?" Sam asked.

Clover sighed."Mac always puts on a brave face. I think this time she can't. Not to rub salt in the wound, but you were always the person that she ran to when something hurt her. You're in uncharted waters. I think she can't talk to you because she knows she would give in to you. She knows if she does, then it's like saying it's okay for you to treat her like you did," Clover said as she leaned back in her chair.

Sam rested his elbows on his legs, lowering his head. The high beginning to kick in harder. He felt a hollow sensation creeping into his chest. He let out a broken breath.

Sam heard Clover get up from her seat. He could feel her walk over to him. Sam looked up as his mother hunched down in front of him.

"Figure out what you want. Is Mac really your future or just what you are used to?"

Clover challenged, pressing her hands on top of his thighs.

"I love her, mom, it's the one thing I am sure of. I would do anything for Mac."

Clover squeezed his legs, getting his attention. She looked into his eyes, giving him a sad smile. Sam immediately knew whatever she was going to say would hurt them both. Him, hearing it and her, having to say it. She reached up, stroking his hair, comforting him. She gulped, then whispered.

"Then let her go, for now."

Chapter 12

MACKENZIE

Giddy wasn't the word she would use. Elation was more like it. Her heart began to pound just as hard as it did when she first saw the Eiffel Tower from the town car earlier that day as they drove into Paris from Charles de Gaulle Airport. Hunter told Mackenzie he had been to Paris a few times in the past.

He'd asked their driver to take them straight to the Arc de Triomphe. He laughed at Mackenzie as she stuck her face out the window, gawking at the Arc de Triomphe de l'Étoile. She remembered grabbing Hunter's hand when she got close to the Eiffel Tower. He mussed up her hair playfully as she felt her eyes water.

Mackenzie had trouble even walking into the Four Seasons. She'd nearly swallowed her tongue when they were led to the Eiffel Tower Suite— a two-bedroom, two-bathroom suite aptly named for its breathtaking view of Paris's most iconic landmark. She stood nervously in the shared living room space.

"Would it make you feel better if I said I tried to get the Prince de Galles, but it was already fully booked for the night?" Hunter questioned.

"It's the most expensive hotel in Paris," Ollie offered.

Mackenzie's eyes widened, and she let out an "eep" sound that made Hunter laugh. Hunter led her to the balcony showing her the view of Paris. He stood next to her, pointing out different points of interest, trying to distract her from the grandeur of their accommodations.

It was night as they walked into the plaza underneath the Eiffel Tower. The light on the top of the tower shone brightly into the sky. They got into the elevator that ran up the middle of the iconic structure, getting out on the second floor. It was surprisingly sparse of tourists tonight. They took a lap around the viewing platform, seeing the city from every side.

Hunter stopped, looked around, and clapped his hands once.

"Perfect!" He exclaimed, pulling Mackenzie to him. He took out his phone and started to scroll through his music app.

"Okay, what song?" He asked, holding his phone to her.

"It should be romantic and slow, right?" She asked, looking through the app.

"Why? It should match how you feel at this moment. Then, skyrocket you into bliss," Hunter said dramatically.

Mac turned to Ollie, who was at present pulling out a small Bluetooth Speaker.

"He can be poetic," Ollie teased.

Mac smiled, typing in something, then handed it back to him. Hunter looked down at his phone and smiled.

"That's amazing," he beamed, playing the song she chose, cranking the volume all the way up.

Handing his phone to Ollie, Hunter held out his hands to Mackenzie and led her into a dance. Mackenzie quickly realized they were doing the foxtrot.

Hunter smirked, noticing that he didn't have to instruct her on the steps.

"Pretty sure every Filipino kid has been taught at least five ballroom dances," Mackenzie said.

"It was part of a fitness campaign in Beijing," Hunter laughed.

To her surprise, Hunter began lip-synching to the song. She laughed as the sound of Neil Diamond's "Forever In Blue Jeans" played.

"How do you know Neil Diamond?" she asked.

"If you can't appreciate Neil Diamond, then we can't be friends," he chuckled.

Mackenzie looked around, noticing people beginning to smile as they watched them dance. It wasn't long before they started cheering. Hunter spun her out and let go. She bumped into the elevator attendant. Just as she was about to apologize, he looked down, taking her in his arms, turning them a few times. He held out his hand, handing Mac off to an older Hispanic woman. Mac twirled the woman around watching her blush playfully, hitting her shoulder.

As the song continued, a few couples started playfully dancing while others clapped along. Mac skipped around the viewing platform, doing a full lap around the elevator before heading back to where Hunter and Ollie were standing.

Hunter laughed. The look on his face was like a mixture of awe and pure happiness. He reached for Mac, pulling her phone out of her pocket and pointing it toward her.

"What's your passcode?" he asked.

Mac stopped dancing to type it in, catching her breath. She could see he was filming. Mac tried to hide her face just as a guy offered her his hand, and the two began to dance. He spun her toward Hunter, who reached out for her with one hand as he continued to film. He twirled her around, then pulled her to him, dipping her dramatically. Just then, a security guard walked up to them, telling them to stop their "unsafe antics." A few people booed as Mackenzie, Hunter, and Ollie apologized for the momentary disruption.

"Number two off your list," he whispered in her ear.

"I can't believe this is happening," she laughed breathlessly.

"That's why I filmed it for proper documentation," he quipped. The song ended, and everyone clapped, then turned back to take in the view again.

"Hunter, saying thank you seems..."

"Then don't," Hunter interrupted. "I don't need it. Seeing another one of your wildest dreams come true is enough."

It took Hunter forty-five minutes to coax a petrified Mackenzie to take the lift to the top of The Tower.

"I have horrible vertigo. If I look down, I get nauseous and dizzy," Mackenzie confessed. Hunter held her hand, helping her step to the edge.

"Then look out, not down," Hunter instructed.

After a few breathtaking moments, they headed down to the second floor again.

Mac touched the cold steel, trying to reconcile herself with the fact that she was actually touching the Eiffel Tower.

"Why Neil Diamond? Your uncle?" Hunter asked.

Mackenzie looked out toward the Arc de Triomphe. "He would always sing it when he heard it and obnoxiously point at me if I happened to be wearing jeans. He was always singing something and poking fun at me," Mackenzie said. She felt the hollowness in her chest again. The sad and helpless feeling she had tamped down. She always missed her Uncle Deano, even more so lately.

"What next?" Mac asked, taking a deep breath, still in a daze.

"We attempt to sleep, then find a café, drink coffee, and eat way too much cheese. We can walk around the rest of the day and do whatever you want. Our flight leaves early the next morning. Oh, by the way," he said, holding out his hand to Ollie. Ollie handed him Mac's list and a pen.

"Put a line through it," Hunter said, looking down at her list.

"We heading back to US soil?" She asked, holding her list in her hand as she crossed off number two.

Hunter gave her an incredulous look. Dramatically swiping the card from Mackenzie and handing it back to Ollie.

"Hell no, we are going to cross number three off your list next."

Chapter 13

SAM

Sam didn't mean to pry; he just happened to see Bianca leaning against the counter of the break room, chuckling softly as she looked down at her phone.

He went about making his coffee, trying to figure out a subtle way to ask Bianca about Mac. It had been four days since she left for wherever she was. He hadn't gone four days without hearing from Mackenzie since high school.

Sam had stopped at her place on the way back home from his Mom's house. He stood outside, looking up at her balcony. Mackenzie was a notoriously early riser, always opening the sliding glass door of her balcony first thing. Her car was parked under the carport, and the door was closed. He knew she wasn't there.

Sam thought about what his mother said about giving Mac space. Still, he couldn't help but check on her place, hoping to see her. He attempted to keep himself busy. Yet, at night, when it was just him lying there, all he thought about was Mac. Was she okay? Did he shatter her heart? Or worse, had she become indifferent to him?

He dialed her number a few times, knowing she wouldn't answer but still hoping she would. For all intents and purposes, Mac had gone silent, only talking to or texting Bianca.

Just then, he heard Mac's laugh, and his heart started pounding. He looked over just as Bianca turned toward him. Thrusting her phone in front of him. It was a short video Mac must have sent her.

In it, he saw Mac laughing; it was night, and she seemed to be on some sort of overlook he couldn't quite place. Someone was spinning her around and around. As the crowd laughed, he heard people cheering her on, speaking what sounded like French. In the background, he caught a glimpse of what he thought to be the Arch de Triumph behind Mac as she spun. He looked down at Bianca, shocked as he realized what the steel structure was.

"She's in Paris?" he asked in disbelief.

"It would seem so."

He watched as Mac giggled, dancing with various men and women. The phone wobbled for a moment as he saw a man's arm stretch out, taking her hand to spin her a few times before dipping her dramatically. Hearing him laugh as he steadied Mac. Mackenzie wanted to go to Paris for their honeymoon, to see the view of the Eiffel Tower at night, and to walk around aimlessly, taking in the sights. She was a romantic at heart. He knew that. He thought it was too cliché. Instead, he convinced her to go to Manhattan even though she was a Southern Californian girl. He had pointed out that they could go to the Met while they were there, knowing she had agreed because that's what he wanted to do.

As the video stopped, Bianca started it over again, almost as if she was pouring salt into a wound.

"Do you know him? Is she okay?" he asked lamely.

Bianca put her phone away, tucking it into her back pocket.

"No, I don't. Again, obviously."

Sam could tell she knew more than she was saying. He had known Bianca since college. He still remembered the day Bianca and Mackenzie met. Bianca and Sam were study partners after discovering they both wanted to get into the Anderson School of Finance at UCLA to get their MBA in Corporate Finance.

One night, he got a call from Bianca saying she was in West Hollywood and was a bit too drunk. She told Sam she felt a little unsafe, asking if he could pick her up. Mac and Sam got into his old beat-up Honda and made their way to Weho. It was best friend kismet right from the get-go when it came to Mackenzie and Bianca. They talked about everything from football to Project Runway, joking about how they were making Sam miserable as they sat at Canter's helping Bianca get sober.

Sam knew that when Bianca lied, she would get overly aggressive like she was now. It should comfort him that Bianca seemed to not be concerned for Mac. All he felt, though, was good, old-fashioned jealousy. Mac always teased him about being carved out of marble. She didn't realize how beautiful she was. Guys would look at her all the time; she just never paid enough attention to realize. The foreign feeling of being truly jealous burned through him.

He gripped his mug until his knuckles turned white. The smug look on Bianca's face made it even worse.

Sam began to walk out the door. Suddenly, Bianca spoke, stopping him in his tracks.

"I remember the night you proposed. You told us it had to be at the Griffith Park Observatory. You said everything needed to be perfect for her. Ezra and I got there an hour before to shoo people away from her favorite spot. Mac always said it had the best view of the Hollywood sign. You had to have a single white rose lay on top of the wall. Made us pack it in an ice chest so it wouldn't turn brown. It was like you were running fire drills preparing us for it. Mac looked like she was going to faint when you got down on one knee."

He turned toward her. Expecting venom, instead, he saw hurt and confusion.

"You were a man possessed. You were never nervous, just excited. You wanted to make that moment unforgettable. You told me Mac had a lot of bad in her life, so it had to be the best that you could offer her. You said you wanted her to walk away the happiest she had ever been, hoping that it dulled a little of the pain she had suffered. God, I admired you for that," Bianca whispered, shaking her head.

"We made bets on which one of you would crack and start crying first. I won because I said it would be you. You knew how incredibly lucky you were to have Mac."

"What happened to that guy, Sam?" she asked, her voice getting small. "Was it the job? The paycheck? The recognition? People suddenly paying attention to you?" Her eyes glanced toward Clarissa's office across from Sam's.

Sam could not help but feel disappointed in himself. Bianca's opinion of him meant the world to him. He admired and respected her. Bianca wasn't judgmental. He couldn't fault her for being that way now. He knew everything she said was the truth. Obviously, he had let her down.

"Once upon a time, you were like my big brother. We have gone through so much together. Still a drop in the bucket in comparison to Mac. No one would have blamed you if you said you wanted to take a break and figure things out. You guys have been in each other's lives since you were kids. I warned you that people in the office were making assumptions. If Mac caught wind of it, she would feel insecure. I tried to say something to you, but you always brushed me off," she paused, " Sam, let me ask you a question?" Looking up at him for a moment. "Are you upset that you hurt Mac or that you got caught?"

Sam stood there saying nothing, shocked.

He watched as Bianca took a sip of her coffee, looking down into her mug. It felt as if she did not want to look at him. It dawned on him how much his actions hurt Bianca, not only because of Mac. At that moment, the gut punching question and unwillingness to even raise her head to meet his eyes cemented the fact that Bianca had lost all faith in him.

"When you and I grew apart, I told myself as long as you loved Mac, it was fine. I thought there would be no way you could hurt her. Not like this. But things change, right?" she finished, turning to top off her coffee before walking out the door.

Sam leaned against the counter, rubbing his hands over his face. He knew in his heart the answer to Bianca's question was that he had hurt Mac. Hating that Bianca felt that he had sunk that low.

However, he could see where she was coming from. The truth of the matter was he never outright questioned their decision to get married right now. But it lingered in the back of his head. He didn't want to admit to himself that he was comfortable being work-driven and admired by his peers. In fact, he liked it immensely. Sam had stopped asking Mackenzie to go to dinners and events more than six months ago. He had told himself Mackenzie would be bored, that his talking about work would make her feel excluded. The reasons now sounded lame in his mind.

He thought back to the drives home they would have, going back and forth from his Mom's house. Mac and Sam used to have silly conversations and make jokes as they drove. They talked about everything from music to movies, laughing the entire way down the Pacific Coast Highway.

Lately, he would be listening to finance podcasts while Mackenzie played games on her phone. The truth that they were in different places in life sunk down deep into his stomach.

Still, he never thought he would be here, getting information about Mackenzie from a third party. Then again, he never thought he would be embarrassed by her either.

Chapter 14

MACKENZIE

Mackenzie walked out of her bedroom into the hotel suite's luxurious living area early the next morning. The sun was just starting to rise. She was pretty sure she had jet lag; either that or being in Paris was giving her a series of adrenaline rushes.

She kept getting up to look out the window or walk out onto the balcony just to see the Eiffel Tower. Ollie had come out a few times to get water or a snack, apparently having trouble sleeping as well.

Ollie opened the door to the set of rooms Hunter was sharing with him. He looked up and saw Mackenzie standing there.

"Hey, Hunter is feeling a bit worn out. He says you shouldn't wait for him. Get out there and enjoy the city," he said, giving Mackenzie a tight smile.

Mackenzie walked closer to the second room in the suite. She could see a silver IV stand next to the bed with what she knew to be saline dripping down into the line. Mackenzie stopped beside Ollie, looking towards him, silently asking for permission to enter the bedroom. Ollie nodded and made his way toward the bar.

In theory, Mackenzie knew Hunter was sick. However, seeing him lying there, eyes closed, breathing a bit labored, drove it home. For the first time, she noticed the hollowness of his cheeks and the dark rings around his eyes. The buzz-cut hair now made more sense. She briefly wondered just how long it had been since he had stopped chemotherapy.

"What are you doing standing there?" His eyes briefly opened, meeting hers. "Get out there and annoy some French people."

Mackenzie plopped down on the bed, lying across the end of it. "So, jet lag is real," Mackenzie said, crossing her arms and laying her head down on them. "I've actually never been anywhere that would cause me to have jet lag. Unlike you," she teased.

Hunter looked down at her, giving her a weak smile.

"Here's the thing I was just thinking: you have seen my list, but we've never talked about yours," Mackenzie stated. "Tell me one of your wildest dreams. You said you were working on number four. What was number one?"

"Ziplining through the Amazon," Hunter answered.

"Whoa...I would faint," Mackenzie chuckled. "How was it?"

"I went to Iquitos, Peru. Did the canopy walk first to really see everything."

"I would never make it across," Mac laughed.

"Look out, not down, remember?" Hunter reminded her. "For a second, I felt like I was on a movie set because it looked so unreal."

Mackenzie watched Hunter close his eyes, smiling at the memory.

"Going down the zipline felt like I was flying. Looking down at the trees in the jungle was the closest thing to euphoria that I ever felt," Hunter said softly.

He looked down at her. She yawned, closing her eyes. "Let me try to get some sleep so I don't look like the walking dead. Then, I will do some gallivanting," she said

Hunter shook his head, playfully glaring at her.

"You forgot I'm a pro at this. Been on your side of things. Don't feel bad or guilty. Please don't feel obligated to post up here," Hunter asked.

Mackenzie smiled up at him. "Then you are well aware I am not going to go anywhere," she said, closing her eyes.

They laid there in a comfortable silence. Both understood the gravity of the situation. They had been through this with the people that meant the most to them in this world.

"Hey, Mac?" she heard him say.

"Hm?" she responded, opening her eyes.

Hunter smiled again. "Thanks," he whispered before he drifted off into sleep.

Hunter felt a bit better later that afternoon.

He insisted that they go to Montmartre. While it was a popular tourist neighborhood, it was still a must see. He said it's how most people envisioned Paris to look like. Mackenzie felt like she was in a dream. She was actually standing in a place that once was home to Vincent van Gogh, Renoir, and Toulouse-Lautrec.

On top of that, there were live artists painting, cobblestone streets, and the white-domed Basilica of the Sacré-Cœur.

"Are you aching to stand in front of one of those easels?" Hunter teased.

"Dear God, no. When I painted, it was always in a hidden place where no one could see. I'm not bold enough to paint in front of others," Mackenzie replied.

"Something tells me you're lying to yourself," Hunter smirked.

Hunter dragged her to 53 rue des Trois Frères to take pictures in the famous photo booth. The four photos looked like a chaotic mess. None of them had caught them looking at the camera. The only black and white photo that looked somewhat clear was a picture of the two of them looking at each other and laughing as Hunter had his hand on the top of her head, messing up her hair.

They sat at a street-corner café, people-watching, eating over-priced crepes, and sipping the best hot chocolate she'd ever tasted.

"You're avoiding the elephant in the café," Hunter teased as they sat side by side nursing their hot chocolates.

Hunter peered over, waiting for her to respond. Mackenzie gave him a small smile. She hadn't mentioned Sam since they arrived in Paris.

However, he was never far from her thoughts. Every time she thought of him, all her emotions jumbled up: hurt, pain, confusion, but never anger. She wasn't angry at Sam. Nothing in this world could make Mackenzie stop loving Sam, which led back to her feeling confused.

"I let Bianca know I am okay. I know she'll tell Sam," Mackenzie said, reassuring him.

"You had mentioned you knew Sam growing up. How long ago did you meet?" Hunter asked.

"We've known each other since I was eight."

"Jesus, that long?"

Mackenzie nodded, wrapping her hands around her hot chocolate.

"Known each other is putting it lightly. We were at the center of each other's worlds. Believe it or not, I haven't gone this long without talking to Sam since high school."

"It has to feel weird not talking to him, then." Hunter finished off his hot chocolate, his eyes fixed on her. Mackenzie looked toward the Basilica of the Sacré-Cœur. Her silence must have been affirmation enough because Hunter changed the subject.

"So, how was it growing up like that? With someone you ended up engaged to. Did you always think, or hope, you would get married?"

"It was strange because we never thought about the future and doubted we would be in each other's lives. I think everyone assumed we were a forever sort of thing. I never imagined Sam falling for me. He's been my anchor my entire life. Telling you our entire story would take more than an afternoon sitting here eating brie and drinking hot chocolate," Mackenzie teased.

"I would say I have time if I did," Hunter said with a smirk. She shook her head, already used to his dark humor.

"You said he was your anchor. I assume it was because of your uncle, right?"

Mackenzie shook her head.

"It was before then. Sam had this sixth sense or something. He somehow was always there to stop me from falling or catch me if I did. It was during high school. We went to LACES, the Los Angeles Center for Enriched Studies. Sam, of course, was a genius, so he was in AP classes. I was with the peons and took art electives, so we didn't have any classes together. If there was ever a time we drifted apart before, it was in high school. I made a friend named Jenni. We bonded because both of us were considered the school freaks."

She looked down at her mug, taking a deep breath.

"Sam was a grade ahead of me, and a lot changed when he went to high school while I was still in middle school. I didn't see him as much that year. That was the start of us drifting apart. Then, the next year, when I got to high school, all the girls hated me and called me a freak and a weirdo. I figured out it was because a lot of the neighborhood kids went to LACES, too, so they knew that growing up, Sam and I were stuck together like glue.

They must have mentioned me and how close we were because almost from day one, girls would point and sneer and talk under their breath every time Jenni and I walked by. I didn't even try to talk to Sam in school. I didn't dare tell him what was going on. I know he would have defended me. I thought it would just make things worse for Jenni and me, with every girl in our high school trying to snatch him up. We were basically strangers for a while."

Mackenzie took a deep breath, "One day, I was sitting in class, and I looked out the doorway. Sam was standing there, motioning for me to come out. The look on his face made my heart sink. He was devastated. I tried to mouth him from my desk, but I couldn't leave. Then the loudspeaker announced that there had been a car accident and to keep good thoughts and prayers for Jenni and her family. I don't remember running out of the room. I just remember Sam holding out his arms and hugging me tight. I just stood there, stunned. I didn't cry—I guess I was in a state of disbelief. I barely remember the funeral, honestly. I just remember Sam standing behind me, his arms wrapped around my waist, holding me as tight as he could. Which was a good thing because my legs gave out a few times."

She looked over at Hunter, shrugging her shoulders.

"After that, he was stuck to my side like glue. I think he knew I was on the verge of falling into the abyss. He once told me he would have jumped in there after me if I did. Like I said, he was my anchor," Mackenzie finished, looking away for a moment.

"Damn, Mac, you've dealt with a lot of loss," Hunter said.

"I mean, pot calling the kettle black, right?" Mackenzie winked, giving him a grin.

Hunter chuckled, heaving a little. Mackenzie crossed her arms in front of her chest. She knew he felt bad about her sitting in the hotel all day and worried he was pushing himself too hard. She'd decided in the short time they'd known each other that he was prideful and hated that he was growing weaker by the day.

"Hunter, maybe we should just go back home," Mackenzie suggested.

"Our flight leaves early in the morning, so don't drink any espresso. It's strong as fuck here. Like I said, we're knocking out your number three," Hunter responded, completely ignoring what she said.

Mac chuckled. "Okay, fine. Number three it is."

Chapter 15

SAM

Why had he agreed to this? Sam thought to himself. It was because he was angry and being petty. Seeing Mac in that video had done a number on him—watching her twirl around without a care in the world while he felt his heart slowly shredding with every step he took. He didn't even remember nodding in acceptance when Clarissa mentioned she had seats at an exclusive five-course gourmet dinner in Santa Monica. She'd told him her friend had bowed out, but he wasn't stupid; he knew she'd hoped he would take her up on it.

The entire office knew Bianca was being icy to him. Also, Mackenzie hadn't been around. She was somewhat of a fixture in their office. She walked over from her office building to his, often enough that her absence was noted. Especially since Mac had made it a point to get to know his co-workers. She made small talk with them if he and Bianca were held up and she had to wait around. He knew they deduced that they had broken up.

Sam tried to justify it, telling himself he needed to practice for events like this to gain more experience with the art of schmooze and whatnot. Nights like these were incredible for making contacts he might call on one day. However, Sam knew he was full of it. Sure, that was part of the reason—but mostly, it was the hurt that drove him.

The jealousy and pettiness dissipated once he got there. He had introduced himself to a few people before Clarissa veered his way. He had gotten drawn into conversations about foreign business markets and even got a few stock tips. The dinner was like nothing he had ever experienced. Mac would rather bleed out of her eyeballs than go to something like this. He was sitting at a table drinking stupidly expensive wine. The only wine Mac drank was a seven-dollar Moscato from Trader Joe's or Manischewitz when his mother decided to observe Shabbat. Things like this were a part of his career now, however. Sam felt the divide between him and Mac widen a bit more.

"How did you like the dinner, Samson?" All his business associates called him by his full name.

"It was different, thanks for inviting me. I have never been to something like this."

Clarissa smiled, looking at him, her intent clear. It made his insides twist. He truly told himself he only thought of her as a coworker. Looking over at her, now realization sunk in. He liked her flattery, her knowledge of the upper echelon of the business world. Even how she was able to work a meeting with an ease he had yet to attain.

For just a moment, he felt guilty for enjoying his evening with Mackenzie's perceived love rival.

"I go to things like this all the time. It's good networking. The next time something comes around, I'll give you a heads up."

Sam blinked a few times, returning her smile.

This was what he wanted, right? To succeed, make connections and network. At first, he told himself it was to make a comfortable life for Mac and him. So, they could go on any one of her crazy adventures, anytime they wanted.

But now there was no Mac. And if he was honest, she wasn't why he was doing this. His reasons were completely selfish. Things had always come easy for Sam. He was at the top of his class in high school and UCLA. It wasn't until he began his career that he felt truly challenged. He got a rush closing a deal. He liked the way people praised his business savvy. Working harder when the C-suite started paying attention to him. Somewhere along the line, all that had overtaken Mackenzie and their future.

Sam looked down at his wine glass, his thoughts wandering to what life would look like without Mac and with someone like Clarissa. They were like-minded and had the same goals. She would get just as immersed in work conversations the same way he did. Would Mackenzie even want to be in his life? Should he start thinking about them going their separate ways? Was that becoming a reality?

He took a sip of his wine, looking over at Clarissa, unsettled that he was envisioning a life without Mackenzie Almazan.

Sam and Clarissa said their goodbyes. For the first time ever, Clarissa reached out and gave him a hug. Instinctively, he returned it. Smelling her perfume again, feeling guilty that he might be attracted to her. She seemed to sense his shift because she gave him a sly smile as she got into her car.

Sam found himself driving past the I-405 on the ramp and through the familiar side streets only locals really knew without the assistance of GPS. Suddenly, he was in front of Mac's bungalow. All the lights were off, so he knew she wasn't there. Mac needed to sleep with a bit of light. She hated the dark. He sat in his car, looking up at the place where he had made so many memories.

First, as a kid, Uncle Deano made them adobo while they watched TV. Then, as an adult, Mac stood behind him as he did the same. Making him swear to secrecy that he would never tell anyone that he made the staple Filipino dish better than her. He never told Mackenzie that Uncle Deano taught him how to make it when he was sick, making sure he perfected it.

"She'll be sad if she never tastes this again the way she did growing up," Uncle Deano told him.

He put his hand on his chest, thinking about how disappointed the man he loved like a father would be in him now.

DeAngelo Almazan was his hero. In fact, he was the neighborhood hero. He helped a lot of the kids. He kept them out of trouble. When they did get into trouble, Uncle Deano would find a way to keep them safe, yet make them understand the consequences of their actions. He'd taught Sam what was important in life. He even talked to him about love when Sam became a teenager. Uncle Deano had known about the massive crush he had on Mackenzie.

"You'll know it's love if you hear a song and it makes you think of her," Uncle Deano teased him after one of the many times he caught Sam gazing over at a sketching Mackenzie.

Sam tried to brush him off, but Uncle Deano was right. Sam never told him that there was a song that made him think of his niece.

Starting the car, he drove the small distance to the now-empty building where Uncle Deano's record shop used to be. There were a few incarnations of businesses that inhabited the space in the last few years. Now, though, it was empty. No one is able or willing to invest in it. In fact, he had heard a major corporation was trying to buy the building but was getting pushback from the city.

He sat in his car, looking into the empty boarded-up building. His eyes tried to make out the corner where he'd spent most of his childhood. He could still see Mac dressed in her cut-off jean shorts, converse with no socks, and whatever thrift shop tank top or t-shirt she had procured.

Him, leaning against the wall, torn jeans and a white t-shirt, reading Bukowski out loud to Mac. Whispering when one of the poems hit a cuss word as she doodled designs on the white rubber sides of his Vans.

Mac still dressed the same way most of the time. And him? He couldn't remember the last time he wore Vans. Another visceral reminder of how much he had changed.

He rested his head against the car seat, looking up at the roof. He knew he'd thrown a Molotov cocktail out that had exploded his life. It killed him every time he thought about the moment Mackenzie looked up at him, asking that question.

"When did I become not good enough for your world?"
The hurt and betrayal in her eyes haunted him. Still, behind them, there was strength; she knew how to guard herself. He just never thought he would be something she had to guard herself against. Sam took a deep breath and started his car, making his way back to his high-rise apartment, still thinking about what life looked like without Mackenzie Almazan.

Chapter 16

MACKENZIE

Mackenzie tried to steady the sketchpad in her lap as she drew. She did not account for how much rocking would occur as she attempted to do number three on her list. She looked over at Hunter, trying her best to capture his side profile.

"You did not come all the way here to draw me," Hunter looked down at her, giving a playful glare.

"Sometimes artistic expression just takes over. Trying to capture the moment. You said you have never been here. The look on your face is..."

Mackenzie shrugged her shoulders, continuing to try to capture his likeness.

"I have been to Rome a few times but never here. For some reason, I thought it would be more private," Hunter laughed, looking off the side and seeing at least four gondolas pass by.

Mackenzie laughed, pausing her drawing to look around. She shook her head, going back to her sketch.

"So, it looks like number three is done," Hunter announced. "It's kinda funny that we just left a city with the same name."

"Venice to Venice," she quipped.

It still floored her that the flight from Paris to Venice was only one hour and thirty-five minutes. For some reason, she always thought they were worlds apart.

Mackenzie had bought a sketchbook and pencils before they left Paris. Hunter offered to pay for them, but Mackenzie insisted on buying them herself. He was already spending way too much on this adventure.

Getting off the plane and walking onto a water taxi was a new experience for all three of them.

Mackenzie was speechless as she tried not to gape at pointed arches and decorative details of the Venetian gothic architecture all around her. She openly gawked at the Byzantine influence of mosaics as they rode by.

"Glad you don't get seasick. Or else you would miss all of this," Hunter said, coming behind her and breaking her out of her state of awe. Startled, she jumped. They both broke out into hysterical laughter. Ollie stood behind them, shaking his head like he was a hall monitor.

Hunter held his hands up in defense upon arrival as they were ushered into the Lido Suite of The Hotel Excelsior. Mackenzie wondered if she once again looked like a fool gawking at everything around her. The hotel was opulent with Moorish architecture. The famous Lido Beach just steps away.

"It's not the most expensive suite," He promised.

Mackenzie shook her head at Hunter, glaring at him. She walked out to the balcony; the beach view, while much more majestic, reminded her of home. The water of the Adriatic Sea was shimmering in shades of blue and green. The Il fattorino who walked them to the room said they were lucky. It was a clear day, so they could make out the Venetian skyline. All three of them walked out onto the balcony to a glorious view of St. Mark's Campanile and the Doge's Palace.

They'd taken a few hours to unwind since they arrived early in the morning. Once they were rested, Hunter arranged for a gondola fairly quickly. Ollie had stayed behind waiting for Parker's arrival, and Hunter let him know he had reserved a gondola for them as well.

Mackenzie eyed Hunter as she shaded, doing linework as best she could. After a while, she put her sketchbook aside and began to enjoy the scenery.

Hunter sat across from Mackenzie, smiling at her.

The gondolier said something in Italian. She watched Hunter nod.

"He said we are going to turn and go under a few bridges."

"So, you speak French and some Italian. How many languages do you know?" Mackenzie asked.

"I speak French, Korean, and Cantonese fluently. Obviously, Mandarin and English as well."

"Were you some genius child prodigy or something?" Mackenzie teased.

Hunter lowered his head. It felt like he was shy; she had never seen him act like this before. She stared at him, things clicking in her mind. He was only thirty and had accomplished so much. His career timeline had to be extraordinary.

"All my life, I have been so focused and driven, even as a kid. Now, I wish I had lived life more. Instead of studying to prepare for it," Hunter said with regret heavy in his tone.

"Anyways, what about you? Do you speak Tagalog?" he asked.

"I was around Filipinos who spoke Cebuano, which is the dialect of Cebu. Weirdly, I understand Cebuano and Tagalog I just can't speak it. My uncle was a part of this cultural society for a few years. They had Fiesta and Novenas. He wanted me to know about our culture. He never taught me either language. He always said he wanted to leave that decision to me."

"Do you speak any other languages? What language did you take in school?" Hunter asked.

Mackenzie felt her face warm. She looked up at Hunter, biting her bottom lip.

"Mandarin," she answered softly. "Same thing, though, I understand it somewhat, but I can't speak it."

Hunter was staring at her in disbelief. "Really? You mean I could have been speaking Mandarin to you this whole time? Were you going to keep that to yourself?"

"No. It just never came up," Mackenzie smirked.

She looked down at her sketch, still not happy with how Hunter's nose looked.

"*Innamorato?*" the gondolier asked.

Hunter looked up at him and shook his head.

Mackenzie looked up, her eyes going to the gondolier and then to Hunter

"He's asking if we are in love," he explained.

Mackenzie knew it would be assumed that they were a couple even though there was nothing romantic about their relationship, which was ironic since they had now been in two cities known for romance. She looked up at Hunter, relieved that he seemed unphased by the question. Her thoughts went back to Sam. He would have labeled this as corny. He would have thought the same about dancing atop the Eiffel Tower. However, she knew if she had asked, he would do it for her. Or at least she used to think.

"Have you ever been in love?" Mackenzie asked.

Hunter leaned forward, shaking his head.

"I was focused on school. Then, after my parents died, I had to oversee the sale of their business. My sister had moved from Houston to Los Angeles, so I decided to follow her. When I got to California, I started my company. A little while later, Xiāng got sick. Relationships were not a priority. Also, I was a shallow asshole," Hunter explained.

"Really? It's so hard for me to wrap my head around that," Mackenzie confessed.

They continued to take in the view around them the conversation stilling. Again the quiet between them was tranquil instead of being awkward.

"Did you always know you would fall in love with Sam?" Hunter asked.

Mackenzie laughed, shaking her head. "Sam was the catch of Venice Beach, always has been. It wasn't a matter of thinking I would be in love. I have been in love with Sam from the moment I met him. I was pretty clueless when I was younger. I guess I never thought he would feel that way about me," Mackenzie answered.

"Who told who first?"

Mackenzie looked up at the sky, smiling sadly. "He did, actually. I was eighteen, and he was twenty. He promised my uncle not to say anything until I turned eighteen. You know, legality and all."

Mac looked down at her finger, the tan line still visible.

"Tell me how it happened," Hunter said gently.

"It was Valentine's Day—before you say anything, I never thought of February fourteenth as Valentine's Day. It is Jenni's birthday," Mackenzie explained.

"Every year, I would disappear and find somewhere to be alone and think of her. Sam would always track me down," Mackenzie laughed.

"That sounds like trying to find a needle in a haystack," Hunter commented.

"Sam knew the places I would go. So, he would just go from place to place. He finally found me sitting on the wall of the Griffith Park Observatory. I had a favorite spot," she explained.

"He sat next to me, not saying anything for a while. I joked about all the Valentine's Days I had ruined for him. He turned to me and said, 'Mackenzie, who else do you think I would want to spend Valentine's Day with? I love you.' I told him I loved him, too. He groaned and took a deep breath and told me, 'Not that way.' I was pretty speechless."

"Is this the part where a love song plays, and there's a passionate kiss?" Hunter teased.

Mackenzie shook her head then closed her eyes, getting lost in the memory. She felt the boat sway as they turned, going under a bridge. Mac opened her eyes trying to compose herself before giving Hunter her response.

"No, actually. He looked at me, laid his hand on my cheek to pull me closer, then kissed me on my temple. I remember turning toward him and seeing his eyes closed. That was the moment I knew Sam Madden was in love with me. My heart exploded. From then on, it was our thing. Saying goodbye or whenever he told me he loved me, he would reach over and give me a kiss on my temple," Mackenzie's voice got small as she gulped down the lump in her throat.

"He kissed you on your cheek," Hunter murmured. He blinked a few times, looking at her. "The day at the restaurant. I remember because of the way you just stood there afterward. It was like you had suddenly turned into stone. You didn't kiss him back. Now I understand why."

Mackenzie nodded. To anyone else, it would not seem like a big deal but that was the moment she knew things would never be the same.

"Yeah, I get how I handled it looks extreme to most. But that told me something, and then it was like something in me snapped. I knew if I had talked to Sam, I would convince myself everything was fine. Sam and I would live in a space where we weren't being true to ourselves. It would diminish us and our love. I couldn't live that way. As heartbroken as I am, I would rather it break like this instead of chipping away piece by piece to the point where we wake up next to each other one day, living totally separate lives," Mac whispered.

"I'm blown away by how brave you are. Most people wouldn't have your resolve." Hunter leaned back in his seat, looking up at the sky.

"I don't feel brave. I feel like it was more self-preservation or an attempt to save some dignity. It's not like I confronted him. Instead, I'm floating on a gondola with a guy that might be a stalker."

Hunter shook his head. "I think a lot of people destroy their relationships because they hold on when they might need to let go. That takes courage," Hunter said.

Mackenzie felt her face warm at Hunter's compliment. She didn't feel courageous. If anything, Hunter was courageous, facing death and still being able to laugh and enjoy life. She didn't want to spoil the mood by voicing her thoughts.

"Honestly, I feel bad for Ollie. He's being dragged across Europe watching me do asinine things," Mackenzie said, changing the subject again and taking attention away from her.

Hunter laughed, pointing at the gondola passing by. "I think he's dealing with it just fine."

Mackenzie twisted her body around to see Ollie and Parker going in the opposite direction, making out as their gondola driver paddled. She knew Parker was going to meet them in Venice, but she didn't know he had arrived yet.

Mackenzie couldn't help but feel happy for them, even though her heart was broken.

"Yeah, looks like he's dealing just fine," she said with a laugh.

Chapter 17

SAM

S am sat on a stool in the Barber Shop, a bar in Culver City. It was an actual barber shop that had a hidden bar behind it. He and Ezra had found it by mistake after popping into the shop for a haircut. Mackenzie called it their man cave.

He looked down at his rock tumbler, swirling the amber liquid inside. It was his third drink, and he was nursing it hard. From behind him, he heard a voice say.

"Red eyes and bourbon, I hope you took an Uber here."

He turned and saw his best friend, Ezra, standing there. Ezra climbed onto the stool next to Sam and ordered a Blue Moon.

"If you are here to pick my brain about where or who Mac is with, I got nothing for you," Ezra said, taking a sip of his beer. "Bianca knows I would fold like a bad hand if she told me, so she didn't. B did say she was good and safe, though."

"Bianca said I wasn't allowed to call her B anymore," Sam muttered softly.

"I see," Ezra replied, taking another sip of his drink. "I guess things are just different now."

"Things or me?" Sam asked.

Ezra took a deep breath, shaking his head while taking another sip of his beer. "I think you are the only one that can answer that."

Sam picked up his bourbon, downing it. Placing his glass on the bar before motioning to the bartender. His thoughts raced, trying to figure out a way to explain to his best friend what he was going through and how he was feeling.

Sam turned to Ezra, who was staring at his reflection in the mirrored glass at the back of the bar.

"Do you remember what you told me when I transitioned?" Ezra asked.

When they first met Ezra, he went by Esmeralda Ramirez, Bianca's college roommate. A lesbian born and raised in Pico Rivera. When Ezra accepted who he was, he told Bianca first. Then he told Mac and Sam together.

"Mac cried in relief because she thought you were going to tell us you had cancer," Sam said, shaking his head.

"I know. Relief from you guys was the last thing I thought I would see. I was so afraid and miserable. I was worried most about you. Wondering if you would be able to see me as a man. I remember looking over at you. You could see what I was feeling. All you said was, 'You need to be able to look in the mirror and see who you are.' You, out of everyone, gave me the confidence to start transitioning with that one sentence."

Ezra smiled over at his friend.

Sam was aware that his reaction worried Ezra the most. That was until Sam explained that in the Talmud, the central text in Judaism and the link between the Torah and Jewish practices and beliefs, actually recognizes eight genders. One of them being Aylonit Adam, which was one who identified as female at birth but later developed male characteristics through human intervention.

"You were my rock, bro. You went with me to tell my father, even though he disowned me," Ezra muttered.

"Maybe the bit about how you did not understand how he couldn't accept you, but he could accept grown men touching little boys in his house of worship wasn't the best idea," Sam quipped.

Ezra laughed. "Probably not. Still, you were there for me. You showed up at the bar I went to in Weho after my support group. Drove me home from my mastectomy and my hysterectomy. Reminded Mac and Bianca that I was going through hormone therapy and testosterone wasn't always pretty. You went shopping for clothes with me, even though my sense of style was always better than yours,"

Ezra took another sip, then patted Sam on the back and turned toward him. "The three of you are why when I look in the mirror, I see me."

Ezra nodded with his chin toward the mirror in front of them.

"You need to be able to look in the mirror and see who you are," Ezra said, turning back to Sam, the same statement he had said to Ezra five years ago.

"Yeah, you've changed, but if you're happy, then who are we to hold you back?" Ezra explained. "If this is who you are now, it's not fair to ask Mac to change or to fight for the relationship."

"She didn't even try," Sam said, letting his bitterness out for the first time since he found all of his stuff on his bed.

Ezra laughed mirthlessly. "You have got to be shitting me. All she has been doing for the last year is trying. You've just been way too in your own head to see it," Ezra finished his beer, waiting for the bartender to slide over another pint.

Sam opened his mouth to protest, but then he realized Ezra was right. A dozen images of Mac trying to connect with him flooded his mind. They used to have lunch in his office, laughing about whatever they watched on TV the night before. They would sit in the LA gridlock, listening to music and ranting about artists and songs while they drove back to her bungalow. She used to jump on his back until he gave in to taking her to whatever obscure festival or event she wanted to go to that weekend.

For the last year, he had business lunches, so she stopped bringing him lunch to his office. He moved downtown to get to the office earlier, so she drove herself to work, sometimes swinging over to pick up Bianca for coffee. They spent their weekends sitting inside while he scrolled the financials, and she would read or just watch the people passing by. She stopped jumping on him; he could only guess it was because of the cost of his clothing.

"Do you remember her birthday two years ago?" Ezra asked.

Sam knitted his brows in confusion. "I remember all her birthdays," Sam answered.

"What did you give her?" Ezra asked.

Sam actually remembered vividly what he got her. He had just received his first hefty commission check. He was excited to be able to give her something of value.

"I got her clothes and perfume," Sam said.

"You got her business outfits from White House Black Market and Tiffany's perfume," Ezra added.

Ezra took a sip of his second pint.

"Do you realize every piece of clothing you have gifted her since then was for work? And perfume? Mac has used peach oil for as long as I have known her. She smiled and thanked you, covering you in kisses. Later, I caught Mackenzie holding one of the dresses up and looking at herself in her mirror. It was when you and Bianca were cutting the cake and pouring drinks. So, you missed it. She had this look on her face I can't describe. Do you think she saw who she was or what you wanted her to be?" Ezra asked.

Sam looked down at his drink. Ezra was right. From that moment on, he bought her high-end designer clothes and shoes. He was so sure he was being an attentive boyfriend. He knew Mac didn't make as much as he or Bianca. She would never ask for his help. So, he thought he was making things easier for her.

Erza punched him lightly on the shoulder. "B is mad because Mac has changed so much to try to be the girl standing next to you. You being embarrassed by her...I don't need to rub it in."

Sam set down his glass, pushing it toward the bartender. The bartender poured him another bourbon.

"I don't know what I was thinking or what came over me," Sam said softly, shaking his head and holding his hand to his chest. "I just knew..."

"That she didn't belong there. Once more, just be honest enough to admit you didn't want her there," Ezra muttered.

Sam tilted his head back, groaning.

"Maybe you have outgrown being Mackenzie's great protector," Ezra said, shrugging. "Maybe you like the world you're stepping into. But let me ask you this question."

Ezra turned all the way around to face Sam. "If you are embarrassed by Mac, how long until you're embarrassed by me?"

Sam felt his eyes widen. "Dude, are you serious?" he asked, completely taken aback.

"Of course I am. It's Mackenzie, your Mackenzie, the girl that you drove through a brush fire to get to when she had recovered from COVID."

Sam felt a shiver go down his spine. Mackenzie had gotten COVID two weeks into lockdown. Sam had been staying with his mom for the first week. Clover's home was fairly secluded. He wanted to be there in case she needed him for anything. He also didn't want to leave Mac on her own. He remembered lining up in his car, getting his nose tortured to make sure he was not bringing the deadly virus to Mackenzie. He had just tested negative and was planning on heading back to Mackenzie's place when she called and told him, at first, she thought she was having an allergy attack. Then, she confessed that she thought she needed to get tested because she couldn't smell her scented hand soap.

Sam had never been more afraid of anything in his whole life. Mackenzie refused to let him come back to the house. He and Clover stayed on video calls with her twenty-four hours a day. Making sure she was okay. Fortunately, her case was mild. She swore she would have thought she had a run-of-the-mill sinus infection if it wasn't for the loss of smell. Sam barely slept. He would wake up in the middle of the night just watching Mackenzie sleep because he had heard people with the virus were dying overnight. He would have pho and acai bowls delivered to her. Watched Chinese dramas, movies, and reruns of her favorite shows. His heart dropped every time she had sneezed or coughed.

Ezra and Bianca would join in at times. All of them tried to hide the fact that they were terrified. Mackenzie had been the first person they knew to catch COVID.

Sam practically flew out the door and, in his car, when Mac appeared on screen telling him she tested negative. Ezra was right, there had been a bad brushfire down PCH. They were common in Los Angeles; this particular one had diverted traffic. It took Sam an hour and a half and driving through flames to get to Mackenzie. That was only three years ago. How had things changed so drastically between them?

"She was your everything. Now she isn't. So, the question is fair," Ezra argued.

Sam hung his head. Ezra was always brutally honest with him. He was also one of the most loyal people he had ever known.

"I don't know what I am doing anymore," Sam said miserably.

"Sam, it's obvious the road you're traveling on might make you leave your past behind. People change; it would hurt if we no longer fit in each other's lives, but I would wish you well. We all would."

"I don't think I need to sacrifice anyone to walk down this road," Sam argued.

Ezra sighed. Sam watched as Ezra opened his mouth to say something then shut it, taking a deep breath. Sam knew his best friend was deliberately holding out on him by the deep breath he took. Ezra was horrible about keeping things to himself. Hence why Bianca didn't tell him anything about Mackenzie.

"Maybe," Ezra commented. "You just have to figure out if you want her there walking next to you, not standing by the roadside."

Sam felt his heart pound out of his chest again.

"Although, it does seem like Mackenzie has let you know where she stands."

Sam shook his head at his friend. "None of this is making me feel better or less confused," Sam muttered.

Ezra laughed. "I said I would have drinks with you, not solve all your problems."

Sam laughed, clinking his glass against his friend's.

Looking down at his phone, the wallpaper was a picture of Mackenzie. It was a black and white photo of her leaning on her balcony, the wind kicking up her hair as she gave him a shy smile. She was always shy when it came to him taking pictures of her. He looked down at it thinking he should change it, seeing the state of things. Yet, Sam couldn't bring himself to do it.

Chapter 18

MACKENZIE

"How are you allergic to shellfish?" Hunter asked, shaking his head in disbelief as they sat on a stone bench on the walkway of the Ca' Rezzonico.

Mackenzie gave Hunter a playful glare. He was referring to how difficult it had been the evening prior to finding a restaurant in Venice that did not primarily serve seafood. Parker had struck gold when he discovered Trattoria Anzolo Raffaele. It was a restaurant in a hidden campi, a less busy square, secluded from the tourist-heavy parts of Venice. The sleepy square had two churches, San Sebastiano and Angelo Raffaele, guarding it. Mackenzie was thrilled to find out from their server that the campi was right by Campo Madonna dell'Orto, the final resting place of Tintoretto, one of Italy's most famous painters.

The server had kindly let them know of some less crowded places to visit. They all agreed it would be a crime if Mackenzie did not see some of the Venetian paintings and art while they were there. So, in addition to visiting Campo Madonna dell'Orto, which also had some of Tintoretto's work, they were guided to Ca'

Rezzonico, a palace that houses 18th-century Venetian Baroque and Rococo styles. Mackenzie found herself standing outside of it for a while. The building itself was a work of art, with beautiful frescoes, sculptures, and architectural details.

Mackenzie and the guys wandered slowly, examining the collection of paintings by 18th-century Venetian artists, including Canaletto, Francesco Guardi, and Giambattista Tiepolo. Hunter wasn't the only one worn out after several hours of walking and standing, so they'd decided to rest briefly on one of the benches.

"It's genetic; Uncle Deano was as well," she said with a shrug.

Mackenzie watched as Hunter leaned back against the white wall behind the bench. He closed his eyes, his breathing a little bit labored. It was not lost on them that Hunter ordered pasta e fagioli, a bean, and pasta soup at Trattoria Anzolo Raffaele the night before. He did his best to keep his spirits up even though they could all see the difficulty he had in finishing the soup.

She knew Hunter was aware that they were moving through the church and palace slowly. Mackenzie had used her knowledge of art to stop them a few times to discuss a painting or comment on the room they were in.

Hunter crossed his arms in front of him. Mackenzie looked down at the wide silver band on his right ring finger, taking his hand in hers.

"What does it say?" she asked.

Hunter's eyes popped open, raising his hand toward Mackenzie. She took his hand by the wrist, examining it further. It was a flat, half-inch-wide ring on top with a Chinese character in the middle. She had noticed it before and was curious about the character and its meaning, but she hadn't asked about it until now.

"Zhou," Hunter said. "It was my sister's, and she wore it on her pointer finger. She had it commissioned from an artist friend of hers. She wore it all the time."

Mackenzie dropped his hand. Hunter started rubbing it against his jeans. He crossed his arms and legs, rubbing his arms as if trying to generate heat. It was not cold, yet she could tell Hunter was.

Mackenzie reached into her crossbody bag, pulled out a beanie, and handed it to him. Hunter took it from her, not making eye contact. She nudged him, making him look at her.

She grabbed the silver chain around her neck, pulling it out. Mackenzie turned to him, holding the coin medallion that hung at the end of it. Hunter leaned over, raising a brow. Mackenzie chuckled.

"Happiness," Hunter said, flipping the coin around. "And a dragon, of course. Interesting, I don't think I have ever seen one in platinum."

Mackenzie nodded, looking down at the quarter-sized medallion.

"A coworker got it for my uncle when he worked at Northrup. He's been wearing it since before I was born." She held it in her palm, closing it for a second before putting it back under her shirt.

"Did you put it on at the hospital?" Hunter asked.

Mackenzie nodded. "I remember the nurse handing it to me after they turned off all the machines. I just put it over my head, letting it drop to my neck. I have been wearing it ever since."

Hunter smiled, nodding. "My sister handed her ring to me the day she passed. I had forgotten about it until later when I got home, sat down, and felt something in my pocket. I tested which finger it would fit on, and voila," he said, holding his hand up again.

"Asians and our jewelry, right?" Mackenzie laughed.

Hunter chuckled, taking a deep breath. Mackenzie wanted him to rest a bit more before they moved on.

"Okay, tell me another thing you've accomplished and crossed off your list." Mackenzie urged.

Hunter laughed. "Make a snowball at the North Pole."

Mackenzie's eyes got wide. "How did that go?' She squeaked.

"Ollie and I made the trip last April. You get there via Khatanga, Russia; from there, you take an AN-74 aircraft to an ice camp named Barneo. It's on a drifting ice floe near the North Pole. Then, you get in a helicopter that takes you all the way to the North Pole. There's this red banner that says North Pole with the number ninety and a degree symbol in the center of it." Hunter explained. "Making a snowball was actually not easy. It's mostly solid ice up there. I got it done, though."

"Just thinking about being zero degrees Fahrenheit is giving me frostbite," Mackenzie laughed.

"Honestly, I questioned my choice on the way there while trying to make the snowball. There was this moment, though, when I was standing with Ollie. Looking out at the ice and snow stretching as far as you can see. Knowing I was standing in a place only a few in this world had ever been. Hearing a few small glaciers break into the water. It was tranquil, I guess," Hunter replied.

"Suddenly, I feel like my list is lacking in depth," Mackenzie joked.

"No, it doesn't. They are your dreams. Don't discount them," Hunter said.

"Have I mentioned I can't believe I am doing this?"

Hunter gulped hard, then cleared his throat. "I wanna ask you a question but I am struggling to find a way to phrase it without it coming off as rude or challenging."

"Please, Filipinos have zero filters. Half the time, the questions are combative," Mackenzie said. "When will you get married, Mackenzie?" she said, mimicking a Filipino accent.

Hunter groaned. "I hate that question."

Both laughed.

"So ask away," Mackenzie urged.

"Are you purposely hiding?" Hunter asked.

Mackenzie gave him a look of confusion.

"I realized something while we were walking around: you were flexing your art knowledge. Seriously, people were standing close so they could hear," Hunter turned toward her and took her hand in his.

"You're already as bright as the sun. But listening to you talk made me feel like you were shining. I could tell it's been a long time since you talked about painting," Hunter said, dropping her hand.

Mackenzie smashed her hands underneath her legs, tilting her head to the side.

"I can't remember the last time I talked about art. It's been a long time since I painted anything. I sketch a lot, but painting on canvas? It's been years," she confessed.

"I'm sorry if what I am about to say is hurtful," Hunter frowned.

"Hit me," Mackenzie said.

Hunter cleared his throat again. "You talk about Sam, your best friend Bianca, your friend Ezra. All the things they are doing with their lives. What about you?" Hunter asked.

Mackenzie leaned back against the wall behind her with a thump. Not knowing how to respond. Hunter's observation floored her. She opened her mouth for a beat as if she were going to come up with a solid example. She realized she couldn't.

"Honestly, I don't know. I have never thought about it that way. Until you said something, I never thought about the fact that I..."

"That you're a support player in everyone else's world, but you don't have one of your own?" Hunter interrupted.

She blinked a few times, letting what Hunter said sink in. He was right. Her life was working and going home, taking cues from Sam and her friends when it came to doing things. The only thing she had going on was planning the wedding.

"Should I apologize?" Hunter muttered.

Mackenzie took a deep breath, shaking her head.

"No, in fact, thank you for asking. I'm not sure if I have an answer for you, though," Mackenzie confessed.

Hunter smiled, "You don't need to give me one. Hopefully, one day soon, you will be able to give an answer to yourself."

Chapter 19

SAM

Work was keeping him sane. He was so busy with negotiations that he could put the thoughts of Mackenzie, where she was and where they were going to be going, in the back of his mind.

Bianca peeked into his office yesterday. He braced himself for her to say something biting.

"She texted. Let me know she was still in Europe," Bianca announced. "I actually talked to her right after, she's safe."

Sam exhaled belatedly, realizing he had been holding his breath.

"Bianca," Sam called as Bianca started to walk out the door.

Bianca stopped, looking at him. He could tell she was wondering if she would have to defend or protect her best friend.

"Thank you for telling me," Sam said. His voice was a little wobbly, emotion getting the better of him.

Bianca gave him a nod.

He saw Clarissa approach his office, stopping just behind Bianca. Bianca turned her head back in Sam's direction, rolled her eyes, and then walked out the door.

Sam closed his eyes. It was the first time Bianca and he had spoken without there being hostility, and of course Clarissa shows up. Bad timing was his constant companion these days. He opened his eyes, taking a deep breath, smiling at Clarissa.

"Hey," he said lamely.

Clarissa smiled, walking up to the front of his desk.

"Hey, so my father and a few of his old colleagues are going to be having dinner at Orsa & Winston down the street. I was wondering if you wanted to go. I was planning on picking their brains a bit," Clarissa explained.

Orsa & Winston was a Michelin star restaurant with a Japanese and Italian inspired menu. He had been there once with some clients. He had been going to a lot of these types of places lately, getting more and more comfortable with being in the environment.

"I have so much going on right now," Sam replied, looking at the pile of folders scattered across his desk.

"Oh, I totally get it. Which is why I invited you. It's a five o'clock reservation, so you could get back to the office if you needed to afterward," Clarissa replied.

Sam sat back in his seat, thinking about the fact that he's been living on takeout. Clarissa's father retired from finance and was an occasional financial advisor for their firm. They had bumped into him once at a charity event. Dinner with him and some of his old colleagues was probably a smart move. Besides, it wasn't like he had anything else to do.

Sam and Clarissa arrived at Orsa & Winston at five minutes to five. The restaurant had a minimalist interior with large windows and sleek wooden tables and chairs. They were greeted by Edward Cargill, Clarissa's father, as they walked in. Sam looked around, only seeing a woman and another girl standing next to him.

"Dad, I thought uncle Stephen and Davis were going to be here," Clarissa asked.

Edward waved his hand in front of him.

"They said they didn't want to battle the traffic. So, I brought your mother and sister instead."

Sam stiffened, glancing at Clarissa.

"I'm so sorry," she said, "I thought this would be more of a professional thing. Please feel free to go back to the office."

Sam felt his chest squeeze. Was it innocent? Or calculated? Either way, it would be rude if he left. Sticking it out in situations like this was Sam's default setting. He wondered if Clarissa had learned that about him.

"I don't mind staying," Sam said, smiling. "That is if it's alright with you and your family."

Edward smiled back at him, letting the host know they were ready for their meal.

"Sam, I swear I didn't know," Clarissa said urgently.

Sam nodded, smiling reassuringly, intent on not making it a big deal. "I believe you. Let's go to the table."

The conversation flowed easily between Edward and Sam. Sam asked a few questions. Got a bit of advice on how to handle high end customers. Clarissa's sister, Sofia, was in marketing.

Her mother was a retired broker. Clarissa came from a well-off successful family who lived in a Brentwood mini mansion.

"So, Clarissa tells me you are brokering a deal with a tech company in Japan," Sofia said, taking a sip of her wine.

Sam nodded. "Yes, it's been a ride. It will be a feather in the firm's cap once it closes," Sam replied.

"Have you ever dealt with Japanese clients? They are a different breed. I guess you have a leg up on the culture and how to navigate through it because of your fiancée," Sofia said, smiling over at him.

"She's not Japanese; she's Filipino," Sam said, trying not to sound snappish.

Margot, Clarissa's mother, cleared her throat.

"I could have sworn that Clarissa said she was Japanese," Margot said.

Sam immediately knew it was a lie. Her mother was just saving face.

"Remember when I had gallbladder surgery. The nurse I had was Filipino," Edward said as if saying that made up for his daughter's cultural ignorance.

Sam felt his insides twist. Suddenly he felt like he was having an out of body experience. He knew Edward was trying to compensate for what happened. He had been in a few situations that tap danced on the verge of being culturally inappropriate; this was blatant.

"Nurses in the Philippines often get recruited by US registries. It's because the training there is much more in-depth and intense than it is here," Sam explained, doing his best not to sound like he was defending an entire culture.

He heard Sofia gasp theatrically. "Oh, I'm sorry, I didn't realize this is a sore subject," Sofia said, giving him a saccharine sweet smile.

He looked over at Clarissa, who had the good sense to look mortified. Then, he turned to see Edward shake his head at Sofia.

"So, Clarissa tells me you graduated summa cum laude at UCLA," Edward said, changing the subject.

"Yes," Sam confirmed. Both he and Bianca graduated summa cum laude. Ezra had teased them about how their sashes clashed with their robes. "It was really challenging but worth it."

"Did you get a Masters in Finance or an MBA?" Edward asked, taking a sip of his water, smiling over at Sam.

"I got my MBA in Corporate Finance then took online night classes to get my Masters in Finance," Sam replied.

Edward looked over at his daughter, raising his brows to convey how impressed he was. He watched the looks between Clarissa and her family. Sam felt like he was being interviewed. Any illusions of this being an accidental family dinner disappeared. Clarissa was getting her family's approval.

"Your parents must be proud." Sam found himself nodding instead of clarifying that only his mother was in the picture. It would lead to questions about his father. The dinner was uncomfortable enough already.

After dinner, Sam walked Clarissa to her car in the parking garage, making sure she got there safely.

"Sam, I'm sorry my sister is a bit out of touch," Clarissa apologized, standing in front of the driver's side door.

Sam laughed, shaking his head. "I picked up on that," Sam said, trying to act like he was unaware of what Clarissa and her family were doing.

Clarissa reached out, squeezing his forearm. "How are you holding up? I'm sorry if I am being intrusive. I'm just worried about you."

Sam looked up, taking a deep breath. "I'm managing. Thank you for checking in, though. It's nice to know you care," Sam said quietly.

"How long have you two been together?" Clarissa asked.

"Since birth," Sam joked, leaning against Clarissa's car and sticking his hands in his pockets.

"It has to feel strange," Clarissa said. "I know it has something to do with seeing her at the Platform that day."

Sam nodded, clearing his throat.

"Hey, you'll get through it," Clarissa said reassuringly.

"Thanks, it's still nice to hear it though. I keep telling myself the same thing."

Clarissa pushed off her car and stood squarely in front of him.

"Sam, full transparency—I mean, you have to have guessed. All the time we spend together. My family knows so much about you..." she whispered.

Sam gulped hard, looking down at her, speechless. He wasn't an idiot. He deduced that during dinner, which was clearly a setup. It felt like Edward's silent approval of him made Clarissa more confident to express how she felt.

"We have so much in common. And we fit, so it's natural to feel this way. I'm about to get transferred out of our department as well. So, it's hard not to feel like all the pieces are falling into place for us."

Sam took another deep breath. He opened his mouth to say something just as Clarissa stepped up and kissed him on his lips. Before he could think, Sam felt his arms go around her. Her lips were soft, and the smell of her perfume and her body pressed against him made him feel a little intoxicated.

Unlike Mackenzie, who only knew Sam, Sam had kissed other girls before. He was older and went on a few dates, so the concept wasn't completely foreign to him.

He felt her deepen the kiss, beginning to slide her tongue into his mouth. Right at that moment, Sam put his hands on her shoulders, gently pushing her away.

"Clarissa, I'm sorry. We shouldn't..." Sam said, panting, still holding her by the shoulders. "It isn't fair to you. I don't want you to feel like a rebound," he said.

Clarissa smiled, stepping away from him. "You realize you just admitted that you think maybe there can be something more." The confidant blonde said triumphantly.

She took her keys out of her pocket and pressed the button on the car remote to unlock the car door. She pressed another button and Sam heard the vehicle start. Clarissa got into the car, smiling at him.

Sam instinctively smiled back. "Be safe getting home," he said.

"Sam, don't feel too bad. You're a great guy. And honestly, you're at a place that Mackenzie can't understand. Not like I do," Clarissa finished as she backed out of the stall and drove off.

Sam stood there feeling as if someone had just filed him. He had kissed Clarissa. He was technically single, so he shouldn't feel too guilty. Yet something about how she said he was going to a place Mackenzie couldn't understand made his blood run cold.

Chapter 20

MACKENZIE

Mackenzie opened her eyes, blinking them, trying to get her world into focus. She heard the guys outside laughing. She got up, slid her feet into the hotel slippers, and walked outside. They all went silent as she walked out onto the private veranda of their suite. Mackenzie smiled, resting her hands on the smooth wooden rail. She laughed, shaking her head, looking out and seeing the blue domed churches of Agios Spyridonas and Anasteseos. Then turned slightly to see the crescent-shaped Caldera of Santorini.

"That's number four off the list," she heard Hunter say from behind her.

Mackenzie turned, seeing him sitting there with an IV line next to him. Parker got up, pulling his seat out, guiding Mackenzie to sit down at the table. It had a bowl of Greek yogurt with honey and dates on each side. There were a few pastries along with a carafe of coffee and glasses of orange juice.

"Did I steal the covers last night?" Mackenzie asked.

Hunter chuckled, taking a spoonful of yogurt and swallowing it slowly.

"Please, that bed is so enormous that I practically need to send a text to talk to you," Hunter joked.

They'd left Venice and flown to Frankfort, where they had an hour-long layover before getting on a connecting flight to the tiny Santorini International Airport. The view out the windows as they landed was like something out of fantasy. It was dusk when she could see the caldera, a collapsed volcanic crater that created dramatic cliffs along much of the coastline of the Aegean Sea. The tiny whitewashed houses of Oia cascading down the cliff sides got bigger and bigger as they descended, all of this surrounded by the blue Aegean. The contrast between the deep blue water and the white cliffs made her ache for oil paints, an easel, and a blank canvas.

They arrived at Luxus VIP Suites, where Hunter had unsurprisingly booked the Grand Blue Dome Suite. The trip was clearly taking a toll on Hunter. He needed Ollie to help him get in and out of the car from the airport to the hotel. Ollie had arranged for a catered traditional Greek dinner to be brought into the suite. They'd sat outside eating saganaki halloumi, lamb kofta with roast garlic and lemon yogurt, and avgolemono soup, debating if they should let out a joyful whoop or just sit there in reverie.

After dinner, Mackenzie listened to the three of them debate about sleeping arrangements, wondering how all four of them would manage with just one sofa bed and the biggest bed Mackenzie had ever seen.

"I'll crash with Hunter," She announced, "The bed is big enough for a family of six." She teased, looking at Hunter and smiling at him reassuringly.

"We can't separate a married couple, right?" Mackenzie asked.

Hunter had shaken his head, the blush that crept up his face slowly fading.

They all sat there finishing breakfast, watching Hunter start to doze off a bit.

"After a nap, we should go visit the churches," Hunter suggested.

Parker and Ollie announced they were going to go for a swim after he had disconnected Hunter's IV line. The bruising on the crook of his elbow had spread across it, the purple and blue looking dark against his pale skin. She watched Ollie and Parker exchange a look before they left.

Mackenzie offered her arm to Hunter. He took it as they walked back to the bed. Mackenzie helped him get situated then plopped into the chaise lounge chair next to his bedside.

"You never told me the name of your uncle's record shop," Hunter said softly.

"It was called Vinyls in Venice," she answered.

Hunter smiled. "Great name."

"It was a great little shop but it struggled a bit before we decided to close it. Vinyls weren't big around that time, not like now. We got a bit of business from dedicated customers. Weekends were always good because of the tourists, but we were barely making it work," Mackenzie said sadly as she looked over at Hunter.

"The one thing I am grateful for is that my uncle was already bedridden in the hospital when we shut it down. I think it would have made doing it so much worse."

Hunter nodded. "At least you had the balls to do it yourself. I hired people to clear out my sister's office. Gave her employees great severance packages and offered them any of the art and furniture they wanted."

She looked over at Hunter. He was staring at the ceiling, lost in memory.

"Sam, Bianca, and Ezra all helped me sell off the stock and close the place," Mackenzie said.

Hunter turned to her and smiled. "So tell me, did you and Sam do all the dances, prom, homecoming, and such? Did you wear dresses that feel like bad fashion choices, looking back?" Hunter asked, his accent getting a bit thicker.

Mackenzie shook her head and laughed. "No, mostly because I didn't want to do any of that. Also, like I said, the shop struggled a lot. I worked there after school and on the weekends."

Mackenzie explained, "I'm happy I did now. I spent a lot of time with my uncle talking music, him asking me about painting."

"Let me guess, Sam worked there too."

Mackenzie shook her head. "No, we couldn't afford to pay another person, Sam wanted to do it for free but Uncle Deano wouldn't allow it. Besides, he was doing all the bookkeeping for his mom's yoga studio."

Mackenzie crossed her legs, putting her hands behind her back.

"I get it, though. Sam sacrificed a lot for me already. He only went to homecoming the one year I wasn't there."

She noticed Hunter's look of confusion. "One year?"

"Yeah, his freshman year, when I was still in middle school. He's actually two years older than me, but I skipped a grade," Mackenzie explained.

Hunter smiled, looking over at her, "Not surprising. You are a lot smarter than you give yourself credit for."

She shrugged her shoulders. "I don't feel like I am."

"You got into UCLA, and that's not an easy feat."

"I got a lot of help from my uncle and Sam. I got in by the skin of my teeth. It was my submissions to the art department that carried me through," Mackenzie explained.

"No matter how much they helped you in the end, your talent and fortitude got you there. Don't forget that," Hunter said adamantly.

Mackenzie looked over at him nodding. He was right; she had always credited others for getting into UCLA. She stopped to give herself a pat on the back for the long hours she put in.

"So why didn't Sam go to any of the dances or take you?" he asked.

"Part of the reason was because it was expensive, at least for us. If I wanted to go, I knew Uncle Deano would make it happen. But high school wasn't a good time for me. Especially after Jenni died. I think Sam knew that, too. So, on the nights of the dances, he would come hang out with me and Uncle Deano at the shop. Playing records and dancing there," Mackenzie smiled, taking a deep breath.

Hunter rolled to his side, tucking his hands under his head.

"The more you tell me about the two of you, the more I understand why you walked away the way you did. A lot of people would argue that, for the sake of history, you should have worked it out. I can see your perspective. You were trying to preserve your history. I still think that's brave. To look at something and knowing the truest thing you know was slowly becoming a lie."

Mackenzie felt an errant tear roll down her cheek and quickly wiped it away.

"Thanks for saying that. I have moments where I doubt myself," Mackenzie chuckled.

Hunter rolled back over onto his back, looking at the ceiling again. She closed her eyes for a moment until she heard Hunter's breathing beginning to sound labored. She looked over at him, seeing that he had his hand up to his nose, blood seeping in between his fingers.

Mackenzie jumped off the chaise lounge, opening the medical tote bag beside the bed, pulling out a towel. She moved Hunter's hand away, replacing it with the towel before helping him sit up. She walked quickly to the bathroom sink, emptying the glass bowl that was filled with hand towels, grabbing a few of them and filling the bowl with water before walking it all carefully back to Hunter's bedside. Hunter sat there, his eyes shut tight. She could tell he was starting to hyperventilate.

"I'm so sorry, Mackenzie," He cried, gulping hard, beads of sweat beginning to form on his face.

Mackenzie knew he was in the throes of a panic attack. She looked through the bag, trying to find Valium or Tranxene. She knew from experience that they were the fastest-acting anxiety medications prescribed for terminal patients. She found a bottle labeled Valium, read the dosage, and took two out. She raised a bit on her knees, grabbing the water bottle from his bedside. Then, she gently pinched his chin and pulled it down, feeding him the two pills, raising the water bottle to his lips, and watching him swallow them down.

"Don't call Ollie," Hunter pleaded. "I don't want to ruin their swim."

"Please, you forget I'm a certified pro at this," she scoffed. "You know what to do next; let's hear it."

He pulled the towel away from his nose as it stopped bleeding and handed it to Mackenzie.

Hunter took a few deep breaths.

"Chaoxiang Zhou," he said, his voice warbling.

Mackenzie watched as he lifted his left leg, raised his right arm, and made a fist with his left hand.

"What do you hear?" Mackenzie asked for the second set of three of the 333 rule, a coping mechanism used for people having anxiety attacks.

Hunter had said his name in the beginning to settle his brain and had moved three body parts. Now, he needed to tell her three things he heard. Hunter closed his eyes, and his breathing began to return to normal.

"The ocean, a bird squawking, and the door curtain hitting the door because of the wind."

"Okay, three things you see," Mackenzie asked.

Hunter reached for her hand, squeezing it and opening his eyes. She watched him look around the room, finding three things he could see. They had talked about her uncle and his sister having panic attacks. She knew he was well-versed in the practice.

"The mirror, the glass bowl..." he gulped, then looked at her. "And you."

Mackenzie took the hand towel she grabbed from the bathroom, dipping it into the glass bowl of water. She wiped the blood off his hand until it was clean then dipped another towel into the water wiping off his face.

She stood up taking the soiled towels and bowl of water to the bathroom. Putting the towel in a waste bin and emptying the bowl in the sink. She laid a clean towel over the waste bin knowing Hunter might feel bad if he saw the bloodied towels then made her way back to his bedside.

Hunter had scooted down on the bed. He raised a clenched fist to his forehead, resting it there, and closed his eyes. Mackenzie watched as he gulped hard, his breathing slowing down to normal.

She sat on the floor resting her back against the side of the bed taking his hand, stroking it softly.

"Mac?" he whispered.

"That's me," she answered softly, looking down at their joined hands. She had been through this with her uncle; panic attacks were very common in terminal patients. She was strangely grateful that she knew what to do at that moment.

"Thank you," he said. Mackenzie squeezed his hand. They sat in silence for a long time. Mackenzie thought Hunter had drifted to sleep until he spoke again.

"I'm sorry. I was hoping you could avoid this part," Hunter said, trying to hide his anguish.

"Would it be weird if I said that I am glad I was here for it? I am finally able to do something for you."

She held his hand in between hers raising and blowing onto his hand softly rubbing it between her own, knowing that touch brought comfort.

Hunter chuckled.

"Weirdly, no," he said, his accent now barely detectable. "Can you do one more thing for me then?"

Mackenzie smiled, looking up at him. "You know the answer to that. Hit me."

Hunter gulped, squeezing her hand.

"Will you come with me to do my number three?"

Chapter 21

SAM

Sam successfully avoided Clarissa most of the morning due to meetings and a few reports he needed to send out. He kept telling himself he shouldn't feel as guilty as he did.

Any self-convincing he did immediately flew out the window every time he looked down at his phone and saw the picture of Mackenzie smiling up at him.

He thought back to when Bianca had confronted him about Clarissa. He knew she was right; his coworkers had been whispering about how much time they had spent together. He just chose to ignore it.

Clarissa came into his office, dropped off a file folder, and left his sliding door open.

"Let's table what happened last night for now until you get yourself into a better headspace," Clarissa said, giving him a sly smile.

"Thanks, I think that's a good idea. I am sorry I let things go too far," Sam apologized, looking up at her.

"It takes two to tango," she said. Clarissa began to walk out the door.

"Clarissa?" he called out.

Clarissa turned around, tilting her head, "Yes?"

Sam leaned back in his chair. "Yesterday, you said something that I wanted clarification on," Sam said.

Clarissa smiled, sitting down on the tufted wingback chair and crossing her legs.

"I thought we were going to table last night, but sure, how can I help you?"

Sam swiveled toward her. "You said I was in a place that Mackenzie couldn't understand. What did you mean by that?" he asked.

Clarissa folded her hands onto her lap. "I mean, as your career grows, she will not be able to provide you the full understanding and support you need to help you navigate big opportunities," Clarissa explained.

"You said you could, though?" Sam asked.

Clarissa bit her lip. "As your circle becomes more exclusive, you need someone who can keep up. Challenge you. As you pointed out, you have an MBA and Master's in Finance and graduated summa cum laude. You have moved up the firm faster than anyone else before you. You need someone who can accent your accomplishments," Clarissa explained.

Sam leaned forward, suddenly irritated. "Are you referring to the fact that she didn't finish her college career? Her uncle got sick and passed away. She had to deal with a lot while he was dying and afterward. I don't think that makes her less smart or supportive," Sam argued.

Clarissa held her hand up defensively. "I'm not judging her," she said.

Sam knew most of the time when people said that judging them was exactly what they were doing.

"Just pointing out that she'll never be comfortable in your social circles going forward as your career takes off. In my defense, you have said so yourself."

Sam felt a stabbing sensation in his chest. He had said that to Clarissa before.

"She was working toward a Fine Arts degree, right?" Clarissa asked.

Sam nodded, waiting for her next statement.

"It's far from finance, right?" she said, shrugging her shoulders.

Sam took a deep breath, calming himself. "Mackenzie has innate qualities that most people will never have. As far as support goes, no one has been more supportive than Mackenzie. Saying she could not contribute to my success is almost insulting. I wouldn't be where I am without her," Sam stated.

He looked up just then and saw Bianca standing in the hallway opposite his door, looking down at her phone. Sam realized she was eavesdropping. He knew most of Bianca's tells. He saw her look up at him. She nodded, giving him a smile as she walked away briskly.

Sam felt a smile creep up on his face. He cleared his throat, turning back to Clarissa. She was looking down at her nails. She raised her head, looking him dead in the eyes.

"I am not saying she didn't help you get as far as you have. Just saying I doubt that she could help you achieve your goals going forward," Clarissa rose to her feet, sighing. "If you are confident that she can then why have I been the one at your side for the last six months?"

Sam stared at her, at a loss for words. He'd always admired Clarissa's savvy and cutthroat attitude, but it felt different now that it was being turned on him.

"I know you are trying to process a lot right now. It's not unheard of to outgrow your childhood sweetheart. Once you accept it, things get easier," Clarissa offered.

She began to walk out the door, then stopped turning around.

"From what I have heard, she's gone silent on you during the most crucial time of your career. It doesn't sound supportive to me. Remember who is here for you. Besides, I'm patient," Clarissa said, smirking as she walked out the door.

Sam sat there thinking about what Clarissa said. How Mackenzie abandoned him just as he was closing the biggest deal of his career. He waited for the feeling of anger to overtake him. It never came. All he felt was the ache of the lack of her presence in his life.

Sam couldn't avoid Clarissa the next day. They had several things they needed to get wrapped up. They were working on a huge presentation powerpoint and going through notes from the legal department.

Sam felt himself getting lost in his work and focused on getting things done. He would be lying if he didn't admit that Clarissa's presence made things go smoothly: pointing out things and acting as the devil's advocate when needed. The two of them truly ran like a well-oiled machine. He also noticed that she would lean in a little closer as she hovered beside him, looking at his laptop. How she touched his hand or rubbed his shoulder.

She had invited him to dinner, which he declined, explaining he was driving out to see his mother.

It was not a lie. He had left work early, calling his mom to let her know he was coming to see her. Clover did not hide her surprise. She told him she would get a couple of sandwiches and meet him at the beach.

At present the two of them were walking along the shore. They had finished dinner and had decided to watch the sunset.

Sam had rolled up his slacks as he walked barefoot next to his mom, feeling the cold water hit his feet.

Clover took his shoes and socks, putting them in her large bag that seemed to be able to hold everything.

"I take it you still have not heard from Mac," Clover said, breaking the silence.

"She's in Europe," he choked out, still trying to process that she was there.

"Good for her," Clover said. Sam looked at his mom, shocked.

"When's the last time Mac's done anything for herself?" Clover asked.

Sam thought about it for a moment, realizing he couldn't think of the last time she had.

"There's this girl at work. Her name is Clarissa. She's been there for me a lot. She pointed out Mackenzie isn't comfortable in my social circles, that she would struggle," Sam explained.

Clover nodded, looking out at the ocean. "Let me guess, sometimes you feel like Clarissa's the better fit. She can move through your circles easier than Mac can. I can see how true that is and why she said it. Have you stopped to think there's a reason for that beyond having the same educational background?" Clover said quietly.

"What's that?" Sam asked. He felt a bit clueless.

Clover snaked her arm around his, holding his forearm with the other one.

"My dear boy," she sighed, resting her head on his shoulder. "Suddenly, I feel like you growing up in Venice Beach was a double-edged sword."

Sam looked down at his mom, even more baffled.

"It was such an eclectic community. And most everyone around you envied your relationship with Mackenzie." Clover said with a smile.

"Mom, I know, trust me. Do you know how many guys I had to threaten to stay away from her even though they probably could have put me in the hospital?" Sam scoffed, shaking his head.

"I remember when a boy volunteered to teach her how to surf. You got up at the crack of dawn and learned how to do it. After you told Mackenzie that you would teach her," Clover laughed.

Sam shook his head, looking out at the ocean. Thinking back on it now, he had felt jealousy when it came to Mackenzie.

"I had to keep the surfers and skaters away from her. Uncle Deano would have killed me," Sam laughed.

"Also, Mackenzie was your favorite person," Clover added. She squeezed his arm again. "Do you know why they all wanted to be close to her?"

"Isn't it every surfer's dream to date a girl that looked like they were from the islands?" Sam laughed.

Clover released him just as Sam stopped dead in his tracks.

"Mom, you can't mean Clarissa is talking about her being Asian?" Sam said in disbelief.

Clover turned toward her son, giving him a sympathetic look. "Have you noticed the only person of color in your company who holds an Executive Director position is the Director of Diversity? I was reading an article about how that was a common occurrence in most major corporations. So, I went to your company website to see if that's the case for you. Sadly, it is. Also, have you noticed how you have been promoted to higher positions and Bianca has not? Even though she referred you for the job there. I understand you are in different departments, but your opportunities should not be that different. She graduated summa cum laude as well. You've been promoted three times already, and you're staring at the fourth. If you look at your social circle now. It looks quite different, doesn't it?" Clover asked.

Sam thought about it, realizing she was right. He'd always regarded himself less as caucasian and more as Jewish. His grandmother and his mom had educated him on the nuisances of both the Jewish faith and culture. Growing up, he recognized that his family celebrated different holidays from everyone around him. He embraced the traditions, acutely aware that his heritage was unique because it was both an ethnicity and a religion. While he didn't go to temple more than once a year, he still observed Rosh Hashanah, Yom Kippur, and Sukkot. Mackenzie had always joined him and Clover on those occasions and even learned to make Haroseth, a dish made from diced apple, toasted walnuts, a touch of cinnamon, and a splash of wine. It was his favorite.

He also knew going into finance as a Jewish male was very stereotypical, but it was something he didn't think much about day to day. And obviously, he knew he was white facing, yet he never claimed to be caucasian. He suddenly realized the magnitude of what it meant that the world around him saw him as white, within the firm and in his life.

He plopped down on the sand, and suddenly, all the subtle hints Clarissa was giving about how Mackenzie couldn't support or understand him made sense. He felt the blood drain from his face.

"Mom, you know I'm not like that," Sam argued.

"I know you do not intend to be, but it's systemic. And part of white privilege is not having to acknowledge it to yourself," Clover explained, sitting down next to him.

Sam sat there stunned thinking back to Bianca asking him at the conference, "What's all this?" Or Erza saying he might have to leave them behind. Suddenly he flashed to how he panicked at the restaurant wondering if Mackenzie's olive skin tone, that he had always found beautiful, played into him feeling embarrassed of her.

Sam hung his head down, shaking it in disbelief. Thinking back to how Sofia acted, everything clicking into place.

Clover sat down next to him in the sand. "I think a lot of people in your field feel like Mackenzie is not the 'right' type of Asian. The Philippines isn't considered one of the super-rich, developed Asian nations. If you are around close-minded people, then they would stick their nose up at her as being not good enough for you. Maybe undeserving of your time and love."

"Mom, there's no one in the world besides you that I love more than Mackenzie," he cried.

Clover turned toward him and ran her fingers through his hair. "Oh, my dear boy. I know that like I know how to breathe. I am merely pointing out an aspect of this that you haven't looked at yet. The good thing about all this is even though you could not see it, you felt that something was off," Clover said, trying to comfort him.

Sam felt his world shift again. They both sat there for a long time not saying a word. Sam looked up at the sky, stunned. Ezra had stopped short of saying something to him at the bar, but was this what he'd meant? Sam hung his head low and felt his heart pounding out of his chest, suddenly afraid of what he was turning into.

Chapter 22

"I still don't know how you managed to snap your fingers and get flights, hotels, meals, and laundry to just fall into place," Mackenzie teased as they sat at the airport, waiting to board the plane.

"If you throw enough money at something, magically, things get done."

Mackenzie scrunched her face in mock disgust. "Apparently, that sounded as obnoxious out loud as it did in my head," Hunter said, taking another sip of his water.

Ollie and Parker had come back about an hour after the panic attack and nosebleed. Ollie naturally felt guilty when Mac and Hunter filled him in.

"I told her not to bother you. Besides Mac's familiar with this stuff, we handled it," Hunter said reassuringly.

Then Hunter announced he was going to do number three on his list. Ollie immediately protested.

"Not the actual thing, but a modified version of it. I'm not dumb enough to try that," Hunter reassured him.

Mackenzie twisted her body toward Hunter. "Wait, you owe me one. Tell me another of your wildest dreams you've accomplished," Mackenzie said.

Hunter nodded and took a deep breath. "Watch an opera at the Sydney Opera House," he said with a smile.

Mackenzie shook her head in disbelief. "Did I mention my list feels lackluster compared to yours?" Mackenzie declared. "What opera was it?"

"Le Nozze di Figaro," Hunter answered. "The Marriage of Figaro."

Mackenzie let out a soft, long whistle. "It's arguably the greatest opera of all time," she said, smiling over at him.

Hunter tilted his head. He looked a bit surprised she would know about opera.

"So, how was it?" Mackenzie asked.

"It's funny. I didn't know much about it. When I got there, I was really surprised at how much it looked like a ship," Hunter admitted.

"Did you wear a tux and sit in a box? Maybe get tiny binoculars?" Mackenzie teased.

Hunter shook his head, gently elbowing Mackenzie.

"No," he responded to her in an exaggerated, whiny tone. Then cleared his throat. "Okay, maybe we did," he muttered.

Mackenzie nudged him back.

"In my defense, they said Box A was the best seat for viewing and sound. Ollie got a kick out of it, though he was worried he was going to fall asleep. He made it through. Honestly, I don't think anyone could have slept in there. They weren't exaggerating when they talked about the acoustics. I felt the music thump in my chest. It sounded intimate as if the singers were right in our box even though they were on stage. The clarity of the music sounded, I guess, pure?" Hunter offered.

"That's a unique one. Not as daredevil as the other dreams you told me about."

"My list becomes more sedate as you get to the bottom. I actually changed the last three after I found out that there was nothing more they could do for me," Hunter said with a sad smile.

"You said you can't finish your list. Why is that?" Mackenzie asked, trying to downplay the latter part of his statement.

"Five to seven, you can't throw money at," he joked.

Mackenzie pursed her lips, wanting to ask what they were; however, something told her Hunter would rather not share. She wasn't going to push him.

Mackenzie looked around the plane in amazement. "So, this was your solution to not having to layover anywhere?" she said in disbelief.

"If I say the throw money line again, will you judge me?" Hunter asked.

"I'll just add, 'that time I flew on a private jet' to the list of the things I can claim to have done thanks to you."

"Did your uncle really have an opera section in the shop?" Hunter asked.

Mackenzie nodded. "Honestly, back then, it was one of our more popular sections. My uncle firmly believed all music was good to someone. He had songs and reasons for everything."

Hunter looked over at her interest. "What do you mean?" he asked.

Mackenzie looked up, trying to think of an example. "He said music was its own language. If you were happy, sad, or angry, there was a song for whatever you were feeling. He had this theory that you can tell you are in love when you see someone, and a song pops into your head," Mackenzie answered.

Hunter gave her a smirk and nudged at her again.

"'A Case of You' by Joni Mitchell," she confessed. "Parts of it are sad, but there is the chorus that says, 'you're in my blood like holy wine and a verse about being a painter. I remember looking up and hearing that part in my head. Sam, he's well in my blood," Mackenzie said.

"How about him?" he asked.

"He won't tell me," she laughed.

Just then, the captain announced they were clear for takeoff. Mackenzie looked out the window, watching as Santorini fell away below them, getting smaller and further away.

She looked over at Ollie and Parker. Ollie was holding Parker's hand. Parker had told her he hated taking off; it was the only time he was truly nervous while traveling.

Hunter closed his eyes for a moment. She noticed he always did that during takeoff.

"Do you get nervous too?" Mackenzie asked.

Hunter shook his head.

"I got a thought one day, and now I just do it. The feeling of rising up in the air," he said.

Mackenzie understood what he was alluding to. She sat there silent, not commenting or trying to change the subject or give words of comfort. Sometimes the best thing to do is say nothing at all.

"You know you have the best sense of intuition," Hunter said, his eyes still closed, head back tilted up to the roof of the plane.

"My uncle always said that about me. He told me once I could probably clean up in the psychic game if I was a charlatan."

She watched Hunter smile, opening his eyes, which were still fixed on the roof of the plane.

"I like that you don't ask me questions like if I am scared. It's nice to say things candidly without judgment or fear. Not having to worry about uncomfortable statements hanging in the air. Having to elaborate about things you would rather not talk about."

Mackenzie grabbed his hand, squeezing it softly. "I figure if you want to talk about it, you would."

"You said the last time you painted on canvas was years ago. Why is that?" Hunter asked.

Mackenzie sighed.

"First, painting is expensive. Plus, I used to paint the pictures I felt really good about, like the one at the coffee shop. I started going there a while ago and mentioned I was a painter. The owner asked if I could paint something for the wall my painting is on right now. Actually, thinking about it now, that's the last time I painted on canvas," she confessed.

Hunter turned toward her. "I am not blowing smoke, I promise you, but that painting was really amazing. They say paintings are supposed to move you. I've seen the Mona Lisa, Starry Night, and Monet's Water Lilies. Mona Lisa did nothing for me. Starry Night did mostly because I am a huge Van Gogh fan. Monet's Water Lilies were pretty, but they didn't move me. Your painting was like seeing the boardwalk through someone's eyes who truly loved the place."

Mackenzie rubbed her lips against each other. "Venice Beach is in my soul," she whispered.

Hunter reached over, tapping her on the knee. "Did your uncle have a song he associated with you?" Hunter asked.

"Of course," she said with a smile. "He told me he used to play it when I cried as a baby. He joked that he didn't realize he was foreshadowing," Mackenzie said.

"What song?" he asked.

"'Tiny Dancer,'" she said with a smile. "Blue Jean Baby, LA Lady," she sang, pointing to her jeans.

Hunter tilted his head, nodding. "Come to think of it, I have never seen you in anything but blue jeans," he chuckled. "Seriously, your uncle sounds amazing."

Mackenzie looked over at Ollie and Parker who were wrapped in each other's arms watching some documentary as the flight attendant poured wine into their glasses. Next he came up to Mac and Hunter and asked if either of them would like a drink.

"Water," both of them said at the same time.

The attendant returned with two ice-cold blue bottles. Mackenzie read the name in the etched glass.

"Antipodes? Never heard of it," Mackenzie muttered, taking a sip. Then, she held the bottle in front of her and studied the label for a moment.

"Ten-dollar water doesn't taste any different, right?" Hunter asked with a smirk.

"Ten dollars a bottle!" she exclaimed. "This puts my Brita filter to shame," she laughed.

They both took a sip, looking at each other and giggling again.

"Do you suddenly crave caviar?" Hunter asked.

Mackenzie sighed. "Sadly, no. I guess I don't have refined tastes." Mackenzie stopped suddenly, thinking of the day at the Platform. Her previous jesting hit home.

"Can I ask, is your uncle the reason why you don't really drink? You said you had wine now and then. But you have been to a few places where you could have really indulged, and you didn't."

Mackenzie nodded, looking out the window. She bit her bottom lip. "So," she said, taking a deep breath. "I lied when we first met."

She watched as Hunter looked at her in confusion.

"Uncle Deano didn't stop drinking after he took me in. He binge drank maybe once or twice a month. He would go and play mahjong all night, drink hard, then sober up. First, it was cirrhosis of the liver that progressed to pancreatic cancer. He was really good about hiding it, but I knew he did it to himself," she said quietly.

Hunter lowered his head. "I told you we came over for my sister, right?" Hunter asked.

Mackenzie nodded in confirmation.

"She had a fairly aggressive form of acute lymphocytic leukemia when she was seventeen. Every doctor in China advised us to go to the US since no one in our family had bone marrow that matched. That's why we moved. MD Andersen in Houston is the best in the world when it comes to treating leukemia. She went into remission, and for a while, they had a handle on it. But when she turned thirty-one, she was diagnosed with myelodysplastic syndrome. A few years later, it developed into AML."

Hunter rubbed his face a few times. "I think she always felt like she was on borrowed time. She was successful, but she was promiscuous. Sometimes really thoughtless," Hunter said quietly. "She had a few scares. I guess she never thought about the consequences."

Mackenzie looked out the window again. "I have never told anyone about my uncle's drinking. I mean, Sam knew. No shock there," Mackenzie joked mirthlessly.

"Thanks for telling me," Hunter said.

"I guess you wash away the negatives when you watch someone you love fight a losing battle," Mackenzie whispered. She shook her head, looking over at Hunter.

"Okay, so let's change the subject," Mackenzie announced.

She pulled out her phone, holding it up to him. "Let's figure out the best way to go about your number three."

Mackenzie and Hunter peered down at her phone.

"Wait," Hunter said, swiping her phone. He smiled and began to chuckle.

Mackenzie could not figure out what was so funny until he tapped on one of the folders on her home screen.

"No," she screamed as Hunter grabbed her phone and held it in the air. Her scream was loud enough to draw the attention of Ollie, Parker, and the attendant.

She reached out, trying to retrieve her phone from him.

"How many of these Vertical drama apps do you have?" he said, laughing so hard that he had to wrap his free arm around his midsection.

Mackenzie finally successfully retrieved it. Feeling her face get hotter by the moment. Hunter finally stopped laughing.

"Sorry, there's, you know, just so many," he said, starting to laugh again.

"I went down a TikTok rabbit hole one day and found a couple of bootleg ones. The next thing I know, I am downloading apps and buying coins to unlock the next chapter," Mackenzie agonized. "Congratulations, you now know my shameful secret." She glared over at Hunter, who was still softly chuckling.

"What, you have no guilty pleasures?" she asked, a bit of animosity in her voice.

"He watches soap operas," Ollie yelled, his eyes still never leaving the screen.

Mackenzie gasped, covering her mouth with one hand and pointing to Hunter with the other.

"Bro," Hunter growled, looking over at Ollie and Parker.

She watched Parker tilt his head up and announce loudly.

"All of them."

"Dude!" Hunter yelled his accent thicker than she had ever heard it. He leaned toward them, raising his hand in the air as if he was going to smack them over their heads.

Mackenzie looked over at him smugly, cocking her brow in the air, laughing at Hunter.

"He even goes to spoiler sites," Ollie added.

"Seriously?" Hunter barked

Mackenzie sputtered, laughing as Hunter picked up a small bag of gourmet nuts, hurling it toward Ollie's head.

Chapter 23

MACKENZIE

They landed at Thessaloniki Airport in the evening and made their way to Cavo Olympo in Plaka Litochoro, Pieria. They decided to stop and eat at Nero, a restaurant in the hotel lobby. Knowing that if they did not eat at that moment they would get to their suites and just pass out.

Hunter and Mackenzie shared a suite once more. Hunter insisted they share the bed when she said she could crash on the couch.

"It's not as big as the one in Luxus, but we still can barely reach each other," Hunter argued.

Mackenzie caved after she laid on the couch and found it uncomfortable enough to know she would toss and turn all night, keeping them both up. Suddenly the constant traveling caught up with her. She woke up the next day, ate breakfast, and told Hunter she was still tired so going back to bed. Hunter echoed her sentiment, also climbing back into bed again.

It was nearly dusk when Ollie shook her awake. They went out on the terrace, all of them laughing about how they didn't realize how tired they were until they got to Plaka.

"Maybe the Gods cast sleep on us," Parker mused.

After dinner Parker and Ollie went back to their room to enjoy their private outdoor jacuzzi. Hunter had insisted they enjoy as much alone time as they could, to treat it like a vacation even though Ollie was technically working.

"They love you," Mackenzie said, watching them leave.

"I have to make up for springing this last-minute jaunt on them," Hunter laughed.

They sat side by side in beach recliners, looking out at the white tents along the beach from the balcony of their suite.

"The ocean is so calm here," Mackenzie commented

.

"I take it that Greece isn't the most popular place for surfing," Hunter joked.

Mackenzie shook her head, chuckling while taking a sip of water. "Have you ever tried surfing?" Mackenzie asked.

"Of course. I mean, all you hear about in China is surfing in California. I'm decent at it," Hunter said, shrugging his shoulders.

"Me too. I mean, I used to be. I haven't surfed in years," Mackenzie admitted.

"What, no time between work and scrolling the verticals?" Hunter teased.

Mackenzie groaned, crossing her arms in front of her. "Listen, everyone has something, right?" Mackenzie argued.

"But most of the storylines are so toxic. The male lead tortures the female lead before realizing he loves her."

"Or the couple that love each other deeply, but for some reason, they have complete trust in the scheming sister or friend making their lives miserable," Mackenzie added.

Hunter crossed his arms, scoffing. "Exactly, they make Chinese men look so stupid and gullible," he spat out.

"Does it make you feel better to know I skip those entirely?" Mackenzie turned to her side to face Hunter.

"Which ones do you watch then?"

"They have some where the couple is super savvy and don't fall into traps. Some are just sweet love stories. A lot of the American ones aren't as savage," Mackenzie argued. "I mostly watch the ones about a character who gets reborn." She felt her cheeks get red.

"Really?" Hunter responded. "Why do you like those?"

Mackenzie looked up at the sky, musing. "They always start off with the heroine making a tragic mistake that causes her death. Getting reborn to a time in her past before everything went bad. Vowing to do things differently," Mackenzie said.

"In my next life," Hunter said dramatically.

Mackenzie eyes Hunter.

"You seem to know an awful lot about them…"

Hunter shrugged. "I might have seen a couple of them," Hunter confessed.

"The fact that you know they are called verticals gave that away," she teased.

"Is there anything you regret that you wish you could go back and do differently? I know everyone does, but anything that stands out?" Hunter asked.

Mackenzie turned, pulling her legs up and wrapping her arms around them.

"Yeah. I wish I could go back and tell my uncle I would be okay sooner. He held on for so long. Toward the end, his stomach was so swollen he looked like he was pregnant. He was in pain every day and didn't want to be doped up. Clover would come and do some meditation sessions with him. They helped for a while, but those last few weeks..." Mackenzie shook her head, gulping hard.

Hunter reached over and squeezed her hand.

"He held on because he was afraid of leaving me alone. I think he thought I wasn't ready to let him go, so he fought to stay alive even though he was miserable."

"I can understand that. My sister worried about me, too," Hunter replied.

"You are probably tired of me saying this, but it was Sam who made me realize what he was doing. The nurse kept coming in asking if she could push more pain meds through, and Uncle Deano kept refusing. I begged him to let them, but he didn't listen. Sam was sitting behind me, arms around me as I held my uncle's hand. Sam reached over and said, 'Don't worry, Uncle Deano, I got her.' That's when it all clicked."

Mackenzie felt tears run down her face, wiping them away furiously.

"I kissed his forehead. Told him I would be fine. Then said *'mahal kita taytay.'* It means 'I love you, dad.' I never called him dad, even though that's what he was. I just felt at that moment he needed to know how I felt. The next time the nurse came in, he let them give him a high dose of Demerol. He passed maybe ten minutes later," Mackenzie said, taking a deep breath. "I keep thinking if I said it sooner, he would not have been in so much pain."

Hunter took her hand again and squeezed, trying to comfort her. Mackenzie gulped hard, clearing her throat looking over at him across their connected hands, spanning the space between them. Swinging their arms a few times. She gave him a look inviting him to share.

"Shocker warning, it has to do with my sister. I regret not taking her out of the hospital before she passed. I think she would have wanted to be at home or at the beach because she hated the hospital," Hunter said.

Mackenzie turned again, this time crisscrossing her legs.

"When we first got the news, I wasn't the best support. I was in denial; I didn't see her as much as I could have. I buried myself in work until Ollie came to tell me to get my head out of my ass. After that, I was pretty much stuck to her side. To the point of annoyance," Hunter laughed, shaking his head.

"I could tell a sterile room wasn't where she wanted to be when she left this world. But again, because I was a train wreck, I was afraid to take her out of hospice, even with Ollie there. So yeah, if I can go back, I would have asked her where she wanted to go and take her there." Hunter sighed hard. "In my next life, right?"

Mackenzie held her hand out to give him a fist bump. Hunter brought up his own fist and tapped it to hers, both laughing at Mackenzie's bro-y move as they lay there looking out at the ocean.

The next morning, they got up and piled into their rental jeep, driving first to Litochoro, a village nestled at the foot of Mount Olympus. They waited for a few minutes to hire a guide named Chrysanthos, who was highly recommended by the resort, to arrive. He introduced himself, then got into the jeep with them, drove them up the winding road, and took them to Prionia, a mountain village at an elevation of 1100 meters.

Ollie kept eyeing Hunter suspiciously. They got out of the jeep and began to walk up Mount Olympus. Ollie was adamant they would only walk for ten minutes and then turn around.

"The original dream was to stand on top of Mount Olympus. But there's no way I can hike all the way up," Hunter said.

Hunter looked around and found a small, flat part of the mountain. The four of them walked up to it as Hunter looked up. Mackenzie smiled, taking his hand and pressing it to the side of the mountain.

He looked up in bliss, then gave a bittersweet smile.

"I would have loved to climb it." He said softly. "Stand on top of it," Hunter whispered.

Mackenzie turned and walked away, giving the three men their moment. Ollie was the one who'd been there when he did his first three. She walked back to the jeep, looking at them from a distance.

"Your friend is sick?" she heard from behind her. It was their guide, Chrysanthos.

Mackenzie nodded, turning toward him with a sad smile. "His dream was to stand on top of Mount Olympus. There's just no way he could make the climb."

"You want to go to the top?" Chrysanthos asked. "It can be done." He pointed to the jeep, looking back at her.

"Really?!" Mackenzie squealed. "You can drive us to the top?" Her heart was pounding out of her chest.

"*Nai*," he responds. "Umm, yes. It is a good time, no snow."

Mackenzie screamed at the guys, motioning them over, letting them know there was a way up.

"Have you driven up there many times?" Parker asked.

Chrysanthos nodded. "Yes, a lot. Very familiar," he said. "It is a bit scary but easy drive for me."

Mackenzie jumped up and down, pulling Hunter into the jeep with her. Chrysanthos drove them about 30 minutes to a town called Kalyvia. He explained the drive was about 13 miles. Warned them that it would be bumpy. Mackenzie held the bottom of the car seat until her knuckles were white.

Hunter gasped. "Your vertigo!" he exclaimed, yelling over the sound of their open jeep jerking, some equipment in the back clanking, and the roar of the engine

"I'll be okay!" she yelled back as they took one of the more than 25 hairpin turns to get there.

Hunter held her hand and yelled, "Remember, look out, not down!"

Mackenzie looked ahead and saw two small cement buildings surrounded by a row of rocks.

"This is Christakis Refuge," Chrysanthos yelled, driving toward it.

The jeep stopped. Hunter grabbed Mackenzie's hand, pulling her out of the jeep with surprising strength. She let him drag her to wherever he was going. Suddenly he stopped, he smiled so brightly it nearly brought tears to her eyes. He raised his arms up in the air and screamed.

"Number three, stand atop Mount Olympus!"

Mackenzie laughed as he hugged her, spinning her around. Her face was aching because she was smiling so hard.

They got back to the resort a few hours later. Whatever Hunter tipped Chrysanthos made him insist he drive them to the airport the next morning.

Mackenzie looked over at Ollie, he was uncharacteristically quiet, hovering more than usual. They got back to their suites and took showers, washing the dust and dirt off them. When she got out of the shower Ollie was already putting an IV line into Hunter's arm, holding out two pills. Hunter took them and swallowed them lying down.

"Sorry, dad's being a bit much," Hunter said, looking up at Ollie.

"They should kick in fast," Ollie muttered, stepping away from the bed and next to Mackenzie.

"He needs to get some sleep. We are on the first flight to Frankfurt in the morning," Ollie said softly before leaving the room.

Mackenzie walked up to the bed, sitting beside Hunter.

"Before I pass out, I just wanted to say thank you. None of us would have thought to ask. I think Ollie didn't object because of how determined you were," Hunter laughed.

Mackenzie smiled down at him. "You have no idea how happy I am that I got to experience one of your dreams with you."

Hunter drifted off to sleep about thirty minutes later. She did not know why, but she felt like she needed to check on Ollie.

She knocked on their door softly. A beat later, Parker opened the door. Mac looked behind him and saw Ollie sitting on the edge of the bed, crying hard. Parker ushered Mackenzie in. Mackenzie knelt down in front of Ollie, putting her hands on his knees.

Ollie wiped his tears away, shaking his head.

"Tell her, baby. She deserves to know," Parker coaxed.

Ollie gulped hard. "Hunter is adamant that he wouldn't be doped up in a bed, barely coherent when it's his time," Ollie said quietly.

"He always said if it got to the point where they needed to push pain meds through..." Ollie began to cry again.

Mackenzie felt herself shaking. "How long until then?" Mac said quietly, closing her eyes she braced herself for his response. Not wanting to hear his answer.

Ollie began to cry again, his fists covering his eyes. Parker sat next to him, hugging him hard and making soothing sounds.

Ollie looked down at Mackenzie. He took her hands in his, kissing her fingers. "As strong as Hunter tries to be. Not long. The pain will soon become unbearable because of how weak his body is," Ollie whispered.

"Ollie," Mackenzie said softly, tears already falling down her cheeks.

Ollie squeezed her hands, then looked at her in anguish. His voice broke as he whispered.

"If we are lucky, maybe a week."

Chapter 24

SAM

"**D**ude, I'm going to have a heart attack," Ezra moaned, slowing his pace to a walk. His hands were on his hips, gasping for air.

Sam stopped a few feet in front of Ezra, shaking his head.

"You're out of shape, bro," Sam joked, walking up to him and grabbing his shoulder.

Sam was a seasoned volleyball player and he used to surf a bit, but nowadays he didn't have time to commit to a beach volleyball team and he lived too far away from the beach to even think about surfing.

Sam and Ezra walked up to their tote bags, beach of them grabbing a water bottle. They made their way up the bleachers catching their breath.

Sam looked around Drake Stadium on the UCLA campus. He spent a lot of time here. Running around the light and dark blue track with UCLA painted on each side of the bleachers. He took a big gulp of his water, leaning back on the bleachers behind the ones he was sitting on.

He looked over at Ezra, who seemed lost in thought.

"What's on your mind?" Sam asked, taking another drink of water.

"I was just thinking about the first year we were all here. Bianca and I would always know where to find you and Mac. You would be running laps. She would have her head buried in whatever sketch she was working on," Ezra smiled, taking a huge gulp of water.

Sam looked around again, envisioning the scene from Ezra's memory. Mac would go through sketchbooks like most bookworms go through books. She could be sitting anywhere, see something—a leaf, a bird on the rail, even people running around the track—and feel inspired to sketch. Sam often snuck up behind her and screamed because she would get so absorbed with whatever she was drawing. Suddenly, something dawned on him.

"Ez, when was the last time you saw Mackenzie paint?" Sam asked.

Ezra turned to him and let out a slow whistle.

"Man, years. In fact I think it was at the fine arts department second year right before she had to drop out," Ezra answered.

Sam straightened up, resting his hands on his knees.

"Canvas and paints," Sam muttered.

Ezra looked over at him in confusion.

"Been thinking a lot about what you said. Her birthday presents. I could have gotten her canvas and paints. She's had her eye on this set at Blick for a long time, but it is over a grand, and she would have never gotten it for herself," Sam looked up at the sky, groaning.

"I have been getting her that Tiffany perfume for the last two years. Come to think of it now, I never smelled it on her either," Sam shook his head, feeling Ezra put his hand on his knee, patting it a few times.

"You know she was always happy to get anything from you, right?" Ezra said.

"I know. I'm just realizing after talking to you and my mom how out of touch I have been with her," Sam said quietly.

Ezra leaned back, watching the people running around the field.

"People outgrow their childhood sweethearts," Ezra said.

Sam whipped his head toward Ezra.

"Clarissa said the same thing to me," Sam said.

"Ah yes, Clarissa, I have heard about her. Bianca calls her 'that thirsty Becky with the good hair.' Is she what's been on your mind?" Ezra asked.

"No," Sam said too fast. He paused for a moment before confessing, "Yes, in a way. I don't know, it's just that she fits my everyday life so easily."

Ezra nodded, looking at Sam. "Mac doesn't, I get it," Ezra replied. "Look, I am not going to lie, a part of me wants to smack the shit out of you for the stunt you pulled. But I more just want to know why," Ezra commented.

"I just remember seeing her and panicking. I was worried the execs from the C-suite might get a bad impression," Sam said.

"Of her or you?" Ezra asked.

Sam looked at his friend, feeling that tightness in his chest was now familiar.

"Me," he confessed. "I don't know when I started leading this weird work-personal double life."

"Probably around the time that you started to be embarrassed by Mac," Erza said pointedly.

Sam got ready to protest then stopped himself. He thought of the countless times he didn't bother to take Mac to some event or dinner with a client. How he easily invited Clarissa because he knew it would be more beneficial.

Ezra stretched out his legs, crossing them over each other.

"Would you believe me if I said I didn't know I was doing it?" Sam asked.

"Of course, because if you were an asshole, you would just start dating that 'thirsty Becky with the good hair'. I think the best thing for you to do is wait for Mac to make the first move. At the very least, you guys can get closure."

Sam rubbed his face.

"If she ever talks to me again." The thought made him feel like his heart was shattering. "She's still in Europe. Pretty sure with a guy," Sam said, eyeing Ezra.

Ezra laughed, "Again, B didn't tell me shit. This is the first time I have heard about her being in Europe. So, I still got nothing for you," Ezra said, putting up his hands.

Sam lowered his head and felt his throat dry.

"Clarissa kissed me, and I kissed her back," Sam agonized.

Ezra let a huge breath out.

"I would be lying if I said there is not a part of me that wants to beat the shit out of you. Technically, you did nothing wrong. Mac broke up with you. You're free now to explore that option," Ezra said, taking another sip from his water bottle.

Sam thought back to what his mom pointed out. He could go down that road, in fact he was already on it. He wanted to talk to Ezra about some of the things his mother pointed out, but he was still trying to wrap his mind around it.

"She's not making a secret about wanting a relationship."

"How do you feel about that?"

Sam shook his head. "I am still trying to figure out if I like her ambition or if I'm just bitter because Mac is off with some guy I don't know," Sam explained.

Ezra uncrossed his legs and sat up.

"You know, anytime you were hanging out with us, we always knew the second Mac walked into the room. You would smile or get up and reach out for her. We joked that it was nauseating," Ezra mumbled.

Sam chuckled, taking another sip of his water.

"Let me ask you this question," Ezra started. "Who do you see yourself reaching out to when you're at your lowest point? When you wake up in the morning and roll over, who do you want to be there?" Ezra asked.

Sam felt the tears form around his eyes, wiping them away.

"You know the answer to that," Sam said.

"No, really think about it, Sam. Not because it's the right answer or because you're afraid the people you love would judge you. Think about it for a while and get back to me," Ezra instructed.

Sam nodded, looking down at his phone. He had changed his screen saver to a picture of the ocean in Malibu. He wasn't sure if he did it out of anger or guilt.

Chapter 25

MACKENZIE

Mackenzie sat in front of Hunter on the floor at the Frankfurt airport, eating a bowl of *Kartoffelsuppe*. They had a five-hour layover, and the four of them said they had to try at least one unique dish there. The German soup had potatoes, key onions, celery, butter, and milk.

"You're not having the soup because of me, right?" Hunter asked.

"No. Have you seen what Parker and Ollie are eating? My stomach hurts just looking at it," she pointed to the two of them sitting at a nearby table.

They had chosen something called *Schweinshaxe*. All she knew was that it was a pork knuckle, and it had a thick layer of sauce under it.

"Besides, this came with cake," Mackenzie said, smiling, holding up a wrapped piece of plum cake.

Hunter chuckled, handing her his slice. Mackenzie took the cake from him. Eating had been a struggle for Hunter this whole trip. Earlier that morning, he'd woken up disoriented for a moment, forgetting he was on a plane. Thankfully, Ollie was prepared and had his meds ready. As she watched him eating, she noticed there was a blueish tint on the skin of his hands.

Mac looked up and saw Hunter had noticed her eyeing his hands.

"I am going to venture a guess that Ollie and Parker told you," Hunter said quietly.

Mackenzie nodded.

"Mackenzie, I have thought about this a lot. And this is my decision. Please respect it. Don't try to talk me out of it," Hunter pleaded.

Mackenzie put her soup to the side, then scooted closer and took the soup from his lap, setting it aside, too. She took both his hands in hers.

"Hunter, you forget I have been through this. I know what it looks like at the end. How it hurts them more than it hurts you. I might not completely agree with it, but I understand. Uncle Deano hated that I used to have to feed him. He'd get embarrassed when he would throw up or, worse, soil the bed in his sleep. Cancer robbed him of nearly everything, including his dignity. If this decision makes you feel like it will help you hold on to yours, then I support it," Mackenzie replied.

Seeing the stunned look on Hunter's face, she squeezed his hands.

"I remember sitting beside Xiāng's bed. There were tubes with bags filled with all kinds of liquids. She was so small. She would wake up now and then and just look at me. Me doing my fucking damnedest not to cry. I didn't want her last memory of me to be crying," Hunter choked out, tears beginning to fall from his face.

Mac dug through her bag, found some tissue, and handed it to him.

She looked over at Ollie, who was beginning to stand up. Mackenzie put her hand up, letting him know she had this. Parker grabbed Ollie's hand gently, trying to get him to sit back down. Ollie did not sit down right away, but eventually he did. Parker brushed his cheek from across the table. Hunter wiped the tears away.

"All I could think was: that wasn't Xiāng. She looked so small and helpless. She was fiery and intimidating. No one would ever look at her and think she was vulnerable. I felt so guilty that the first thing I felt was relief when she passed. Knowing she didn't have to be that shell in the bed," Hunter gulped.

Mackenzie put her hands on his knees. "You know my uncle kept the End of Life Option Act from me," Mackenzie said.

She read about it a little while after her Uncle Deano passed. California had an act that permits patients diagnosed with a terminal disease to request aid-in-dying drugs from their doctors.

She watched Hunter's eyes widen.

"The same with me. I am pretty sure like my sister, your uncle didn't want to scare you," Hunter offered.

"That and he was worried about me. He needed to make sure I would be okay," Mackenzie explained

.

Hunter took one of Mackenzie's hands, rubbing them between his own and blowing lightly.

"We do that too," Mac laughed, referring to the action he had just taken.

"Everyone does in China. It's a strange way to bring comfort, but it does," Hunter said.

"Unless your breath stinks," Mackenzie laughed, trying to bring a bit of humor into the heavy conversation.

Hunter laughed loudly, holding his stomach, coughing a few times.

"Mackenzie, I don't want to hurt you, but..."

"Your doctor has filed the paperwork," Mackenzie finished.

Doctors were required to file paperwork in order to enact ELOA.

Hunter took a deep breath and nodded.

"Ollie's really upset about the decision, but Parker has helped him understand," Hunter said, looking over at them.

Mackenzie nodded, looking over at them.

"From what Ollie has told me, you and Parker are his only family. Sure, you pay him to take care of you, but he loves you," Mackenzie replied.

"I'm worried about when it happens," Hunter said. "I am glad he has Parker." Hunter smiled at the two of them.

Mac looked up at Hunter. "I know you said I didn't have to say thank you. But I am going to anyway. Thank you, Hunter, for everything," Mackenzie said.

Hunter reached down and pinched her cheek. "Just remember to always be the sensational person you are. And if you can, try to stop hiding," Hunter asked.

Mackenzie chuckled, picking up her soup again spooning out a biteful. She looked over to see Hunter struggle; he was shaking. Mackenzie took a seat next to him. Without saying a word, she lightly supported his wrist helping him steady his arm to continue eating.

They got on the plane, making the trip from Frankfurt to LAX. The line at customs was a nightmare, so much so that Hunter begrudgingly agreed to sit in a wheelchair. Mackenzie could see how hard that was for him. She still remembered how adamant her uncle was about pushing it himself. Until he didn't have the strength to argue.

Ollie and Parker stood in front of them, waiting in the long queue; both looked slightly uncomfortable.

"I told you guys to use the bathroom before we got off the plane," Mackenzie scolded.

Ollie turned around, rolling his eyes.

"Go to the bathroom. We will hold your spot," Hunter said.

Ollie and Parker made their way across the few roped-off areas and toward the bathroom. Hunter reached out to Mackenzie, taking her hand in his.

"You mind if we drop you off? Or have you called Bianca to come get you?" Hunter asked.

Mackenzie looked down at Hunter. She had so many things she wanted to say to him before they said goodbye. At that moment she realized she did not want to leave him. Mac bit her lip trying to figure out a way to say what she wanted to say. She decided just to go with the direct approach. She squatted down holding the arms of his wheelchair.

"So, here's the thing," Mackenzie started. "I have another week before I have to face the masses. And well, as much as I love Venice, I would be just wandering the streets or cooped up at my house watching vertical dramas. I was wondering if I can hang with you guys."

Hunter took a deep breath and said, "Mackenzie, I don't know if I can let you do that."

"I mean, it's that, or I am just asking Ollie for your address and forcing my way in every day," Mackenzie said dramatically.

Hunter grabbed her by the wrist. "Mac, I don't know when I am going to do this. I don't want you to regret it," Hunter whispered.

Mackenzie smiled up at him. "I promise I won't, Hunter. I would regret it more if I just left. Let me play Hooky from my life for a little longer," Mackenzie said, giving him a playful wink.

She didn't want to admit she was terrified he would say no. While the rest of her life was riddled with uncertainty, this was the one thing she was sure of. Something about the look on Mac's face must have gotten to Hunter. She watched as tears filled his eyes.

"Promise if it gets to be too much, you will leave. Don't feel obligated to stay," Hunter choked out as he wiped the tears away.

Mackenzie felt her own eyes start to water. She got up, still bent, giving him a hug. She pulled away holding her hand up in the scout sign, three fingers raised and together with her pinky and thumb bent down.

"*Wǒ fāshì*," Mackenzie said, winking, knowing it meant 'I swear.'

Hunter chuckled through his tears. "You still remember some Mandarin. Or is it the vertical dramas? Seriously, how much do you watch those things?" Hunter asked.

"Probably as much as you watch your soaps," Mackenzie said a bit loud.

Hunter shh'd her while trying to dramatically hide his face. Mac held her hand out with her pinky and thumb extended. Hunter shook his head doing the same. She hooked their pinkies together and pressed her thumbprint against his.

"That's better than signing a contract, right? At least that's how they make it look."

Hunter started to laugh but it brought on another coughing fit. He finally caught his breath long enough to get his question out.

"No, seriously, how many do you watch?"

Chapter 26

MACKENZIE

"This is what you call downsizing?"

Mackenzie looked around Hunter's two-bedroom house on Laurel Canyon in the Hollywood Hills. The inside had high vaulted wood ceilings with angled support beams cut into them, track lighting, and hardwood floors. It looked like something that would be on the cover of Architectural Digest. She followed Parker, Ollie, and Hunter deeper into the house.

Hunter wheeled his luggage into a small bedroom on the ground floor. The bed was enormous, taking up most of the room. The rest of the bottom floor was all open living space. She heard Ollie and Parker coming back downstairs.

"Make yourself at home," Ollie said, making his way to the kitchen. He pulled out a pint of vanilla ice cream, dumping it into a blender. He disappeared as he bent down. She heard him rummaging for a bit until he popped back up with a can of Ensure.

Belatedly, she noticed there were fresh bananas on the counter. Someone must have come in and stocked the house before they arrived. Mackenzie realized Hunter had not come back out. She walked toward his room, knocking on the open door. Mackenzie saw Hunter sitting there with a towel seeped in blood, holding it to his nose. She turned toward the bathroom, drenching a towel in warm water, then wrung it out. By the time she reemerged, Hunter's nose had stopped bleeding. She walked up to him, handing him the wet towel, and then plopped herself down on the bed.

Hunter looked white as a sheet. She noticed that his skin had sunk in a little more around his eyes. Before they started their adventure, Hunter looked like he might be a little sick. Now, it was more obvious.

"So, are you a billionaire?" Mac asked in a teasing tone.

"Not quite, but if I'd kept going on the path I was on, I would have been," he said. Mackenzie rolled over to the far side of the bed as Hunter tossed the two towels in a wicker basket by the bed before he stretched out on his back.

"To be honest, a lot of it comes from my sister and my parents. Then I sold my company a year ago," Hunter explained. "It's not the greatest feeling in the world to know you have a fortune because your family is gone."

Mackenzie rolled over on her side.

"I get that. My uncle had a few really big life insurance policies. Plus, his 401K from Northrup is now in a trust. Getting the money made me feel a little sick," Mackenzie replied.

Mackenzie looked around his bedroom. She knew everything was on the high-end side. The other thing she noticed was that his room looked sparse besides the bottles of medications and what looked like a picture of him and his sister. There was nothing on his dresser. No pictures on the wall. It was as if someone was just moving in or about to move out. Little reminders of how Hunter had already made plans for when he was gone.

"Your place is really nice," Mackenzie said.

"It was actually one of my sister's properties. It was her favorite, so I didn't sell it," Hunter said, smiling. "Sometimes it makes me feel like she's close."

"Do you know where I go when I want to feel like my uncle's close? It's strange, but it makes sense," Mackenzie said.

Hunter turned to look at her, inviting her to continue.

"Amoeba Records"

Hunter nodded, smiling, turning on his side to look at her. "I could see that."

"It's like I hear him when I am rifling through the records. Telling me some odd fact or the meaning of a song. Or a tidbit about the artists," Mackenzie smiled.

"Do you ever visit his grave?" Hunter asked.

Mackenzie shook her head.

"He told me not to. That's not where he wanted me to think of him. He said he was getting buried just in case the Catholic religion and Filipino superstitions were right. He wanted to at least try to get into heaven," Mackenzie laughed.

"My parents believed in reincarnation. My sister was an atheist. Something I didn't tell the cemetery in China. She's with my parents," Hunter said.

"What do you believe?" Mackenzie asked, her voice small, not sure if this was something he wanted to talk about.

"I'm agnostic," Hunter proclaimed. "So, I guess it's 'we'll see what happens.' However, I wouldn't mind having another crack at life. Maybe I will do it better the next time around."

She watched Hunter roll to his back, the sound of the blender no longer echoing. She turned around, facing the foot of the bed, rolling onto her stomach. Ollie walked into the room with a milkshake in a tall glass with a straw sticking out of it. He sat on the side of the bed by Hunter, looking over and seeing the bloody towel but not mentioning it. Instead, Ollie held the glass in front of Hunter, angling the straw so he could drink it without having to get back up. Hunter did not fight him. He took a few sips and then put his arm over his eyes.

Just then, Parker came in and jumped onto the massive bed, pulling out a pillow so he could sit up and lean against the baseboard.

"I'm so fucking tired," Parker moaned.

"Not me. I'm wired," Ollie chimed in, putting the milkshake on the bedside table. He held Hunter's wrist up as he checked his pulse, looking down at his watch.

He stayed there holding the shake, making sure Hunter finished the whole thing. Mac observed the three of them. They were trying to act nonchalant, but it was impossible to ignore the reality they shared. Hunter's choice at passing soon hung in the air.

Hunter reached up and gave Ollie a small smack. "You guys order something to eat," Hunter said. Parker pulled his phone out of his back pocket, asking Ollie and Mackenzie what they wanted. They settled on subs. Hunter closed his eyes, almost immediately falling asleep.

Mackenzie and the guys quietly left the room. Parker immediately put his arm around Ollie.

"I have to get my shit together," Ollie muttered. "I should be handling this better."

Mackenzie sat on the barstool as Ollie and Parker stood in the kitchen.

"There isn't a right way to handle this," Mackenzie replied, looking toward Hunter's room.

Parker reached over, grabbing Mac's hand.

"Mac, seriously, thank you for coming back with us. Hunter didn't have many friends to begin with. He was always working. When he got the news, he distanced himself from everyone. I think he didn't want them to feel bad or obligated to ride this out with him," Parker said.

"You coming into his life in general," Ollie smiled. "It was the best thing that could have happened to him."

Mackenzie chuckled, shaking her head.

"Yeah, huge sacrifice letting someone take me jet-setting across Europe," Mackenzie said, holding the back of her hand to her forehead dramatically.

She didn't know why she heard it, but somehow, she heard Hunter's erratic breathing from where she was lying on the couch. She popped up right away, stumbling into his bedroom. Hunter was lying there, drenched in sweat, curled in the fetal position. Mackenzie picked up the few bottles of medication sitting on his bedside table, finding his Valium. She took the water bottle and climbed on the bed next to Hunter. Hunter blinked a few times, looking up at her. Mackenzie was on her knees on the mattress, holding out the two pills. She watched him put them in his mouth and swallow them, his hand shaking so hard that some of the water spilled onto the bed. Mackenzie took the bottle back from him, placing it on the table.

Mackenzie could tell he was too far gone for any coping exercises. Hunter reached for her. Mackenzie laid on her back letting his head rest on her chest as Hunter still laid in a fetal position. Mackenzie stroked his hair softly.

"You're okay, Hunter," she whispered. Feeling him twitch a few times. She heard him whimper, his sweat and tears dampening her shirt. She lay there, continuing to hold him, stroking the top of his head. She felt his breathing slowly return to normal.

"Not yet, Mac. I'm not ready, but I have a few more things I want to do," Hunter confessed.

She hugged him tighter.

"Then we will make sure you get them done."

She wasn't sure how much time had passed. Hunter straightened up, apologizing profusely. Mackenzie gave him a 'tsk.' They were both still on the bed, Mackenzie on her back and lying in reverse. She scooted up so she could cross her legs against the headboard behind them. They sat in silence, in turns. One of them randomly asked a question here or there.

Mackenzie told him about her bout of COVID-19. How she got it right off the bat. How it affected her friends and Sam.

"I can't believe you haven't said anything about that until now," Hunter said, shaking his head.

"Again, minuscule to what you are going through."

"Still, I remember when it first happened. Everyone was in a panic. I couldn't even peek my head out the door because of misconceptions about the virus. People acting like somehow just because I was Chinese, I was a carrier," Hunter said with a shake of his head.

Mackenzie nodded in agreement, then shrugged her shoulders.

"Everyone in my life was terrified. So, if I was afraid, I couldn't show it. I was scared when I first got the results. After that, I did my best to keep a smile on my face so they wouldn't worry."

"Do you think that's when it started?" Hunter asked. Mac knew he was referencing her pattern of hiding in everyone else's worlds.

"I think it started before that. It was easier to just tuck myself away in everyone else's world than deal with the pain of losing my uncle and closing the record store in the same month. Getting COVID just amplified it. Everyone was so scared of me. I guess

I felt like I had rocked their world, so I needed to help make it steady again. Now, thinking about what you said, I realize it was just an excuse to stay hidden."

Hunter didn't say anything in response. After a brief lull, they started talking about music. The topic led them back into the living room, where the far side wall was hidden behind Hunter's massive record collection. The shelf ran the length of the wall.

Hunter walked over to the shelf and pulled out a few of his favorite vinyls so they could listen to them. He told her the sound-track to Jerry McGuire was probably his favorite in the collection. Informing her that Jerry McGuire was the first movie he watched where he didn't need subtitles.

They debated when Mackenzie stated that disco was the best era. Hunter said it was protest rock, as he called it, the music of the sixties and seventies. They laughed at how it was so uncool to admit they loved Neil Diamond growing up.

After a while, Hunter started to get tired again. The two of them went back into his bedroom. Mac once again lay the same odd way she had been doing before, with her feet toward the headboard. She had caught there were times that Hunter seemed afraid to close his eyes and did his best to try to look at her. She had figured out this position was the easiest for him to do.

Mackenzie looked up at the ceiling and then looked over at Hunter.

"You said you had things you still want to do. Care to share?" Mackenzie asked.

Hunter reached down, squeezing her hand.

"You'll see."

"Is there anything you would want to do one last time?" Mackenzie asked.

Hunter took a deep breath and exhaled.

"Probably get laid."

Mackenzie gasped, clapping a hand over her mouth, eyes wide. Hunter laughed. He held his hand up.

"It's not a request. Even if I wanted to, it's in retirement," Hunter chuckled. "Just answering your question."

"I thought you said you've never been in love," Mackenzie said. Hunter laughed again.

"Being in love isn't a prerequisite to sex. At least for most of us," he teased. "I have had relationships sort of, hooked up with a girl or two. Mackenzie, I wasn't a good guy. I was pretty driven and shallow."

Mackenzie swung her legs off the back wall and then sat up cross-legged. "That's hard to believe, but I'll take your word for it."

Sam crossed Mackenzie's mind just then. She wondered how much he would change. He had been so focused and driven as of late. He wasn't as jovial as he used to be. Hunter must have sensed she was thinking about Sam.

"I know if you have that, it was only with Sam. Going to venture a guess that you guys were each other's first. I remember my first time. It was so awkward."

Mackenzie felt herself blush, nodding.

"Are you going to gag if I told you our first time was perfect?" Mackenzie said, clearing her throat.

"Nausea comes with the territory right now," he joked. "No, I won't. I think that's great."

Mackenzie smiled.

"Who was your first?" Mackenzie asked.

"Annabelle Beddoe. I was at Oxford. She was from Wales," he said. "Pretty sure she just wanted to bang me because I am Chinese. See if the stereotypes were true."

Mackenzie gasped again, reaching for a pillow and smacking his legs lightly.

Hunter laughed again, holding his stomach as he did. The heaviness of their situation was momentarily forgotten.

Chapter 27

SAM

S am heard the sound of a mug being placed on his desk. He looked up, expecting to see Clarissa. Instead, it was Bianca.

"Hi!" he said lamely, looking at the mug in front of him. He picked it up and took a sip.

"Don't worry, I left the arsenic at home. Too many witnesses," Bianca took a sip of her own coffee. "Just wanted to tell you, I heard from Mac. She's still okay."

Sam nodded. "Thanks, Bianca," he said, hoping he sounded as sincere as he felt.

Bianca shrugged her shoulders, taking another sip from her mug.

"You look like shit Sam. Get some sleep," Bianca said before she turned on her heels and walked out the door.

Sam sat back in his chair, closing his eyes for a moment. He hadn't been sleeping well at all. No one else at work seemed to notice. However, Bianca was different, they both knew what they looked like after pulling all nighters to finish assignments. Or when they would sit with Uncle Deano all night making Mac go home and rest before heading straight to class.

He looked out the glass wall of his office. Things were so different now. Sam or Bianca used to come into each other's workspaces and bitch and moan. Sometimes he would pass her desk, whispering that the Lakers sucked just to get a rise out of her.

Seeing the two of them walking down the hall was a common thing back when they first started. They often went to the break room together, joking or taking friendly digs at each other. Now Sam wasn't allowed to call Bianca 'B.' They passed in the hall, not even looking at each other. Sam held his hand to his chest, feeling the pain of losing someone he loved like a sister.

Just then, his cell phone vibrated in his pocket and rang. He put his phone to his ear.

"Hello, Sam speaking."

"Hey," he heard. "It's Mac."

Sam felt his heart pound out of his chest. He had taken the call blindly, not even seeing who had called.

"Mackenzie," he whispered, feeling tears form around his eyes. He nearly whimpered in relief. The fear that she would never speak to him again being temporarily quelled.

"I just wanted you to know I am okay. I am sorry for worrying you."

"Mac, listen," he said, clearing his throat. Suddenly his office phone rang loudly. Sam looked down, seeing it was his boss's extension, he was paralyzed for a moment.

"You better get that. I'll reach out later," Mackenzie said, her tone making it clear that she would be the one to call. He heard her disconnect. He shut his eyes tightly. As he picked up the handset of his office phone

"Sam speaking," he choked out, clearing his throat.

"Sam, this is Jack," he heard. "We were wondering if we could meet you in the west conference room in about thirty minutes."

"Sure, no problem," Sam said, nodding, even though he knew Jack couldn't see him. He wondered all the while what he might have done wrong.

As soon as he hung up, Sam tossed his cellphone on his desk and swiveled in his chair until the back was facing his desk. He put his hands on his knees trying to figure out which call made the room start spinning.

Sam walked into the conference room, he saw his boss, Jack Anderson, sitting on one side. Hayes Alexander, the Vice President of Acquisitions and Clarissa sitting next to him. Sitting at the head of the table was their CEO Carter Benson. Carter started his firm when he was a year or two younger than Sam was now. Sam both admired him and was intimidated by him.

Sam closed the door and stood by it.

"Good afternoon," Sam said stiffly, giving them a nod, still trying to figure out what was going on.

"Breath, Samson," Jack said, smiling at him. "Take a seat."

Sam pulled out the chair next to Jack. Carter leaned back in his seat, pointing at Sam, the man exuded authority.

"Been hearing some really great things about you, Samson," Carter said.

Sam straightened back up in his seat. Carter's praise made him feel like he was going to explode.

"It's pretty much a done deal with Ozora Dynamics. We have been chasing them forever. They were very impressed with you."

Sam cleared his throat.

"I'm glad to hear that, sir," Sam responded.

"They would like you to go to Japan and present our proposal to their Board of Directors. Hayes and Clarissa will be joining you. While you are there, we'd also like you to meet with a few other potential clients. Plan on being there for ten days, including travel. We'll make all the arrangements," Carter said, getting to his feet.

Sam nodded, feeling numb, wondering if what just happened was real.

"Gentlemen, and Clarissa, we'll huddle a few times before you go," Carter added, and with that, he strode out of the conference room. Everyone but Hayes started to get up to go, too.

"Samson, a word?" Hayes said, gesturing for Sam to sit back down.

Sam dropped back into his chair, putting his arms on the table and clasping his hands together.

Hayes mimicked Sam's pose.

"How long have you been at the firm, Sam," Hayes asked.

"Four years, sir," he said.

"You are the fastest rising Senior Commercial Acquisition Specialist we have ever had in the company," Hayes said smiling "The commission you will make on this deal is triple your salary."

"Yes, sir. Thank you for the opportunity," Sam said

Hayes sat back in his seat.

"It's not common knowledge, however, that Theo, our senior acquisition manager, is leaving the company," Hayes said. "Carter feels that you might be the man to fill his shoes."

Sam took a deep breath. He was told that closing this deal would almost surely get promoted to Acquisition Manager. This would be a step higher than that.

"I'm floored, obviously," Sam chuckled.

"Let's see how the trip to Japan shakes out," Hayes said.

Sam nodded.

Hayes made a motion to stand, then snapped his fingers.

"Oh, I almost forgot. Not to delve into your private life, but I hear there have been some changes lately," Hayes said.

Sam gulped hard.

"Um, yes, I'm still figuring out a few things. It hasn't affected my work," Sam replied.

It was common knowledge Sam was engaged, and many people around the office knew Mackenzie from when she'd stop in to see him or Bianca. These days, the rumor mill was working overtime, with Mac suddenly not coming in to see him and Bianca's icy attitude toward him. He had no idea if Clarissa had told anyone about what happened that afternoon at the Platform.

Hayes stood up.

"Change can be a good thing. You have a bright future. Make the right kind of work connections. Who knows, better opportunities that are much more beneficial could be right around the corner."

Sam smiled tightly, shaking Hayes's hand. He opened the door, letting Hayes go first, then made his way down the hallway to his office. Something about the way he'd said "change" made the hair on the back of Sam's neck rise. He knew Clarissa got her position here because members of the C-suite were friends with her father. Suddenly, he felt rage hearing Hayes say "better opportunities" in his head, knowing he was implying that Mackenzie somehow had been holding him back.

Sam walked into his office and pulled his tie a bit down suddenly feeling like it was choking him. He wondered if Mac wasn't the only change Hayes was implying looking toward Bianca's cubby seeing a bit of her afro hair sticking out beyond the border. He thought about Hayes's phrasing "the right kind of work connections." The buzz of being told he was going to Japan and was in consideration for Senior Acquisition Manager being sapped away.

He looked down at his phone and saw Mac's number. He swiped her contact photo. It was of her hand partially covering her face as she smiled at him. Sam could not help but smile back at her image. He fought the urge to call her and tell her the news.

The shock of hearing Mackenzie's voice suddenly overtook every other emotion at that moment. Hearing her voice always made him smile. This time it made him feel like there was a vice grip around his heart squeezing it to the point of pain.

Hayes mentioning his commission made him remember what he'd intended to do with it. Sam had planned to use a good portion of his commission on their wedding and honeymoon. With the money he was getting, he could have given Mackenzie the wedding of her dreams. Sam sighed, shaking his head. Mackenzie didn't have some idyllic vision of their wedding. Sam realized he had. Somewhere in the back of his mind, he'd imagined their wedding was going to be a statement of achievement and status from him, not a personal life-changing event.

Sam turned around, opening his laptop diving into his emails, burying himself in them, his eyes occasionally drifting to his phone. Every so often he would unlock the screen and see Mackenzie's contact photo. Wanting desperately to call her. After a while he heard Clarissa come into his office. He looked up at her and smiled.

"Excited?" she asked, standing a bit away from his desk.

"Yeah, my mind is kind of blown," he admitted as Clarissa stood there eyeing him.

He looked up at Clarissa then down at his phone seeing Mac's contact photo. The tragically poetic moment was not lost to him.

Chapter 28

MACKENZIE

Mackenzie was aware of this odd, familiar feeling. Twenty-four hours had passed, but time felt irrelevant. Instead of hours, it was measured by how frequently Hunter would wake up and have a bit of energy.

When he got up, Mackenzie always had a question or comment she would ask or make. Hunter would do the same. Most of the time, Ollie and Parker were there as well. They were careful not to bring up old memories. Mackenzie had made that request. If Hunter wants to share stories, let him take the lead.

"He doesn't need us to make him feel like he's in a living wake, and we are all eulogizing him," Mackenzie said softly while the three of them stood in the kitchen eating pizza.

They were careful to not eat in front of Hunter. His sense of smell was out of whack and food aromas made him nauseous.

Mackenzie stepped outside, staring at her phone. All of this reminded her of Sam being there like this when Uncle Deano died. She didn't know if it was guilt or selfishness that motivated her to dial his number.

The phone rang twice. Before she heard Sam's voice.

The business tone indicated to her that he didn't pay attention and looked to see who was calling.

She heard him whisper, "Mackenzie." Not a second later. His voice sounded strained with a tinge of pain. She knew what she did, running away, going radio silent on him, and taking off with a guy, gutted Sam.

She felt herself retreating, secretly relieved another call cut their conversation short.

She looked back and saw Hunter sitting at his desk printing out something, taking a few pages off the printer, then folding it into an envelope and handing it to Ollie. She felt her heart thud the way it would every time she was reminded that he had limited time.

Mac opened the sliding door then threw herself on the couch. Hunter looked over smiling as he took a bite of the dish Mackenzie had made that he insisted on calling *congee*.

"We call it *arroz caldo*," she informed him.

Hunter cock his brow up, looking at her. "It's clearly a rip-off on *congee*." He was right; the two dishes were nearly identical. It was rice porridge with ginger and chicken wings. In China, seafood was often used.

Mac lay on her stomach. Hunter swiveled in his chair to face her.

"Either way, it's good."

"One of the girls my uncle dated briefly taught me how to make it," Mackenzie explained.

"How old were you when you figured out people weren't actually your Auntie or Uncle?" Hunter asked.

"Right?" Mackenzie laughed. "I was six, and we went to the Filipino bakery where the same girl my uncle dated worked. I remember looking up at him and asking. "Uncle Deano, isn't it wrong to date your sister?"

The three guys laughed for a good bit. She was glad that there was a lot of laughter.

"I had no idea our cultures intersected so much. It's eye-opening," Hunter commented.

"You have Chow mein, we have *pancit*. We both call every adult Auntie or Uncle. Also, I don't think I have ever been to a Filipino gathering without the sound of mahjong tiles being washed."

Hunter chuckled when Mackenzie said "being washed." It was the term used for mixing tiles before a new game began.

"Filipinos are a mixed bag when it comes to outside cultural influences. Chinese, Hispanic, even American in fact most people in the Philippines can't have a conversation without slipping a word of English in what they are saying," Mackenzie explained.

"Really?"

Mackenzie nodded and then shrugged her shoulders.

Just then, Hunter's phone rang. He looked at who it was and immediately got up, walking out of the room. Mackenzie sat up, picking on a frayed throw pillow. Ollie came over to sit next to her and whispered.

"He has to give a verbal request to the doctor twice in forty-eight hours in order to get the meds."

Mackenzie nodded, feeling the tears form around her eyes, furiously wiping them away.

Hunter walked back into the room, plopping down on the other side of her. He nudged her shoulder. She turned toward him, smiling as best she could

"Are you curious as to why we didn't go and do number one on your list since we were so close?" Hunter asked.

"No, I mean, it really never dawned on me. I was already worried about how much you were spending."

Hunter waved a hand at her concern, then took a deep breath. He looked at her, taking one of her hands in his.

"It's the one you thought of first so it means the most to you. I want you to go and do it on your own," Hunter explained, "After..."

"I'll try," she said, interrupting him, as if stopping him from saying it staved off the inevitable.

Mackenzie heard the chimes of the doorbell looking over toward the house's entrance. Ollie went to answer it as a Filipino man in scrubs walked in with a messenger bag at his side.

"Hey, Manny," Ollie said with a turn toward Hunter. Mackenzie saw the look of confusion on Ollie's face.

Manny made his way over to Hunter, shaking his hand as he put his tote bag down. He pulled out a bag of saline and two smaller IV bags filled with cloudy liquid. Ollie walked over to bring Hunter's IV podium to them.

Manny started a line and then put up the other two bags.

"It's just something to give me a bit of oomph to my step," Hunter winked.

Mackenzie nodded, watching Manny work in the lines. Ollie had told her that Hunter said he wouldn't let himself get to the point of needing medication and painkillers via IV. Obviously, he had changed his mind.

"I need to stay up tonight," Hunter explained.

"Let me guess, I'll see, right?" Mac said with a smirk.

She watched Manny check the IV line once more. Hating that she was feeling dread instead of excitement. Thinking back to when Hunter said he still had things he wanted to do. Tonight, not only obviously being one of them, but also the start of a heinous countdown.

A few hours later they drove down the hills getting onto the 101 then to the 110. Mackenzie looked up at Sam's high rise apartment complex for a moment knowing he wasn't there. Sam didn't leave until it was dark these days.

She looked around and saw that they were exiting. Making their way up another hill.

"Hunter, why are we going to Dodger Stadium?" Mackenzie asked.

Hunter looked at her with an expression that gave nothing away. She chuckled, gasping as they drove right onto the field. Two men stood off to the side holding walkie talkies. Ollie stopped the car parking it. Both he and Parker opened their doors obviously knowing what was going on.

Mac saw a large red and white checkered picnic blanket with something that looked like a wrapped present sitting in the middle. As she got closer she realized it was a cake box. Parker and Ollie sat down, making themselves comfortable, and opened the box that held a fresh strawberry cake. At one point, during one of their random conversations, they all agreed that fresh strawberry cake was their favorite dessert from the bakeries in Chinatown.

"No knife, just forks," Ollie said with a shrug and he began to dive into the cake.

Mackenzie sat down, holding her arm out to steady Hunter, as he lowered himself to the blanket. Hunter got situated, holding his arm up in the air, giving the two men a thumbs up. Just then, Mackenzie heard a large crackling sound, looking up as a firework exploded in the air.

Mackenzie gasped loudly as fireworks exploded above them. There was a steady sound of whizzing as rockets shot up the air. Huge booms erupted before the sky lit up in star-shaped bursts of colors. She turned to ask Hunter how he pulled it off. Then, he just chuckled.

"Throw enough money at it, right?"

"I just wanted to see them one last time," Hunter whispered. It was the first time he had said one last time. "You should see the sky in China during Chinese New Year. The fireworks are nonstop."

They all sat watching the show when about four minutes into it they heard "Run" by Snow Patrol blared through the speakers.

Mackenzie continued to look up, the song hitting her hard, unable to check her tears. She felt Hunter's arm wrap around her, the other hand wiping her tears away.

"I need you to promise me something?" Hunter whispered the sound of the fireworks, making it hard to hear. Mackenzie continued to look up at the display and nodded her head.

"Promise me that if you decide to be there, you will allow yourself to feel what you feel. Don't bury it. If you do, you'll keep hiding underneath all the things you are holding in. Please don't make me another pain that you can't let go of," Hunter said.

Mackenzie took a deep breath and then nodded adamantly. Belatedly, she realized she started a chain reaction. Ollie and Parker were wiping away their tears as well. Mackenzie scooted away from Hunter a bit before laying on her side, resting the top of her head against Hunter's thigh. Cocking her head up, watching the fireworks, trying to stop herself from crying. She felt Hunter run his fingers through her hair. Mackenzie closed her eyes for a moment. Hating that the beautiful display of colors meant the countdown had begun.

After the fireworks stopped and they regained their composure, everyone sat on the field eating the cake in front of them. They arrived back at the house around nine. Hunter went straight to his room.

Mackenzie and Ollie watched Hunter sleep from the doorway. Manny had come back over and set up an oxygen tank. Hunter let him put the nasal cannula in and almost immediately fell asleep.

"It's more for his own peace of mind," Manny explained. "His breathing is okay."

Mackenzie ushered Ollie toward the balcony. Opening the sliding glass door, not bothering to close it. Ollie gave her a tortured look. "He has to make another call the day after tomorrow," He muttered.

Mackenzie felt the tears once again, feeling helpless. Suddenly, she had a thought she turned to Ollie grabbing his arm. "Ollie, let me see his list," Mackenzie said.

Ollie blinked a few times then nodded. He walked over to Hunter's messenger bag, opening it. He pulled out a piece of cardstock making his way back over to her.

Ollie handed Mackenzie the weathered piece of cardstock paper folded in half. She read the list, then looked up at Ollie. She smiled at him.

"I need your help."

Chapter 29

SAM

"Hi," Sam said, completely stunned as he looked down and saw Clarissa standing outside his door holding a bottle of wine. He had no idea how she knew his apartment number. He mentioned living in this complex pretty openly but he never told anyone the exact location. He knew there was no way Bianca would have told her.

He watched as Clarissa held up a bottle of wine.

"I thought we could hammer out a few ideas for the meetings with potential clients. Relax for the night. Everything has been really intense lately.

The day before yesterday Clarissa declared she was going to start her "campaign" as she called it to win over Sam. He had little to no choice in regards to the time they were spending together. There were a few uncomfortable moments that bordered on sexual harassment. It was not as if he could report her to anyone.

"Sorry. My mom is here," Sam said.

"Oh, I would love to meet her," Clarissa smiled, straightening up a bit as if ready to make a good impression.

Sam put his hands behind his back.

"Sorry, she is actually lying down with a headache. Driving from Malibu is pretty hard on her."

Sam was impressed with himself for a moment. He was really awful when it came to making up excuses on the spot. Mackenzie always teased him about not having a poker face.

He watched as Clarissa stepped back and nodded. "Save this for another day then," she said, giving him a wink. "Tell your Mom I said hi and I look forward to meeting her." As if it was a given.

Sam waved, watching her walk down the hallway. He closed his door once she was out of view. He pressed his forehead to the door, then lightly banged his head against it, letting out a groan.

He turned, walking toward the kitchen. Still in disbelief that she had shown up there.

"Headache, huh?" Clover said she was leaning against the kitchen counter, arms and legs crossed.

"Sorry, mom," Sam said.

Clover Madden hardly ever went anywhere that wasn't right by the shore. She hated how Los Angeles had become so congested. Sam had called his mom telling her the news about Japan. Clover phoned the next day, letting him know he would have a hard time going anywhere without his passport. Sam offered to drive down and get it. Clover suggested she go to his place instead.

Clover grabbed the two plates of crispy tofu slabs and cabbage slaw, walking toward the dining room table. Then went back, grabbing a gravy bowl that smelled like peanut sauce. Sam was used to eating home cooked vegan meals made by his mom.

He sat down, resting his elbows on the table. He rubbed his face a few times. Then, looked over at Clover, who had just sat down.

"Do you think I will be meeting her soon?" Clover asked, holding her fork in her hand and cutting into the golden rectangle of tofu.

"How would you feel if I said yes?" Sam asked.

He watched as Clover shrugged her shoulders. "I would say it's quite soon, but if you were adamant about me meeting her, then I would," Clover replied.

"Would you?" Sam said, not knowing where the bit of bite in his voice came from.

Clover put her fork down, leaning back in her seat.

"I would if it meant that much to you. I would be lying if I didn't say I feel like I am betraying Mackenzie. You can understand that."

Sam tilted his head back, looking at the ceiling.

"Mac called the other day," he said quietly.

"Did she sound like she was okay?" Clover asked.

"It was a really short call. My boss called before I could say anything," Sam explained. He felt the painful emptiness stab through him again. Sam put his right hand over his heart as if somehow the action would make the pain stop.

Clover looked over at him; the pain on his face must have been evident. She reached across the table, grabbing his hand.

"I feel awful for the two of you," Clover said quietly.

Sam looked down at his food, took a bit of the slaw, and chewed on it slowly.

"You know, there were a few times that felt like maybe the breakup was a good idea. Then all it took was for me to hear her voice," Sam laughed mirthlessly.

"Clarissa and I spend so much time together. Sometimes, it just feels logical," he sighed, hanging his head down.

"Someone in the C-suite made a remark that made me feel like, one, they are downing Mackenzie, and two, they are pushing me towards Clarissa."

Clover leaned forward.

"How do you feel about her?" Clover asked.

"It's easy, we relate, and everyone is right. We make a great team. She has supported me through this whole deal," Sam replied.

"No, my dear boy, how do you feel about her?" She put her hand over her heart. "What do you feel about her in here?"

Sam thought about it for a moment, trying to figure out what he felt about Clarissa.

"I don't know," Sam said, watching his mother smile.

"What is that smile for?" Sam asked.

Clover laughed, shaking her head.

"I am just wondering when you are going to stop chasing your own tail. You have been going in circles since Mackenzie broke up with you."

Sam clasped his hands together, sighing.

"She broke up with me, mom. It feels unreal even saying that," Sam groaned. "I deserved it, though. In a weird way, I am proud of her. No one should treat her like that, least of all me."

"It's interesting to watch you defend her against yourself," Clover laughed.

"Sometimes I feel like I am on a fast train barreling down the tracks. And when I look out the window, I see Mac, Bianca, and, even, Ezra standing there as I whizz by them. Everything feels so this or that. It's driving me crazy thinking I can't have both," Sam explained.

"Then maybe you should ask yourself why you can't. If you have to make a choice, which side means more to you?"

Sam buried his head in his hands.

"It's not an easy choice," Clover continued. "I know I never mentioned him, but your father went through something similar."

Sam never really thought about his father. He knew the story: he was from the East Coast and he came from old money. He had met Clover when he was on vacation and ended up staying for a year.

Sam's Grandfather pressured his father to return to the family and abandon his pregnant girlfriend. Their precious son could not marry someone like Clover Madden. Besides her being Jewish, she did not fit the mold of who they wanted their son to marry. He had to choose between Clover and his inheritance. He chose the latter. When his family found out Clover was pregnant, they gave her a large sum of money to ensure Sam's father's name stayed off his birth certificate. Sam always felt like that was an insult to his mother. Clover, being pragmatic, always said it was for the best. She had dated a few guys after Sam was born. No one seemed to click. Sam was six when his mother figured out her lack of forte when it came to dating men, which was, in fact, that she wasn't attracted to men at all. If they had stayed together, they would have broken up when Clover came out. Then, it would have been a mess. Still, it bothered him that his father gave him up and never looked back. Choosing prestige and fortune instead of staying in his son's life.

"Mom, I don't want to be like him," Sam said softly.

Sam blinked a few times. The realization that he unwittingly had followed in his father's footsteps.

"I can't do it, mom," Sam said. "I can't see my life without Mackenzie. And I really don't want to."

There it was; he finally admitted it. He knew it made him sound weak, but he didn't care.

"It's not an all-or-nothing kind of thing. It's possible Mac could still be in your life, just not as the person you are with. So, I will ask you again. Do you think I will be meeting her soon?"

Sam shook his head. Clover looked out the window.

"Fireworks," she said. "I wonder where they are coming from.

Sam turned and looked, watching them explode, "Probably Dodger Stadium."

Chapter 30

MACKENZIE

Mackenzie would love to say that time moved slowly. But it didn't, and that was heartbreaking. The 48-hour wait time was over. Parker, Ollie, and Mackenzie were tearing themselves apart. Hunter, on the other hand, was almost serene. He'd decided and accepted his fate.

Mackenzie sat in the back of the car, looking over at Hunter. His eyes were closed. The bits of moonlight that came through the window of the car made his face look ashen white. From this angle, she could see the way his cheekbones stuck out because of how his skin sunk underneath them, forcing her to admit how frail he was. He was dressed in a black tuxedo vest and black long-sleeve Armani dress shirt that hid the angry bruises left on his arms from where IV needles were poked through his skin. Mackenzie could not help but notice how the shirt hung loosely on him. She wondered how the guys convinced him to get dressed up and go out. She worried he would think it was a last-ditch effort to get him to change his mind.

Whatever they said worked because he complied. Mackenzie looked down at the white silk slip dress that Parker had shown up with earlier today. He also gave her a pair of stiletto heels with diamond straps across the top and red soles. She knew that Parker had taken them out of the box in order to make her feel better.

The drive was short. Parker turned into a massive driveway and parked the car.

"We're here," Hunter and Mackenzie said at the same time.

They looked at each other, confused, then at the boys.

"Great minds," Ollie said with a wink.

They all got out of the car. Hunter grabbed Mac's wrist, guiding her to an open door. She gasped, putting her hand over her mouth. Seeing the side door of the normally locked-up mansion open.

"Did you really think we wouldn't get you number five with it being a stone's throw away?" Hunter laughed.

She walked into the manor, still disbelieving she was actually inside Graystone Mansion. Instead of peering through the windows like she had ever since she and Uncle Deano first made the discovery. It was Mackenzie's favorite place in all of Los Angeles. Also, the site was number five on her list. They walked down the hallway and into the ballroom, where white strings of light were all around them, and the French doors were covered with white curtains.

She stopped looking into the ballroom. Turning to Hunter in amazement.

"I did tell you my sister had connections to the place," Hunter smiled. Ollie reached over and in front of her putting down a Bluetooth speaker. The Michael Bublé version of "Save the Last Dance for Me" filled the air. Mac looked over at Hunter taking her shoes off. She was afraid to scuff the ballroom floor of the historical landmark. She walked to the center of the room and began to twirl around laughing as the song played.

"Number five off the list," Hunter said, walking up to her about halfway through the song. He took her hand in his and twirled her around much like he did at the Eiffel Tower.

They stood there for a moment. Mackenzie knew standing with her took a bit of effort for him. Hunter took her in his arms swaying back and forth.

"There's a storm behind your eyes," Hunter said looking at her.

Mackenzie knew he was right. Her emotions kept flipping from joy to sorrow. She took a step forward, hugging him tightly, ignoring how she could feel the definition of his bones.

"Wait, what was that about earlier when you announced we were here? Did the guys tell you?" Hunter asked.

Ollie, Parker, and Mackenzie smiled at each other.

"You'll see," Mackenzie said, giving him a wink as Ollie walked up to him.

Parker walked out of the ballroom, and after a few moments, she heard the French doors opening and the curtains coming down.

Hunter looked out onto the terrace. His eyes wide.

Ollie guided him outside. Mackenzie stood at the doorway, watching Hunter's face light up. For a moment, he didn't look gaunt.

Two Christmas trees stood a little distance apart. Both of them strung with white lights and covered in silver and red ornaments. There was white cotton fake snow covering most of the floor with giant ornaments resting on them.

Hunter kept looking around, unchecked tears falling from his eyes. She could see him smiling from where she stood. It was a heartbreakingly beautiful moment.

Ollie guided Hunter into the space between the two trees. Then, he gently turned Hunter toward Mackenzie. She smiled, picking up a small bouquet of flowers. Hooking Parker's arm through hers as they walked toward Ollie and Hunter.

Hunter wiped the tears from his eyes.

Mackenzie gave him a watery smile, gulping hard.

"Number five and number six," she said quietly.

"Ollie here, got ordained online. It is not legal, but you know, you improvise."

Hunter laughed, nodding. He looked over at Mackenzie, who was facing him.

"Your number seven. Cross it off your list," Hunter said softly.

Mac shook her head as her eyes watered. "I shouldn't get credit for that one. I was just fortunate enough to be sitting on my bench," Mac chuckled, remembering the start of their grand adventure.

Hunter laughed weakly. "Of course you should. You altered my life. So, seven on your list is done," Hunter declared.

"Crossing things off your list was selfish, maybe a bit arrogant," Hunter confessed. "But watching your eyes light up the moment right before one of your dreams was about to come true. Hearing you laugh. It changed me. Thank you."

Hunter looked suddenly serious.

"I can't let you give me this moment," he said. "Vows and all belong to someone else."

She had been conflicted about it at first. She thought about Sam and how it might hurt him. She flip-flopped back and forth, and that changed the moment the medication arrived. It went from something she had to do to something she wanted to do.

Mac opened her mouth to protest, but Hunter stopped her before she could, saying, "Ask me what you did in the gondola in Venice."

Mackenzie thought for a moment, then looked over at him. She wiped the tears away.

"Have you ever been in love Hunter?" She whispered

Hunter reached over, cupping her face, his hand shaking. The fervent look in his eyes let her know the trembling was not solely caused by his weaken state.

"Yes, and she is as bright as a bonfire flame. She lit up my dark world like fireworks. She can be brave and terrified all at once. Her laugh grabs your heart. And when she looks over and smiles at you," Hunter choked for a moment, then cleared his throat.

"I know she's not in love with me. It doesn't matter; in fact, I am glad she isn't. I wouldn't want her to hurt more. Strangely, I'm in love with her because of the way she talks about the one she loves. I always thought people were blowing smoke when they said if you love someone, you just want to see them happy. It's the truest thing in the world."

Hunter used his thumb to wipe away her tears. Mackenzie watched as he looked down. He pulled off his sister's ring, smiling at Mackenzie as he slid it on her pointer finger.

"You're the best thing to ever happen to me Mackenzie Almazan," he said pressing his forehead to hers. All four of them were crying.

They drove back to the house in silence. Hunter held Mackenzie's hand, stroking it. No one got out of the car for a solid fifteen minutes. Hunter patted the top of Mackenzie's hand.

"There's still time," Hunter said, giving her an out.

Mackenzie shook her head. Hunter opened his car door. She heard Ollie choke up and take a moment before getting out of the car.

Hunter walked into his room. Mackenzie stared at the dark hallway, waiting for him to emerge. It felt like hours before she saw his silhouette walking slowly toward her. Hunter walked past her, suddenly stopping. He was shaking so hard she thought his legs would give out.

Mackenzie reached for his hand, squeezing it softly. Hunter looked back and smiled. He opened the sliding glass door and took a step out onto the balcony. Ollie walked over to Hunter. Wrapping his arm around him. Hunter smiled at Ollie. He allowed Ollie to take on the bulk of his weight as he slowly walked him further out onto the balcony. It was fitting Ollie had been there through it all. Supporting him through his sister's death, his leukemia, and now, physically, as Hunter took his last steps.

Mackenzie saw a futon and blanket in the corner. Hunter leaned over, swaying, nearly falling, as he attempted to get on his knees to lie down. Parker steadied him, helping him lower himself onto the futon. Mackenzie quickly swooped in behind him, pulling Hunter to her.

Hunter smiled, looking up at the stars in the sky.

"Funny, I always said I wanted the stars to be the last thing I see. Turns out I was wrong," He reached for her weakly as Mac took his hand in hers once again, helping him press it to her cheek.

"Remember number one on your list. Don't forget to look out, not down."

Mackenzie nodded, trying her best not to cry. She stroked Hunter's head again, pressing a kiss to his forehead.

"Mac," he said, smiling up at her. "I know you probably know this but in China there's a saying called *bái yuèguāng* from a novel. It means 'white moonlight.' Talks about a red and a white rose. The white one is 'moonlight in front of my bed.' It means you can look at her beauty and love her from afar but she was never meant to be yours. Still you love her from the purest part of your heart."

Mackenzie nodded, feeling him slouch down in her arms more. Hunter gently grasped her.

"Thank you for being my *bái yuèguāng*. Something else I never thought was real. Yet here you are."

Hunter looked over at Ollie, giving him a smile. Ollie sat down, putting his arms across Hunter's legs.

"Xièxiè, Da Ge," Hunter said, *"Xièxiè."*

The three of them knew separately that he said, "Thank you, my brother, thank you."

Ollie gave him a watery smile.

"I knew you would learn eventually," Hunter teased, his voice sounding breathless.

Mackenzie gulped hard. There was so much she wanted to say to him, but at the same time, she didn't want him to sit in this sadness.

Hunter took a deep breath, smiling at her.

"Close your eyes, Zie Zie," he said. Mackenzie whimpered hard, feeling both of them lurch forward for a moment. She heard Hunter take a few breaths, then felt him lift a shaking hand. She felt her lips tremble as Hunter's hand shook with the effort. She did not know if his hand paused, trembling in the air, because he was scared or too weak to lift it. Mackenzie felt another hand cross in front of her, handing Hunter a small vial. She was sure it was Parker because she could hear Ollie crying a small distance away, his body hunched over Hunter's legs.

Parker let out a small wail as she felt Hunter gulp a few times. She opened her eyes, seeing Parker holding Hunter's wrist. He kissed Hunter's hand, trying to control his painful moans.

Mackenzie took a deep breath looking at the two men. Silently conveying Hunter's last memory of them, should not be of this. All three of them pulled themselves together. Mackenzie looked down at Hunter. His eyes would drift shut then he would open them again. He gave Mackenzie a weak smile.

"Number eight, in my next life... in my next life..." Hunter closed his eyes as if he were trying to gather the strength to tell her his number eight.

She smiled down at him, "In our next life, come find me so I can be there for your number eight."

Mackenzie held his frail form a bit tighter. She did not know how or why but suddenly she felt a sense of urgency. As if she knew what she was about to do, needed to be done just then.

"Number seven, Hunter," she whispered, seeing a slight look of shock on his face. She lowered her head, their lips a breath away from touching, and whispered, "Chaoxiang. *Wǒ ài nǐ.* Chaoxiang. *Wǒ ài nǐ.*" Repeating it to make sure he heard. Somehow, knowing it was time, wanting the last thing he heard to be that he was loved in his native tongue.

She pulled away slightly to see him look up, giving her a smile. Tears freely falling from his eyes as she gently wiped them away. She lowered her head again. First, she gave him a small peck then another, the third time she kissed him deeply. Feeling his lips quiver, keeping her eyes open as he looked into hers.

She felt Hunter shudder. Smiling as best as he could through their kiss. She kept her lips pressed to his and felt him exhale into her mouth. She took the air into her lungs. Holding her breath watching Hunter, he closed his eyes feeling him go limp in her arms.

She felt Ollie shaking Hunter's legs, weeping violently. Parker hugged his husband from behind, doing the same.

Mackenzie whimpered. Not wanting it to be true. She gulped hard, breathing through her nose, trying to hold Hunter's last breath inside. There were things that needed to be done. She had to be there for Ollie and Parker. Already building an emotional wall to tamper down the pain. Suddenly, she remembered her promise to Hunter. To let out whatever she was feeling. She held him tight, crying, rocking him back and forth. The pain of losing him ripped her to shreds. First, she let out a silent scream, emptying her lungs, unable to catch her breath. She took a huge gulp of air that wailed so loud that it made her chest hurt. She felt a hand on her arm. She screamed out in pain. Like she wanted to when Jenni died. Like she wanted to when her uncle's hand went limp in hers.

Mackenzie kissed Hunter's forehead and howled out all the hurt and pain she was feeling right at that moment. Keeping her promise to the man who'd made her wildest dreams come true.

Chapter 31

SAM

"I still don't know if this is a good idea," Sam said, getting out of Ezra's car.

"When have I ever steered you wrong?" Ezra asked.

"Do you want the shortlist?" Sam replied.

Ezra walked over to Sam's side, cupping his shoulder and dragging him with him. They could hear the sounds of Earth, Wind, and Fire getting louder as they got closer to the backyard. Sam could not help but smile when they entered through the fence. There was an older black man on the grill. Boys playing basketball on a cement slab in the corner. Women came in and out of the house, joking around and dancing as they put food platters down on two long white tables.

"Sam, Ezzie!" they heard. Sam smiled as Bianca's mother Ms. Eddy came closer, hugging Ezra first then Sam.

Sam had no idea where they were going when Ezra asked him to "run an errand" with him. It took him about ten minutes to figure it out. Today was, Mr. Noah, Bianca's father's birthday. Sam immediately took out his phone to try to find a present for him.

He was already boiling in lava with his daughter. He couldn't show up empty handed.

"Sam! You in?" he heard Marlon yell out. Sam waved at him and the other five of Bianca's cousins. Bianca was the only girl in her family. Which meant growing up with like five bodyguards wherever she went. Ezra, Mac, and Sam had been coming to Bianca's family cookouts for years now.

"Maybe later," Sam yelled back. He would occasionally play a game of three on three with them.

"Hell nah, dawg, it's been way too long. You owe us a game!" Marlon said, bouncing the basketball before turning around and continuing the game.

Marlon was right; it had been at least a year since he came to a Jones event. Mac usually came and represented both of them.

"Hold on," Ms. Eddy said, looking behind Ezra and Sam. "Where's my baby?" she asked, obviously looking for Mackenzie.

Sam really was terrible at making up excuses on the spot. He tried to think of something to say hoping Ezra would bail him out, but nothing came out.

"She's in San Diego, mom," they heard Bianca say as she moved a few plates around to put down a bowl of potato salad on one of the two long tables that were now covered with food. "An old friend of Uncle Deano's is here from the Philippines."

Sam blinked a few times in shock. He had deduced Bianca had not told her family about their broken engagement. She could have called him out right then and there if she wanted to make this a very awkward time for him. Yet, Bianca was saving face.

"There are my boys!" Mr. Noah said, walking up to them and giving them both guys a hug. "Where's my baby?" he asked just as his wife did.

"She's in San Diego," Ms. Eddy answered.

Mr. Noah smiled and nodded. "It's been a long time, Samson," he said. Mr. Noah was the one person who could call him by his full name without Sam cringing.

"It has, sir. I'm sorry work's been taking up a lot of my time lately," Sam said, looking over and seeing Bianca rolling her eyes.

Ms. Eddy watched her sister, Ms. Stella, walk over from the grill with a plate of BBQ chicken and ribs. "You boys need to go fix yourself a plate before those heathens over there see that meat's come off the grill," Ms. Eddy teased.

Sam nodded, walking over to the table. Bianca was the only one in their group that grew up in a two-parent household. Ezra's mom died when he was born. Mac and Sam grew up the way they did. The Joneses were the couple that Sam admired the most.

When Bianca announced in her sophomore year of high school that she wanted to go to college, The Joneses both took on second jobs to start a college fund for Bianca. They told Bianca she wasn't allowed to work a part-time job in high school or college; they wanted her to concentrate on her studies, much to Bianca's dismay. She vowed to make things easier on them once she established herself in her career. In fact, it was only recently that Bianca moved out of her parents' house off Crenshaw in South City. Bianca insisted on contributing to the household.

The Joneses had to practically kick her out. The one thing she was able to do was make sure her parents made the right investments so they could both retire. Mr. Jones still worked a part-time job at Home Depot because according to him retirement was boring. It was evident where Bianca got her drive and determination from.

Sam and Ezra sat at one of the card tables, eating what Sam thought was the perfect meal. They sat there munching away as Ms. Eddy and Ms. Stella kept coming by with the food. He knew better than to refuse.

It went on until Bianca's uncles told the two women to stop stuffing the boys because the older men of the family needed the square card table they were eating at to play dominos. They took the table from them as Sam and Ezra sat there watching them set out.

"I thought Ms. Eddy said they weren't allowed to play dominos anymore," Ezra said, looking at the men who shuffled the domino titles away.

"No, they aren't allowed to play Spades," Sam said, correcting Ezra. The last time they played Spades, they got so loud and heated that cops who were patrolling came into the backyard to tell them they were being a nuisance. Sam wasn't completely blind to things. He'd angrily asked the cops if it was truly necessary for them to start asking for IDs to run them to see if any of Bianca's cousins had outstanding warrants. Mr. Noah had diffused the situation with expertise, which made Sam feel terrible, knowing this was the norm in their neighborhood. After that incident, Ms. Stella declared Spades was banned from family events.

They heard the scraping of a plastic chair as Bianca sat down with them. Her chair moved closer to Ezra's than Sam's. She placed a small cooler on the ground in front of them, opened it, and pulled out three bottles of San Miguel beer. The three of them started drinking San Miguel beer after hearing Uncle Deano talking about the beer brand made in the Philippines. Maybe it was because San Miguel was their first go-round of beer that made them feel like nothing tasted as good.

Sam cracked open his beer and took a big swig, trying to calm his nerves.

He nodded over at Bianca and said thank you. Bianca gave him a gruff, "you're welcome."

"Okay, so let's get the Mackenzie-sized cloud hanging over us out of the way," Ezra announced.

"She actually called me the other day," Sam replied "It wasn't a long call. She apologized for worrying me. And told me she was all right."

"Like she owes you an apology," Bianca muttered.

"Please, girl," Ezra said. "You told me yourself that you let Mackenzie know that Sam was tearing himself inside out, and he looked like shit because he wasn't sleeping. You're the one that suggested she text or call him," Ezra stated.

Sam whipped his head toward Bianca, "Really?"

Bianca sighed, then nodded, taking a sip of her beer. "I didn't want Mackenzie to feel guilty if you dropped dead from exhaustion," Bianca answered. "Also, you did look like shit."

"Thank you, Bianca. I just wanted to hear her tell me she was safe. Not that I didn't trust you. I just needed to hear it for myself."

They all sat there in silence, drinking for a little while, watching the guys play basketball and laughing at the animated game of dominos.

Sam inhaled hard, then exhaled slowly.

"Listen, I think we could all agree what I did to Mackenzie was a dick move," Sam said.

Bianca started to open her mouth.

"Also, I have been an insensitive prick to her at times since I got my first promotion. This last year, it was constant."

Bianca closed her mouth, apparently satisfied by his verbal flogging of himself.

"I haven't been aware of my attitude and all the prejudice that was going on around me. I am not going to make excuses for my behavior. I definitely did that thing where I thought I was exempt from privilege because I had an Asian fiancée, and the two closest people to me are Black and Hispanic. I just wanted to acknowledge that I see it now and that I have a lot of work to do."

Bianca looked over at Ezra and then Sam.

"Thank you for saying that," Bianca said.

"Gotta tell you it was painful watching you change," Ezra confessed, taking a gulp of his beer. "But you were climbing to the top of the corporate ladder. Hell, you still are. If that's what makes you happy, then like I said before, who are we to stop you. That includes Mackenzie."

"I have been thinking a lot about how life looks without Mac," Sam said.

"And what would it look like with 'thirsty Becky with the good hair'?" Bianca asked.

She had a front row seat at Clarissa's "campaign" He could tell looking at Bianca that it both angered and pained her.

Sam nodded not wanting to lie to his friends. He had been doing a lot of lying to himself already, he wanted to be honest with them.

Bianca put her beer down and crossed her legs, folding her arms over her chest. Sam knew she was getting ready to defend Mackenzie against anything negative he might say.

"Mackenzie has been with me all this time, but I realized now I stopped being with her," Sam muttered.

"Explain," Ezra asked.

"When was the last time Mackenzie painted? Do you guys know if she still has her LACMA membership?" Sam asked. Clover had gotten Mackenzie a membership to the Los Angeles Museum of Art during their first year of college. Before that, Mackenzie would only go the second Tuesday of each month after three, when it was free.

Ezra and Bianca looked at each other and then at Sam.

"That's what I mean. I haven't been aware. I stopped paying attention in general. When I think back to that day at the Platform, all I see is the look on her face. It was like she suddenly came into focus in the worst way possible. On some level, I knew I had lost her," Sam sighed.

Bianca took another sip of her drink.

"I think we are all guilty of that. She's always there for me when I want to do something. Thinking about it now, she hardly ever asks me to do something with her. The wedding was the first in a long time," Bianca mused.

"Since we are pouring lemon juice into the paper cut. It's the same with me. Anytime I need help at a work event, she's right there. I can't remember the last time I did something for her," Ezra said. "Shit, we are all assholes."

Sam held his hands up.

"I'm only throwing shade on myself," Sam declared.

"Do you want her back?" Bianca asked.

Sam cleared his throat. "I can't ask her to come back if I haven't figured out where I am going. I've been dragging Mackenzie through my world for a while. It hasn't been fair to her," Sam explained.

The three of them sat there in silence once again. They all turned their chairs toward Mr. Noah as he started opening presents. Sam looked down at his phone, asking Bianca for her dad's number so he could send him a link. Bianca let her dad know that Sam's present was on his phone.

"My goodness!" Ms. Eddy exclaimed, jumping up and down.

"What did you get him?" Bianca asked.

"Middle of the court floor seats," Sam smiled.

Bianca gasped. The Lakers were practically a religion in the Jones house. However, her dad had never gone to a game at the Crypto.com Arena. He always said why he would sit in the nosebleed seats when he had a better view from his television.

Sam stood up as Bianca's parents made their way over to give him a hug.

"You couldn't have saved that to the end, bro?" One of Bianca's cousins yelled. "Now all our presents look like trash." Everyone laughed as Sam waved his hands in the air apologizing.

Bianca walked Sam and Ezra to the car when they announced they were leaving.

"Bianca, I want you to know I am recommending you for my position when I get moved from there. I know it's a little different from what you are doing now, but there's not another person that I feel could do the job better than you," Sam said.

Bianca looked at him, stunned.

"Thanks, Sam, I won't let you down if I get it. It will help my two-year plan along."

"Two-year plan?" Sam asked.

"I plan to leave the firm and open my own small business investment firm and try to help out people in the neighborhood and anywhere else in LA. If I'm gonna keep things real, watching you move up the ladder made me realize I don't want to be there for much longer, plus, well you know, there's a ceiling when it comes to me."

Sam didn't know what to say. Just then Ezra walked up to them with two huge plates covered in aluminum foil, he opened his car door putting them in the backseat then walked up to Bianca giving her a hug. They all heard Bianca's phone ringing.

Bianca pulled out her phone; whatever she was looking at made her gasp. They watched as she madly swiped her phone.

"Everything okay, B?" Ezra asked.

Bianca nodded. "Yeah, I just forgot I need to do something. See you guys later."

Sam and Ezra watched her turn around running into her house. As they were buckling up to leave, they saw Bianca race out of her house with her keys in her hand and bag over her shoulder. She ran to her car, starting it and taking off.

Sam looked at Ezra in alarm.

"Sam, if Mackenzie was in danger, B would tell us. Whatever else is going on, she knows we love Mackenzie. It's probably something else."

Sam nodded, watching Bianca's car disappear from their view. Something inside of him knew it had to do with Mackenzie.

Chapter 32

MACKENZIE

Mackenzie opened her eyes to see it was late afternoon. Her eyes were burning and swollen. She had no idea how long she sat there holding Hunter. She remembered someone pulling her up and carrying her away. They laid her in Hunter's room on his side of the bed. She could hear Parker talking to someone and a bit of activity, and then the house went quiet again. She realized she had been lying there for a day and a half, only getting up to use the bathroom or drink water. At one point, Parker came in with some soup, which she managed to eat a few bites of before falling back asleep.

Parker let her know the mortuary came and got Hunter.

"Hunter wouldn't want you to see that," Parker said quietly, pushing the bowl toward her, trying to get her to eat more before he left to check on his husband.

Mackenzie turned her head, burying her face on Hunter's pillow. She took a deep breath, inhaling his scent. Hunter always smelt like Only The Brave cologne. He said he thought it was poetic.

After laying there for a little while longer, she sat up in the bed then made her way to her suitcase in the living room. It was open, her clothes all neatly folded inside. One of the guys must have done her laundry. She chuckled thinking of how Hunter laughed at her because she had trouble wrapping her head around hotels doing laundry.

Mackenzie pulled out one of her shirts and a pair of jeans. She went to the bathroom to take a shower, washed her hair, and then got dressed. She felt the painfully familiar feeling of time going at a snail's pace. It had been like this when Uncle Deano passed. Every moment was a constant reminder that Hunter was gone. Back in the living room, Mackenzie folded the white satin slip dress she wore two nights ago and put it in her suitcase. Just then, she heard the door open, and she lifted her head to see the guys walk in. Her eyes drifted behind them, imagining for a moment that Hunter was following, about to come through the door at any minute.

Ollie must have caught on because he walked over to her, pulled her up, and hugged her tightly. The two of them cried for a moment before separating and making their way to the kitchen.

She couldn't taste the food. She was aware she was chewing and then swallowing, but nothing else.

"I was a mess, too. Parker had to deal with it," Ollie explained. She could tell he felt guilty. Parker hugged Ollie from behind, giving him a kiss on the cheek.

The more Mackenzie thought about it, the more she realized that Parker had been holding all of them together fearlessly, down to him being the one who was brave enough to steady Hunter's hand so he could drink down the meds.

Mackenzie looked back at her suitcase.

"Mac, you can stay as long as you want," Ollie said. "You could even move in if you wanted to."

Mackenzie laughed. Hunter had told her he had transferred the deed to the house to Ollie a while ago.

Mackenzie smiled, drinking down some water, realizing how parched she was.

"Thanks, but I have to go back to work the day after tomorrow," Mackenzie explained.

She could not help but look out at the balcony.

"Is there anything I can do to help?" she asked.

"Hunter actually took care of everything. He always joked that he had time to set things in motion once he..." Ollie stopped, still struggling to say that he was gone.

"What did he always say? Throw money at something?" Mackenzie said, shaking her head.

She got up, hugging both of them. Then, she walked over to her suitcase, zipping it up.

"Mac, seriously, you don't have to go," Ollie pleaded.

Mackenzie gave him a reassuring smile. She wanted to give them alone time without worrying about her. The two of them had known Hunter so much longer than she did. They needed time to process everything and deal with their grief.

"Let us take you home," Ollie asked.

Mackenzie shook her head, pulling out her phone and scrolling through her ride-share app.

"No, really, I am okay. I promise to come by in a few days." Mac stated.

"There is actually something you can do," Parker piped in.

"We're taking Hunter back to China. He told us to ask you if you could come with us," Parker explained. "He didn't ask himself because he didn't want you to feel pressured into saying yes to him. He did buy a refundable ticket for you, just in case."

"Of course he did," Mackenzie took a deep breath. "Just tell me when to be at the airport."

She lifted her suitcase, seeing her ride was five minutes away.

"Mac, if there is anything you want. Hunter would insist you have it. He had already told us that he wanted you to have his records. "

Mackenzie knew better than to argue as she looked over at Hunter's huge vinyl collection. She understood why he would want her to have it. Mackenzie looked down at the Zhou ring on her pointer finger and then glanced around the room. She walked up to his desk and picked up his gray hoodie. The one he wore practically the whole time they knew each other. She held it out to the guys.

Parker and Ollie nodded. Mackenzie's eyes drifted to the top of his desk. She saw the weathered piece of cardstock. She picked it up, turning to the guys. They both walked over. Mackenzie grabbed a pen holding the cardstock in place. Slowly, she drew a line across the last three items on his list. Then, she smiled, pressing it to her chest. She turned toward them, clutching Hunter's wildest dreams list.

They hugged her.

"Of course," Ollie said, giving her permission to take the list without her even asking.

"He would insist on it," Parker chimed in.

Mackenzie walked toward the door, Parker taking hold of her suitcase and rolling it out before she could protest.

Mackenzie didn't know why, but she felt the need to shower again, washing her hair once more, even though she had already done so earlier. She thought maybe it was because taking a shower at her bungalow helped her get settled back into her world.

She threw on a tattered pair of boxers and a pair of slouch socks. As she went to grab a shirt, she saw Hunter's hoodie on top of her luggage. She pulled it over her head looking down as it dropped onto her. She laughed at the way she swam in it.

She opened her sliding door, looked out at the beach, closed her eyes, and let the sea breeze hit her. Mackenzie walked back into the house, thumbing through her record collection and finding the album she was looking for. She placed it on the record player, putting the needle down, then made her way out back onto her balcony as the first song played. She sat on the wooden floor, looking up at the sky. She smiled as "The Night We Met" by Lord Huron played. Mackenzie pulled her knees up to her chest and just sat there for a while.

She heard someone working the lock of her front door, then opening it. The familiar jingle of their keys and bracelets putting Mackenzie at ease. She heard her fridge open then some rummaging in her cupboards. A few more moments passed before she saw Bianca step onto the balcony.

Bianca sat in front of Mackenzie cross-legged putting down the two wine glasses. She cracked open the bottle of Moscato that she had put in there while Mackenzie was gone. Then poured it into each glass.

"I still do not know how you find the perfect wine goblets. I mean, each one holds half of this bottle," Bianca said. She finished filling them out and then passed one to Mackenzie. Mackenzie took it, took a sip, and turned toward her friend.

"You know, I take it?" Mackenzie asked.

Bianca nodded.

"I had my phone set up to give me notifications to ding me if anything came up on Chaoxiang Zhou," Bianca explained.

"He went by Hunter," Mackenzie said quietly, looking down at her wine glass before taking another sip.

"Then I looked at your location and saw you were home."

Mackenzie shook her head.

"To be fair, I have known you were back from the second your pin showed back on my screen. I saw you weren't home. I figured you were with him."

"FBI. Fuck, Bianca's Investigating strikes once more," Mackenzie laughed.

Mackenzie took another sip of her wine.

"We weren't messing around," Mackenzie stated.

Bianca gave her a blank look.

"This is me, and I know you. I know you weren't," Bianca replied, taking a sip of her drink.

"Not saying we weren't intimate because we were, but not physically. He's here now," Mackenzie said, holding her hand to her heart. "It wasn't passionate or intense. We just got each other."

"You okay to tell me the deets?" Bianca asked.

Mackenzie smiled and nodded.

"I think that's just what I need."

They sat on the balcony as Mackenzie told Bianca about how they met. Then about listing her wildest dreams and all the other things they did. She told Bianca about Parker and Ollie promising to have them meet her soon. Every once in a while a tear would fall from Mackenzie's eyes. Bianca would wipe it away then ask another question about their adventures.

"I was happy to complete his list," Mackenzie whispered.

"You sure you are okay to go back to work? I am sure if you explained to your boss he would give you a few more days."

Mackenzie shook her head.

"No, in fact, I'm resigning," Mackenzie announced.

"Because of Sam?" Bianca asked.

Mackenzie shook her head and smiled. "Because of Hunter."

"Sam was at my house today," Bianca revealed. "He came to daddy's birthday party."

"How is he?" Mackenzie asked as she felt a pang in her heart.

"He's figuring things out for himself," Bianca stated.

Mackenzie could tell Bianca wasn't telling her something but didn't have the energy to pry.

After a few hours, Bianca announced that she was going home. She hugged Mackenzie tightly and ordered her to call if she needed anything.

Mackenzie sat on the floor of her balcony for a little while longer. She reached into the front pocket of Hunter's hoodie, pulling out the weathered piece of cardstock. Smiling down at it, tracing the lines through each number.

"You finished it, Hunter," Holding it against her knees, she read the list out loud.

1. ~~Zipline in the Amazon~~

2. ~~Make a snowball at the North Pole~~

3. ~~Stand at the top of Mount Olympus~~

4. ~~Watch an opera at the Sydney Opera House~~

5. ~~See Christmas one last time~~

6. ~~Marry someone who loves me~~

7. ~~Have a kiss be my last breath~~

Chapter 33

SAM

Sam would be lying if he said he didn't get up a bit earlier and took more time grooming and getting dressed. He knew Mackenzie would be back at work today, and there was a chance he'd run into her in their office building if she was with Bianca.

He debated wearing her favorite blue and green tie, the one that she said brings out the color of his eyes. He decided it would feel too calculated. Somehow, his choice of wearing her favorite seafoam-colored shirt didn't feel as bad.

He tried not to jump every time he heard the ding of the elevator. Hoping he would see Mac trailing behind Bianca. After about 45 minutes he decided to grab a cup of coffee from the shop they always frequented. Hoping to run into her. He took his laptop with him and sat at a corner table by the door. After about 25 minutes of answering emails and busy work, he spotted Mac walking into the shop, standing in line fiddling with her phone.

He stopped, his heart racing at the sight of her. Belatedly, he realized he felt her presence before she got there. It was some strange sixth sense he had. He would feel her right before he saw her. Suddenly, his heart stopped pounding, and a sense of calm came over him. It was weird that anytime Mac was around, he felt centered and at peace. Even now, just knowing she was close made him feel whole even though they weren't speaking. He watched as she grabbed her drink and then made her way to the condiment station, doctoring her coffee with sugar and half and half.

He remembered the countless times he'd watched her make her coffee. Stand outside the kitchen of her tiny Venice Beach apartment. Laughing as she talked to herself or danced around the kitchen humming some tune. Thinking how lucky he was that he was the only guy that got to see her like that.

Sam heard the ding of opening the door again as Clarissa's voice cut through his revelry. Sam moved his chair slightly out of Mac's line of sight. Clarissa was talking to another coworker about their trip to Japan. He watched as Clarissa eyed Mackenzie. She spoke a bit louder, talking about Sam and all the time they spent together. Cringing when she mentioned their dinner date the other night. He couldn't help but notice a vicious smugness in her voice. Had she always been like that to Mac? Why didn't Mac ever say anything?

Or was it because Clarissa felt she had the right to mark her territory. As if she was putting Mackenzie on notice, letting her know how close they had gotten since she was away.

He watched as Mac straightened herself, turning around. He noticed it right away, sitting where she could not see him, but he could see her. There was something different about her. Something he couldn't quite place. An air of sadness drifted around her. He wondered briefly if she was sad about their breakup. Somehow, he could tell that it wasn't related to him. The urge to walk up to her and hug her was overwhelming. Whatever it was, he knew there was an underlying sense of grief surrounding her.

He watched as Mac looked over at Clarissa. "Clarissa," she said. Clarissa turned around with the same poise and air of elegance she always carried Yet, today it felt pompous to him.

"Best of luck," Mac said smiling. To most it would seem sarcastic, but he felt Mac's sincerity. She tilted her head giving Clarissa a genuine smile. So sincere that he felt a stabbing in his heart. As if she had resigned to the reality that he was no longer hers.

Something about the grace and resolution in her actions caused Sam to feel as if the world he was frantically trying to rebuild was crumbling. He found it hard to breathe for a second. When he heard Mac speak again.

"Someone told me recently that you should always acknowledge people who are brave enough to go after something they want. So, I wish you the best. I hope the trip to Japan is a successful one."

Just then, Mac turned and caught sight of him at his corner table. Sam saw her jump slightly, and he quickly got to his feet. He felt his cheeks warm.

Mac knew he'd been eavesdropping, and there was no use in denying it. He took a step toward her. They stopped between the condiments station and the tables, staring at each other for a moment.

"You're back," he said.

"Sort of," Mackenzie said quietly. "I gave my two-week notice."

Sam felt his blood run cold, "It's not because of me, is it? Mackenzie, I don't want to make things hard on you."

Mackenzie shook her head, looking up at him.

"It's because of me," Mackenzie said. "This working at an accounting firm is not what I was built for."

She looked down, the same sad smile appearing across her face. "This isn't where I am supposed to be."

"Sam, stand up, meeting in ten," he heard. He looked up to see Clarissa standing at the doorway of the coffee shop. She must have spotted him at the same time Mac did.

Sam opened his mouth to say something. "Sam?" Clarissa repeated. He could tell she was irritated.

"Yeah, let's go."

Back at the office, Sam found himself looking toward the aisle in hopes that he would see Mackenzie making her way to Bianca's workspace. Bianca and Mac probably hadn't seen each other in a while, and he was sure they would go to lunch together. He looked so much that he was afraid someone would notice. The only time he stopped was when Clarissa invited him to a working lunch with Hayes.

He stood in the break room afterwards staring at his phone with Mackenzie's contact information up. The knowledge that she was once again four blocks away made the ache to see or talk to her go into overdrive.

"She told me she's working late today," he heard Bianca say. Sam blinked in surprise. Bianca stood to his side as she poured herself a cup of coffee, jerking her chin toward his phone.

"You didn't even hear me come up, did you?" Bianca asked, shaking her head. "Mac told me she was going to work until rush hour was over. Jack's looking for you as well."

Sam cleared his throat, straightening up and grabbing a mug for himself.

"Thanks for letting me know," Sam replied.

"This is going to sound weird coming from me. But you need to get your head in the game. You obviously sacrificed too much for this deal. Still, don't let it be all for nothing," Bianca said, taking a sip of her coffee before leaving the room.

Sam looked down at the time; it was after 6 p.m. He didn't have much time. Ezra was going to pick him up around nine to take him to the airport. Sam had wanted to leave earlier; however, he had meetings about the itinerary for Japan. Sam was briefed on the clients they were hoping to sign. He also had to go over things with his colleagues, who would be taking care of his workload while he was away. He could see Clarissa lingering and then giving up when it appeared that Sam's last conference call would take a while. He left his office just as it started to get dark. He walked quickly to Mac's office, the ten-minute walk feeling more like five. He was worried he would miss her. One of Mac's coworkers saw him standing at the door, letting him in. He walked over and saw Mackenzie sitting at her desk typing away. Her whole section was empty; her team had left at five. Sam adjusted his messenger bag and walked over to her cubby.

"Hey," he said, making Mackenzie jump.

"Shit, sorry," she chuckled, shaking her head. "I was just in the zone. I have a lot of work to catch up on." Mackenzie looked up at him and smiled. It made his heart stop. "I know you are heading to Japan at midnight," Mackenzie said.

"Yeah, for twelve days. I was hoping we could talk when I get back?" Sam asked.

"That goes without saying," she smirked.

Sam smiled back, torn between feeling awkward and wanting to stay and talk to her.

"Well, I should get going," Sam announced.

"Hey, Sam," he heard her say as he began to walk away. Sam turned around and saw her standing up.

"I know how important this is to you. Best of luck," she said, smiling at him

"Thanks," Sam responded, feeling lighter than he had in a long time.

Chapter 34

SAM

"So I think I overstepped," Clarissa said as they sat on the plane. "Showing up at your place that night uninvited was wrong. I won't do it again."

Sam looked over at her, giving her a nod of recognition. He could tell by the look on her face that she was expecting a different response.

"I overheard Mackenzie saying she is resigning from her job," Clarissa commented.

"Yes," Sam confirmed. Suddenly feeling protective of Mackenzie.

"I heard her say to you that she wasn't made for her firm."

"Yes, she did," Sam said, leaning back in his seat.

"I think it's really great to have a sense of awareness. You know, understanding when things aren't for you or when you don't fit in."

He felt his insides twist. Seeing the difference in the way Mackenzie said it as opposed to how Clarissa was commenting on it.

"Yes, Mackenzie has always been brave," Sam said, putting in his earbuds and listening to an audiobook Mac had recommended a while ago. Trying to convey Mackenzie was a topic that would not be discussed.

Japan felt unreal to Sam. It was like Manhattan and Vegas combined. Yet there were places that were traditional and ancient.

They spent most of the trip with Ozora Dynamics then had back-to-back meetings with other potential clients. Sam had trouble adjusting to the time. He went back to his room every night to try to get some rest and go over notes on their next clients.

Clarissa had suggested they check out the nightlife or maybe do some sightseeing. Both Hayes and Sam seemed to be afflicted with jet lag, so they would respectfully decline. It wasn't until Ozora Dynamics had signed the contract that Hayes insisted they go out and celebrate. Hayes wanted to go to a Michelin Star restaurant. They ended up at Wakasugi. Hayes and Clarissa both said they wanted to try Fugu, blowfish. Sam declined, telling them he wasn't that much of a risk-taker. Blowfish, if ill-prepared, could be poisonous.

Hayes asked Sam what he would choose to eat on the menu. Sam suggested they leave it in the expert hands of the chefs behind the counter where they were sitting. Hayes picked up his chopsticks, holding them awkwardly.

"I never had a knack for these," Hayes said. "Sam, how do you get the smaller things off a plate?"

"I'm not great at this either," Clarissa chimed in. "How do you do that?"

"It just takes practice," Sam said, hoping to God they wouldn't ask him to demonstrate.

"When did you learn to use chopsticks?" Hayes asked.

"I would think since you were a kid, right, growing up with Mackenzie?" Clarissa said.

Sam tried his best to keep his composure.

"China, Japan, Korea, Vietnam, and a few other countries use chopsticks. Mackenzie is Filipino." Sam said, trying to hide the irritation in his voice.

"Oh, what do they use?" Hayes asked.

Sam gripped the counter. He was the one who actually taught Mackenzie how to use chopsticks, and his mother was the one who showed him how to use them when he was five. It was common for Jewish families to go and eat Chinese on Christmas Day.

"A spoon and fork," Sam answered, trying to contain his incredulous tone.

Both Clarissa and Hayes laughed. Sam sat there trying to figure out what was so funny.

Sam desperately tried to get out of going out to drink. Hayes did not have it. They started at Gen Yamamoto, a high-end bar. Hayes and Clarissa are both drinking saké. Sam opted for Yamazaki whiskey. He would never order it because of the cost. He decided to be petty and order it since they were spending a company dime.

His hopes that this very painful night was over went out the door when Hayes said their next stop was a club since they had turned Clarissa down a few times. Hayes decided on NinjaBar Asakusa. Sam suspected it was because of the name rather than the recommendation they had gotten.

The three of them walked down the stairs into the basement club. There were a lot of tourists. Because of that, the level of being obnoxiously drunk went through the roof. He wouldn't say Clarissa and Hayes were sloppy, but they were loud and talking to other patrons. Sam sat down at the table nursing Nikka From The Barrel, another Japanese brand of whiskey.

Hayes laughed, sitting back down with Sam as Clarissa belted out a karaoke song.

"Loosen up, Sam. You're going to have to get used to enjoying yourself on trips like this," Hayes said.

Clover Madden would be having a fit so big that no amount of meditation would help her. Clover taught Sam to respect other cultures and appreciate the nuisances.

"Still suffering from a bit of jet lag," Sam said.

"Well, tomorrow you can sleep since our flight leaves late at night."

Hayes insisted on buying Sam another drink and then a few shots. Sam wasn't drunk, but he had a nice buzz. Clarissa grabbed Sam, yanking him to dance with her. She was dancing around like a maniac. Not in the way Mackenzie danced the few times she had gotten drunk. Even drunk, Mackenzie had a grace that made him want to hold her close and kiss her. So unlike the embarrassment he felt just then with Clarissa. Thankfully, a group of girls pulled Clarissa into their little dance circle.

Sam sat down, relieved. He turned to talk to Hayes. Then saw Hayes's focus was on a Japanese server.

"There's something about them, right?" Hayes said.

Sam felt his stomach turn. "They're exotic and, from what I hear, passionate. I can't find the right word for it."

"It's called Asian fetishization," Sam muttered, knowing Hayes couldn't hear him.

"Give me tips on how to start a conversation," Hayes said drunkenly, swinging to Sam.

"I wouldn't know," Sam yelled over the music.

"How did you nab your ex?" Hayes asked.

"She's not Japanese. She's Filipino!" he shouted, using the sounds of the loud music to mask his utter irritation.

Hayes just chuckled, calling the girl over, trying to talk to her doing that speaking loud in English thing that Sam hated. As if talking louder would make them suddenly understand English.

Mercifully, Clarissa said she was ready to go back to the hotel. Sam's buzz had completely disappeared. Hayes suggested Sam walk Clarissa to her room. Sam offered Clarissa his arm trying to navigate her to her room. Hoping to get her there quickly so this night would finally be over. Once they got there Clarissa pulled out her key, swiping it and opening the door.

"Come in for a drink," Clarissa asked, throwing her arms around Sam's neck.

"No, it's late," Sam said. "See you tomorrow."

Clarissa gave him a sly smile.

"Fine, be a gentleman," she said. "We'll get there soon enough."

Sam watched her close the door, suddenly feeling like he wanted to vomit. He got to his room, lying down until the nausea dissipated. He suspected it was because of Clarissa's comment about getting there soon. Sam looked out his hotel window. The thought of this being the rest of his life completely revolted him. If he was honest, all he wanted was for Mackenzie to be there with him.

They got home two days later, Sam was glad he had to check his bag because of the *sake* he bought for his friends. Clarissa offered to wait with him at baggage claim, but he let her know that a friend was picking him up. Ezra had insisted on it since he lived a stone's throw away from LAX. As he waited for the carousel to start spitting out bags, he texted Ezra letting him know he'd arrived.

Sam got into Ezra's car after he put his bag in the trunk. Ezra looked over at him.

"Dear God, you look like shit. When was the last time you slept?" Ezra asked.

"I can't even tell you, bro. But I brought you something from Japan, and from Hawaii since we laid over in Honolulu."

"I knew there was a reason I kept your sorry ass around."

Sam chuckled, looking out the window. "You think it would be a bad idea if I drove over to Mac's tonight?" Sam asked. He was anxious to see her. Give her the present he had bought for her.

"It would be a horrible idea since she's not there," Ezra said.

"She's with Bianca?" Sam said, sinking down in his seat, the fatigue finally hitting him.

Ezra glanced over at his friend and then looked back at the road.

"What are you not telling me?" Sam asked, feeling nervous suddenly.

"She's not here, as she is not in Los Angeles. She left town again."

Chapter 35

MACKENZIE

Mackenzie could not help but think about how Hunter used to tease her and say, "Throw money at it, and magically, things get done."

How else could they have gotten Hunter's ashes, a death certificate, and other essential paperwork like all their travel visas taken care of in less than two weeks? As Mackenzie promised, she stopped over to see Ollie and Parker on the way home from work a few times. On the seventh day, the guys asked if Mackenzie could come and spend the night. The Chinese believe the soul of the deceased returns to his or her home seven days after death. To ensure the soul finds its way, a red plaque bearing an inscription was placed outside the house. They were to remain in their rooms and scatter flour across the door.

Mackenzie, of course, agreed. She found it comforting and odd to be in Hunter's room that evening. She wondered if there was any truth to the tradition. That somehow Hunter's soul came back for a day. Mackenzie was pretty sure she talked herself into believing it. She kept smelling whiffs of Hunter's cologne throughout the night.

That morning, they told Mackenzie that the death certificate would be there in three days. They planned on flying out the next day. Thankfully, Mackenzie's boss did not take offense to her leaving before the two weeks were up. He even made sure she got paid for all her vacations and her quarterly bonus. She told Bianca where she was going and when she'd be back, letting her know she would check in.

The three of them arrived in Beijing around noon after flying for almost nineteen hours with a layover in Hong Kong. To Mackenzie's surprise, Parker spoke conversational Mandarin. According to Ollie, every once in a while, Hunter and Parker would speak Mandarin to say things they didn't want Ollie to hear. While Ollie learned a few phrases here and there, he'd never gotten to the point of being able to keep up with the two of them. Mackenzie was positive that Hunter booked them at the Bulgari Hotel Beijing. Five Star Luxury with laundry service just to make her both squirm and laugh. At least it wasn't the suites. Still standing in the Superior Room made Mac feel like she was in a museum. She could almost hear Hunter laughing at her. They brought Hunter's ashes to the cemetery the next day, then took a day to try to get their internal clock back in order.

The day after that was Hunter's funeral. Mackenzie stood there with Parker and Ollie. She stared at the black and white picture of him and then looked at the images of his sister and his parents. They brought fruit, incense, and joss sticks to lay on all four of their graves. The funeral director gave them a brief explanation of how to honor Hunter. Both Ollie and Parker did one bow holding joss sticks. Mackenzie decided to bow three times; she liked the idea of showing respect to Heaven, Earth, and all life. She looked at the four graves in front of them. Happy she was able to be here when Hunter was reunited with his family.

"Are you family?" an older man who appeared to be a groundskeeper asked in English.

Ollie nodded, "Yes, he's our brother."

The older man pointed at Mackenzie.

"Bái yuèguāng," Parker answered. The man smiled and gave her a slight bow as he walked away.

Mackenzie looked up at Ollie. He wrapped his arm around her, giving her a hug and then kissing her forehead. They stood there for a while in silence. Ollie made a motion to leave. Mackenzie bent down over Hunter's headstone and whispered, "Chaoxiang. *Wǒ ài nǐ.*"

The three of them stayed in Beijing for a few more days. Mackenzie wanted to visit the places Hunter told her about.

The noodle shop, he and his sister would frequent when she would come back to visit him. She wanted to stand before the stone arch at the entrance of Tsinghua University. Remembering Hunter telling her that standing there at the entrance the first day of orientation was the proudest moment of his life.

She wanted to take Ollie and Parker to eat hot pot. Because according to Hunter it was the single best thing anyone could have. They sat there trying not to embarrass themselves while Parker and Ollie told Mackenzie stories about Hunter.

The next morning Parker and Ollie knocked on the door to her hotel room. She opened it letting them in. Both gave a low whistle looking around her room. "He totally did this to get under your skin," Ollie laughed.

Parker sat down, letting Mackenzie know he was about to send her an email. Mackenzie opened her inbox to see what Parker had sent.

"Hunter said if you came, then you needed to do this before you went back home. If you don't want to, we can make other arrangements," Mackenzie chuckled, shaking her head.

"It's okay. I will do it."

Three days after a 16-hour flight with a layover in Vienna, Mackenzie found herself sitting at an iron table drinking a strong cup of coffee. She chuckled to herself, typical of Hunter to make her do this on her own. Going solo felt comforting at times. The silence away from everything and everyone gave her a lot of time to think. Other times, she would see something that she wanted to comment on, wishing Ollie, Parker, and, most of all, Hunter were there.

Mackenzie looked down at the letter she had just written, reading through it one more time.

This wasn't what I thought I would be writing when I thought about doing this. It isn't because I am not brokenhearted. I am completely. Losing two people I love in different ways in the span of a few weeks is making me feel a kind of pain I never had. I told Hunter that when we first met, I felt like there were pieces of me floating around. Like I didn't feel whole. Strangely now, somehow, in the midst of all the pain, the pieces have started to fall into place. Along with pieces I thought I had lost. Pieces I didn't know I had. I feel sad but centered. To the point where I feel pangs of guilt that it took Hunter dying to help me start to feel whole again.

If Hunter had helped put me back together, Sam would have helped me build who I am. Somewhere I lost that. Looking back now I can understand how I lost him. Knowing and loving Hunter didn't take anything away from Sam. Seeing him again made me realize I couldn't imagine a life without Sam Madden in it. Sam is still sitting in the center of my heart. I don't think that will ever change. Even if he has moved on.

All of this has taught me to slow down. Life isn't about just living. It's about living out loud. I guess what I want to say is if you read this and write back to me, remind me to love myself. Don't be afraid of feeling hurt or pain. Find myself again.

Mackenzie looked at what she wrote one more time before folding it up and putting it in an envelope. She sat there for a few more hours sketching the building in front of her. A few people stopped to look at her work and compliment her. When she was ready, she walked over to a red wooden box and stuck the envelope inside.

She got up and just started walking around, not having a plan, just taking into everything. She knew now why Hunter asked her to do this on her own. Being alone in a completely different place where she knew nobody reminded her that life, her life in particular, was something she needed to live for herself and not for anyone else.

She sat at the Piazza delle Erbe, staring down at her list, smiling down at her number one. She took a pen and drew a line through it. Reading her now finished list out loud the same way she had read Hunter's.

1. ~~Leave a letter at Casa di Giulietta~~

2. ~~Dance atop the Eiffel Tower~~

3. ~~Sketch on a gondola in Venice~~

4. ~~Wake up to the blue domed churches in Santorini~~

5. ~~Twirl in the Greystone Mansion ballroom at night~~

6. ~~Ride the paddle boats at Echo Park~~

7. ~~Do something life altering for another person~~

Chapter 36

SAM

It took everything in him not to march up to Bianca's desk and ask where Mackenzie was. Why did she keep leaving? Who was she with? Meetings and catching up on work that had piled up while he was gone gave him something to focus on.

Around noon, he heard the soft tapping on the glass door to his office as it opened.

"Clarissa, I'm eating in today," Sam said, not looking up from his laptop.

"That is going to take the wind out of her sails," he heard Bianca say.

Sam's head snapped up, staring at Bianca.

"She'll be back in about a week or so. You know I am not going to tell you where she went. I think she needs to tell you herself," Bianca explained.

Bianca put her hand up in front of her as if telling Sam to stop.

"I know it goes against everything you think is right. But listen, give her a few days before you do that thing where you barge in like a bull in a China shop, okay? A lot has happened to her both good and bad so please trust me on this."

Bianca turned around, exiting Sam's office. Sam turned his chair around, tilted his head back, put his hand over his mouth, and made a muffled scream. He rubbed his face so hard he felt the skin of his face burn.

Just then, there was another knock on the door. He hoped it was his food and not Clarissa.

"Yeah," he said, turning his chair back around.

"Sam Madden?" a man said.

Sam nodded looking up seeing a courier with a cardboard sleeve in his hand. The courier held out his tablet.

"Please sign here," he said.

Sam signed the tablet with his finger then looked up at the courier expectantly. He was pretty sure it was from legal, they told him they would be sending over some contracts to look at.

The man handed him the sleeve then gave him a wave walking to the door closing it on the way out.

Sam whipped away the perforated seal, pulling out an envelope.

The envelope was made of cardstock paper, he turned it around seeing the initials CZ inscribed on the lip. Sam looked down at it confused trying to figure out if it was an invitation or some sort of summons.

He used his letter opener to tear through the top pulling out several pieces of paper. Sam unfolded it, seeing it was a letter. He knitted his brows and began to read.

Sam,

You're probably wondering who I am. Allow me to introduce myself. My name is Hunter Zhou. You might have heard my name from running in somewhat the same circles. You must be wondering why I am writing to you. I'm the guy who absconded with your ex-fiancée for two weeks. Before you go all ape shit, this is not me boasting or trying to pour salt into a wound. Truly. I guess I want you to know she didn't take off with some creep. Know she was taken care of and safe. As cliché as this is going to sound, by the time you read this, I will have passed. That honestly kind of sucks because, for the first time in a long time, I truly wish I had more... well, time.

Time to give me a genuine chance to steal her heart from you. Believe it or not, when I met Mac, it was never my intention to fall in love with her. Just take a few of her wildest dreams and make them come true. You know better than anyone that it is impossible to spend time with her without her reaching in and grabbing hold of your heart.

Mac's going to need some support. Because she is Mac, and she is a great judge of character, I have to believe you just lost your way. Forgot what was truly important in life. Stupidly thought there was something better than her. As if that existed.

I'm not going to apologize for whisking her away. Honestly, my time with her has been the best part of my life. So much so that I hate to think about it ending. I cannot describe how jealous I am that you have known her for so long. You, having so many moments with her. How mad I am thinking that you are just going to walk away and not fight. Knowing as I write this, I am fighting a losing battle for more moments with her.

So yeah, I think you are an idiot. Sorry, I had to throw that in there. I digress. As I stated, my life is over and she's going to be left to deal with that. She's going to need someone that won't judge her or jump to conclusions. I truly hope you're the person she can rely on. As narcissistic as this sounds, she is going to be in a lot of pain.

She loves you, if you are wondering. She never said she was angry at you. Hurt, yes, but not angry. She gets this look in her eyes when she talks about you. You guys growing up together in Venice Beach. You are in the center of all her milestones. She loves you so much that I wanted to punch you because I was jealous. As much as I hate to admit it, you own her heart. Which is ironic since watching the way she spoke about you made me fall in love with her even more. You know how the saying goes. When you truly love someone, you care more about their happiness than your own.

So, just in case you need reminding, here are a few things about her that make her so incredible.

First, her laugh. When it's real, she laughs with her whole body. It's unbridled and will make you laugh as well. She thinks it's too loud so she tries to subdue it. But when something truly amuses her, watching her laugh is like watching fireworks light up the sky.

Strangers walk up to her and start random conversations. And when they do, she gives them her undivided attention. Maybe it's because they can see the light inside of her, and it attracts them. Still, you have to laugh because it happens nearly everywhere you go.

When she smiles it both breaks and fills your heart. Because if you mean something to her. It's a smile she only gives to you. And you know it. Like you are sharing a secret that no one else in the world gets to know.

You might not need the reminders. Still, I wanted to say them to someone that would understand how it feels to love Mackenzie Almazan. Also because I can not vocalize them to anyone else, not without making this already difficult time even more unbearable for the people around me.

If you have not stopped reading this, let me give you a piece of advice. Google me. I was successful and well-known in the tech world. I made a lot of money, on top of having lots of money to begin with. I had the house in the hills, the luxury cars, and an endless string of people trying to stroke me off or stab me in the back. I was ruthless at times, shallow, and, well, a snobby little prick.

All of what I had and achieved meant nothing when I got my diagnosis. I couldn't throw money at it to make it go away or call in a favor to help me negotiate. I spent most of my life setting goals and reaching them. Being admired by my peers and running in elite circles.

If I am completely honest, back then, I wouldn't look up if I saw Mackenzie walking down the street. And if I did, my snotty, arrogant ass would think she would never fit in my world.

Sound familiar?

I'm telling you this so you don't make a huge mistake. Nothing I have ever done or achieved feels as good as the time I got to spend with Mackenzie. I am hoping you get your head out of your ass and are not going to waste this opportunity to fix things. I truly hope you are letting this sink in and not lost in some machismo haze—this letter isn't me challenging you man to man. I truly hope you see my intent. Writing this is probably one of the last things I could do for her.

Take her back to Paris. Climb the 300 steps of the Sacre-Coeur Basilica. I couldn't do it. I know she wanted to but acted like it wasn't a big deal. Let her see the view. Remind her to look out, not down.

Get it right.

Because trust me, if you don't, someone else will come around and claim her.

Sam felt his eyes well up with tears. At first, he was angry. The more and more he read, the more Hunter's words slammed him in the stomach and ripped out his guts.

He read the rest of the letter then immediately googled Hunter Zhou. The first hit he got was news of his passing. After that he was mentioned in articles both in the US and in China. He found himself mourning a man he never met, someone he would absolutely hate to let around Mackenzie because he knew Hunter would blow him out of the water.

His eyes drifted back to one of his sentences.

Because trust me, if you don't, someone else will come around and claim her.

Chapter 37

MACKENZIE

Mackenzie felt like a wet noodle when she got home from Verona. She texted Bianca and Ollie, letting them know she was back and would probably be lying in her bed for the next few days. She stared at her phone, debating whether or not to text Sam. She knew his office had a lot going on, and he was in the middle of all of it. Mackenzie closed her eyes, remembering his gruff voice or short text when he was knee-deep in work. She decided she would wait until she didn't feel so wrung out.

She collapsed on her bed, looking over at her bedside table. There was a picture of her and Sam. It was the year they met. She was eight, and he was ten. They were both on his skateboard, smiling over at Clover, as they went by. Mackenzie picked it up, looking at it again. In all the years she had the picture, she hadn't noticed a small detail.

Mackenzie had her arms wrapped around his waist to make sure she didn't fall off. It was the first time she saw his hand over hers, holding them tightly. Just in case she let go.

She touched the picture, putting it back down. After a few moments she felt her eyes drifting shut as she fell asleep. She woke up at noon the next day with a pounding headache letting her know she slept much longer than she normally had.

She grabbed some Aleve from her medicine cabinet walking to her fridge for a bottle of water to drink it down.

Mackenzie looked up and saw one of the first paintings she had ever done hanging next to the fridge. She was always embarrassed when she saw it. It was her attempt to be painterly and extremely sloppy.

Yet, Uncle Deano insisted on hanging it up. She smiled thinking about how Uncle Deano seemed to always slip in that Mackenzie was a painter into conversations with people he just met.

Mackenzie ordered takeout because she was lazy and hungry. She sat on her couch, looking at the sketchbook she bought in Paris. She thumbed through finding the sketch she did of Hunter in the gondola. She picked up her pencil and started cleaning up the lines. She found herself being hyper-focused on fixing the sloppy sketch. She closed her eyes a few times to envision him sitting there next to her.

She pulled out the small photo they'd taken in the photo booth in Paris. It was the only one they took together. Hunter told her he wasn't a picture person; Mac knew it was because he didn't want her sitting around rifling through photos, dwelling. She heard the door, meeting the takeout guy before sitting back on the couch, eating her food. She felt her phone vibrate.

"Don't take this as an insult, but you're the last person I expected to call me first."

"That's because Bianca is doing her best not to hover, and Sam is still trying to get his head out of his ass," Ezra said.

Mackenzie shook her head, taking a bite of her food.

"For someone who says that you're his ride or die, you sure take jabs at him."

"It's our dynamic. You sitting on your couch eating chili cheese fries?" Ezra asked.

Mackenzie looked down at the box of chili cheese fries.

"You got cameras in here?" he asked.

Ezra laughed.

"It's your go-to comfort food," Ezra said. "So, I purposely didn't ask too much. Bianca wasn't volunteering information."

"It's because you can't keep anything from Sam," Mackenzie piped in.

"True. I am not going to ask you where you were or what you were doing. Just asking if you are planning on taking any more trips out of town," Ezra explained.

Mackenzie held her phone between her shoulder and the side of her head, taking another bite of her apparently predictable choice of food.

"Not that I know of," Mackenzie chuckled. "Why, Ez, you missed me?"

The phone went silent for a second.

"Ez, you still there?"

She heard Ezra sigh, "I told myself I wasn't going to tell you this because it feels like emotional blackmail. I'm asking just in case I have to babysit Sam again."

Mackenzie stopped eating, sitting back on her couch.

"Babysit?" Mackenzie said.

"Mac, he's been a mess. From the first time you left until now. He told me you were in Paris and sent a video of you dancing at the Eiffel Tower. My man scrolled through Tik Tok trying to find videos that might help him figure out who you were with," Ezra explained

Mackenzie took another bite of her fries, closing her eyes as she leaned back on her couch.

"Honestly, the most cheery I have seen him be was when he asked me if it would be a bad idea to go to your place the night he got back from Japan. It quickly turned into him throwing a fit, asking where you went," Ezra explained.

"Ez, I'm sorry he worried and that you've had to deal with it, but I am not sorry I went," Mackenzie said. "He hurt me, Ez."

Mackenzie took a deep breath, trying to shake away the shame she felt when she realized Sam was embarrassed of her.

"I know, baby girl. I am not justifying what he did or making excuses for him. I just wanted you to know you were never far from his mind," Ezra said softly.

"Thanks for letting me know. If I am honest, I admit I wondered if what he was feeling was guilt because he was relieved," Mackenzie admitted.

"If I am honest, I don't think he knows what he was feeling either," Ezra said. "Listen, I have to go. My date is here. Call me if you need anything, Mac. Love you."

Mackenzie looked down at her phone shaking her head thinking about what Ezra said. She sat there debating about sending Sam a text. Suddenly she realized she was no longer employed and would not be seeing Sam everyday. Mackenzie looked around her bungalow trying to figure out what to do next. She got up and walked to her painting again, staring at it.

She hadn't painted in so long. Mackenzie looked at a single key hanging on the key rack. She grabbed it and her house keys, locked up, and headed downstairs.

Mackenzie walked to the garage door, undoing the lock and sliding the door over. She looked around the garage. It was dusty, thankfully, most everything was under dust cloth. She walked to the first one, pulling it off her sketching desk. Then the other revealing two easels. She kept going until all the dust cloths were off.

Mackenzie walked around the small garage that her Uncle Deano called her painting studio. He had set it up for her with the help of Sam and Clover. She used to spend hours here. But that was years ago. She grabbed a broom sweeping away the dust and sand. Living close to the beach meant sand blew into just about everything. She always had to remember to cover her work.

She went upstairs to get cleaning supplies. Mackenzie returned and folded all the dust covers. She cleaned the dust and grime off everything. The task took hours. Mackenzie looked around the now clean studio. She was going to have to get new brushes and canvases. Luckily, oil paints lasted decades or else she would be dropping a pretty penny.

Mackenzie went back upstairs after locking up the garage to wash the dirt and grime off of her. She searched the food cupboard, finding Udon soup. It was something quick and easy to eat for dinner. She heard her phone ding and walked over to it, seeing Ollie's name above the text.

"Don't freak out. You are going to get a text from Hunter's phone at 7:55 p.m. Make sure you are at home."

Mackenzie looked at the text, completely flabbergasted. She assumed Hunter had arranged to send her something else. She ate her Udon, the time crawling now that she was waiting for 7:55 to hit. She jumped even though she knew the text was coming. She smiled, seeing "Probably Not A Stalker" on the screen. Her heart raced as she opened the text.

"Go out to your balcony now. Click the link below at 7:59."

She did as instructed, wondering what the hell was going on. She clicked the link at 7:59. "Run" by Snow Patrol started playing almost immediately. Mackenzie smiled, looking out at the night sky. Suddenly, she heard a pop in the distance. She looked toward the Venice Fishing pier and saw a firework explode in the air. Mackenzie gasped and chuckled at the same time watching the fireworks go off one at a time until it got to the chorus. Fireworks shot up and out rapidly making her laugh and cry at the same time. The fireworks show lasted the duration of the song, unlike the 30-minute display at Dodger Stadium.

Mackenzie sat down on the floor of her balcony, smiling and crying all at once. After a while, her phone dinged again. "Probably Not A Stalker" appeared on the screen. She laughed as she read the text.

"Just reminding you... look out, not down."

Chapter 38

SAM

Sam knew he was taking a risk. He knew he had to. He parked his car and walked down the street with his messenger bag over his chest. He peered through the glass, seeing Mackenzie standing there. Sam stepped into the small laundry mat around the corner to Mac's house. It was Wednesday, her laundry day. She always said it was because no one else does laundry in the middle of the week, so she had the place to herself most of the time. It was true, he thought Mackenzie was their only patron that Wednesday night. The door chimed as he walked across the threshold. Mac looked up from moving her clothes from the washer to the dryer. She had a slightly stunned expression on her face.

"I see Wednesday is still laundry day," he said nervously.

Mac smiled, continuing her task. Walking over to the bigger washer to move her sheets over. She pulled her lips in for a moment then gave him a smile.

"Routine is a good touchstone," she replied.

Sam approached and leaned against one of the tables.

"Mac, I wanted to say I'm sorry," Sam said, putting down his bag,

Mackenzie walked up next to him, hopping on the table and sitting with her legs crossed, knees bent, and facing outward. His mother would call this position Baddha Konasana. Sam watched as Mackenzie bit her lip and then blew off the strands of hair that had fallen over her eyes.

Sam had to hold his wrist in order to prevent himself from reaching over and doing it for her. Mackenzie bowed her head taking a deep breath.

"Please, it's okay. I'm sorry as well. I left you holding the bag. It wasn't fair to you. I guess we should talk about..."

"Not that," he said, cutting her off. Mac looked up at him. He took a breath and continued turning his head toward the street.

"I mean, I am sorry about that more than I can say. But right now, that's not what I am saying sorry for."

Mackenzie tilted her head, looking at him, "What are you apologizing for?"

"I'm sorry about Hunter," he said quietly as he turned his head to look at her.

He watched as she blinked rapidly in confusion as if she was trying to figure out how he knew about Hunter.

"Bianca?" Mac asked in disbelief.

Sam shook his head, "You know she would cut out her tongue before betraying your confidence."

Mackenzie kept staring at him, trying to figure out how he knew. Suddenly, she looked up at him and smiled, shaking her head.

"The letter was to you."

Sam nodded in response.

"Is it weird that I am jealous?" Mackenzie chuckled. "I was hoping it was for me."

Sam scooted closer to her, watching her body stiffen as she laughed. He watched as she changed her sitting position to lean against the top of the washing machine behind her, pulling her legs to her chest. When Mackenzie was upset, she always pulled her body into a small compact position. Normally he would just reach over and hug her. He knew he couldn't do that now, not after what he did.

"If I was in your shoes I would hope for the same," Sam said, crossing his arms in front of him.

"Full disclosure, I was pissed as I started to read it. By the end of it, I just couldn't keep being mad. I felt grateful," Sam confessed.

"Grateful?" Mackenzie asked.

"Yeah, grateful that he was the one that you were with. Don't get me wrong, I was jealous as fuck," Sam said

Mackenzie started to laugh.

"Sorry, just I haven't seen you so out of sorts in a very long time," Mackenzie explained. "Sam, it wasn't like that."

Sam shook his head, "It wasn't like that for you. He wrote that he fell in love with you."

Mackenzie took a deep breath, searching for the right thing to say.

"I don't know if it's sympathy or me disassociating, but I'm happy for him," Sam said.

Mackenzie looked at him, confused once more.

"You're a great choice to be in love with in general, but in his case, at the end of his life," Sam said.

Mackenzie shook her head in disbelief, "That must have been some letter."

Sam laughed, tilting his head back and looking at the ceiling.

"You have no idea."

"We went to China to bring his ashes back. He wanted to be laid to rest with his parents and his sister."

"We?" Sam asked.

"His assistant, Ollie—he's really more like a brother—and Ollie's husband, Parker."

Sam cleared his thoughts, "I read about how his parents died in a car crash, and his sister died of leukemia as well."

Sam put his hands up, "He actually told me to Google it."

"And if he didn't?" Mackenzie asked.

They looked at each other and started to laugh, knowing the answer to Mackenzie's question.

Sam pressed his lips against each other.

"I get it now," Sam said quietly.

"Get what?"

Sam gave Mackenzie a small smile.

"There's this whole part of your life that I don't know about. That I am not a part of."

Mackenzie opened her mouth to say something, but Sam continued before she could, "I know it wasn't intentional, not like with me." Mackenzie gulped hard.

Sam crossed his arms tighter against him. He wanted to apologize for what he did. He stopped himself from doing it. Right now, he was here for Mac and her grief.

Sam cleared his throat. He reached out to her, putting his hand on her knee.

"Just wanted you to know if you ever need someone to talk to about him or how you feel, I'm here."

Mackenzie blinked a few times, looking at him wearily.

"You mean it?" she asked quietly.

Sam nodded, knowing that she held people at a distance when someone passed, having gone through it twice with her. He was the only one she would let over the wall. If she needed him, he would be there.

"Thank you," she said.

Sam pulled his bag around opening the flap, "I got you something from Japan."

"Is it a mug?" Mackenzie laughed.

Sam shook his head, taking out a black lacquer box. He'd wanted to get her something more than a mug or a t-shirt. He wanted Mackenzie to know he thought about her. It had to be something she would consider getting for herself and not what Sam would think she wanted. He remembered, almost losing hope and about to give up, he stopped in front of a shop. It was the shop he didn't know he was looking for. Sam walked in, looking around, trying to decide what exactly to get her. He stopped and spoke to the shop's owner. Using his limited vocabulary to convey what he might be looking for. The owner walked down the aisle, coming back with the black box in his hands.

Mackenzie took it from him, resting it on her lap as she opened it. She looked at Sam in disbelief.

"The shop owner was kind enough to help me not look like an idiot."

He wondered if Mackenzie had heard him. Her eyes were fixed on the paint brushes on one side and the calligraphy pen and brush on the other.

"The owner said they are called *Fude*. He said the brushes would be good for *Yamato-e, Kanō*, and *Nihonga*. The calligraphy brush and pencil can be used for *Sumi-E*. I remember you took History of Asian Art. In fact, I am pretty sure I have heard you talk about *Sumi-E*," Sam knew he was rambling, but he was nervous since Mackenzie hadn't said a word.

He watched as she ran her hand across the brushes, looking at each of them.

"Sam, this had to cost a fortune," Mackenzie whispered.

"I need to make up for two years of terrible presents," Sam said, flicking her nose lightly.

"They weren't terrible," Mackenzie said, wiping the tears away from her eyes. She closed the box, still guarding it in her lap.

"Don't be nice. As Ezra and Bianca would say, they were ass."

Mackenzie started to laugh hard, making Sam laugh just as hard. He reached for her as she leaned back holding her stomach, worried she was going to fall off the table.

He brought his bag around, reaching into it to get another box.

"I had a layer over in Honolulu," He pulled out a box of Mauna Loa milk chocolate covered macadamias. Opening it for Mackenzie offering her one.

Mackenzie took it and sighed, "These poor things are not going to make it out of here. I better be frugal about them."

Sam smiled, chuckling as he pulled out an identical box of what they were eating, then another one of Hawaii Host chocolates and two bags of Hershey's with macadamia nuts in the center. The girl at the candy stall in the airport let him know they were only available in Hawaii.

Mackenzie shook her head, still wiping the tears out of her eyes.

Sam watched her, waiting a second before he dug out a few bags of Li Hing Mui gummies and watermelon sours. Mackenzie had an insatiable sweet tooth. He couldn't decide what to get her, so he tried to get a bit of everything she liked. He still could see Clarissa and Hayes standing there, shocked as Sam asked to check his carry-on. He had three bags of chocolate and candy. Bianca and Ezra each got a box, and he got the rest for Mackenzie.

"Besides, chocolate has endorphins. It makes people happy," Sam said, Mackenzie giving him a playful glare because it was something she often said.

Sam hopped on the table, legs swinging. He picked up another piece of chocolate biting into it.

"This feels like some weird Seudat Havra'ah," Mackenzie stated.

Sam laughed. Mackenzie was well versed in Jewish traditions and customs. This one in particular since Clover had prepared one for her when Uncle Deano died.

"It is a meal of condolences, in a way," he said.

Seudat Havra'ah was the Jewish practice of serving a meal to mourners after returning from the cemetery following a funeral. They called it a "meal of comfort," which felt fitting since nothing comforted Mac more than chocolate, except maybe cake.

"So, tell me about Paris," Sam said. He knew Paris was the place Mackenzie had most wanted to go. He couldn't be angry about it. It was his own fault that she experienced it without him.

Mackenzie smiled at him, taking a bite of the chocolate in her hand.

"Only if you tell me about Japan."

Chapter 39

MACKENZIE

Mackenzie knew she could only go so long before getting a text from Clover Madden. Her text simply said, "It's been six weeks." Mackenzie responded by letting her know she would be there Friday morning. Usually, it was only an overnight visit; however, since she wasn't working, she could spend a whole day with her.

Mackenzie wasn't surprised when Clover announced upon arrival that they would be meditating with an intense yoga session afterwards. By the end of it, Mackenzie was covered in sweat.

After a long shower Mackenzie stepped onto the patio. Clover was sitting in her chair enjoying a joint. She offered it to Mackenzie who shook her head. Clover gently put it out and turned toward Mac.

" So, what did you like most about Paris?" Clover asked.

Mackenzie reached for the glass of fresh squeezed lemonade that Clover had put in front of her. She took a sip then put her glass back down.

"Musée d'Orsay," Mackenzie said smiling. Hunter had offered to take her to the Louvre. She wanted to go to Musée d'Orsay instead.

"I could see that. The impressionists are the ones who got you to discover your gift," Clover smiled while taking a sip of her own glass of lemonade.

Mac held her glass in her hand, rimming the top of it with her finger. She wasn't sure how much Sam had told his mom. She was also worried Clover would be upset about her taking off with a guy who wasn't her beloved son.

"Want to talk about it, beautiful girl?" Clover asked.

Mackenzie looked over at the woman she loved like a mother, then proceeded to tell her how everything unfolded. By the end of her story Clover had reached over holding her hand stroking it gently.

"What can I do for you?" Clover asked.

Mackenzie smiled, shaking her head.

"Just this," Mackenzie said. "For most of my life, you and Sam have been doing all the heavy lifting for me. I think this road is one I have to travel on my own."

Clover laughed, "You were always so much more intuitive than most people. Unlike my dear boy. It took him chasing his tail for a bit to figure he needed to look in the mirror and dig down deep."

"Clover, please know I wasn't trying to hurt him or get back at him," Mackenzie said.

Clover squeezed her hand again.

"Of course not. Although if you were that was a bed he'd made himself," Clover said.

"It wasn't romantic like that."

"But there was love, right?"

Mackenzie looked down, picking at her nails. Still apprehensive about talking to Clover about her time with Hunter.

"I remember the day Sam met you. He had come racing through the house all sweaty, holding a bag of skateboard wheels. He went into the garage and put softer wheels on his board," Clover explained.

Generally, hard wheels were for use at skate parks and street skating on obstacles like ledges, rails, and gaps for better sliding. Soft wheels were more for cruising around just to ride for a bit.

"What you probably didn't know was Sam had told me he had lost interest in skateboarding. In fact, he hadn't been to the skate park in weeks," Clover said, smiling at Mackenzie.

"Really?" Mackenzie asked.

Clover nodded in confirmation, "When I questioned whether or not he decided to take up skateboarding again, he told me he had made a new friend, and her board was really flimsy. The next day, he took off early, board in hand."

Mackenzie laughed, shaking her head, "I remember he'd promised to teach me a few more tricks, then said he couldn't because he forgot to change the wheels."

"He was terrified of you hurting yourself. Slowly, I realized there was something special about his friend Mac."

"Taking care of you helped mold who he was. He just didn't realize the care you needed didn't revolve around money or finances. Yet, suddenly, that was what his world was," Clover looked out toward the ocean.

"I just want him to be happy," Mackenzie said quietly.

Clover leaned back in her chair, taking another sip of her drink.

"Sam is learning that success and happiness don't always go hand in hand. Just remember, Sam finding his way doesn't mean you have to help him figure that out. You can be there to support him. It doesn't mean you have to compromise who you are. Remember, you are important too."

Mackenzie smiled at Clover, nodding in affirmation.

Mackenzie had somewhat awoken to the sound of the squeaky door of Clover's guest room opening. She could tell it was still dark outside, and wondered briefly if Clover was waking her up to greet the morning. Clover had done that on occasion. It wouldn't shock her if this was the case. It wasn't until she felt a hand rubbing her elbow that she realized who it was. Sam had learned tapping on Mac or shaking her often made her jump. He had learned this was the safest way to get her to rise and shine without having her scream the house down.

Mackenzie rolled over just as Sam was turning on the small bedside lamp.

"Hey," she said, still a little confused.

"Hey," Sam answered back.

Mackenzie blinked a few times seeing he was in a volleyball tank top and a pair of sweat shorts. Belatedly, she realized the only time she ever saw him like this was when he was going to or coming back from working out.

"Is everything okay?" Mac whispered.

Sam nodded.

"I was just wondering if you would want to come with me somewhere," he asked nervously.

Mackenzie got up and tried to figure out what was going on. She found herself nodding. The one lesson she learned from her time with Hunter was that she did not always need to know all the details.

"Let me just get dressed."

A few hours later, Sam and Mackenzie sat drifting in the ocean. Both straddling surfboards. Mackenzie preempted the endeavor by telling Sam it had been years since she had been on a board. He laughed and said it was the same for him.

Surfing wasn't like riding a bicycle. For the most part, both fell or missed waves. Paddling was harder than they remembered. Finally, after some rough go's and laughing at each other hysterically, they manage to catch a few waves.

"I wonder if people on the shore think we are filming some sort of comedy sketch," Mackenzie pondered.

"At least you got the hang of it again faster than me," Sam laughed. "Then again, you were always better at this than me."

Mackenzie smiled, leaning forward on her board.

"In your defense, you have only been surfing two weeks longer than me," she smirked.

Sam whipped his head toward her, eyes wide.

"You know that?" he asked, his voice a little shrill.

Mackenzie laughed.

"Of course I knew that. You had never mentioned anything about surfing the entire time we had been friends," Mackenzie said. "And when that guy."

"Caspien. His name was Caspien. It was like his parents decided in the womb he was going to be a surfer," Sam muttered.

"When Caspien volunteered to teach me, suddenly you said you could teach me yourself. You used the whole 'her uncle would worry if it wasn't me' card on the poor guy," Mackenzie laughed. "Also, all the bruises and scrapes you had started to show up with was a dead giveaway."

She watched as Sam's face reddened in embarrassment.

"I didn't mind though. Like always I was just glad to be with you," Mackenzie said, giving him a smile.

"Mac, I know you would rather die than ask for help. I know you quit your job for good reasons. But if you need me to help you while you figure things out, please let me know."

Mackenzie splashed him, "I'm good. I have a brilliant friend who made my tiny portfolio much more lucrative than I thought it could be. Plus, I have some extra money in my savings."

Mackenzie pulled in her lips, looking away. She knew Sam would put two and two together. The money in her savings had been earmarked for their now-canceled wedding. Mac looked around, looking out at the endless ocean behind her. She remembered Hunter saying he had learned how to surf as well. She briefly wondered what he was like before he got sick.

"So," she heard Sam say. "I know you said you didn't fall in love with him. Thinking about it now, do you still think that?"

It didn't shock Mackenzie that somehow Sam deduced what she was thinking. They both could read each other like a book. She watched as Sam lowered his head as if bracing himself for her response.

"Sam?" she asked, trying to get his attention. Sam raised his head, looking over at her. "I've only been in love once in my life."

Sam's face lit up in what appeared like happiness and relief.

"Do you know I was in love with you years before I said it? I mean, on some level, I have always been," Sam confessed

Sam leaned back, stretching his arms behind the board and propping himself up.

"It was at one of my volleyball games after Jenni died. Back then, you always acted like you wanted to meld into the hallway walls. You despised that your voice carried. I spiked a ball and got a match point. I heard you scream so loud I thought the building shook. I remember looking up and thinking I'm in love with Mackenzie Almazan, I'm going to..."

Sam stopped short, stifling what he was about to say. But Mackenzie knew what the next words out of his mouth would be.

"Do you know when I realized I was in love with you? "Mackenzie asked.

Sam shook his head, waiting for her answer.

"The moment you reached out wanting me to hand you my skateboard."

Sam smiled and laughed, splashing her.

"Not going to lie. I did love Hunter. He made me look down my own path. Help me start walking down it again. I think, in the end, it was that he took with him a part of me that I needed to let go of. And he left a piece of him behind for me to hold onto," Mackenzie looked down, smiling.

"I can see that," Sam said quietly. "I wish I could help you more or give you a bit more comfort."

Mackenzie splashed toward him, making him hold his hands out in defense.

"You, and this, help more than you will ever know."

Chapter 40

SAM

Sam could barely hide his disappointment that he didn't see Mackenzie sitting on his mother's porch the next time he came over to spend the night.

Talking and hanging out with his mom was always great but he hadn't seen Mackenzie in three weeks. Even then it had been with Bianca and Ezra. Ezra wanted them to meet his new girlfriend. While they hung out it wasn't as if he was able to get one on one time.

They texted back and forth nearly every day. Mackenzie called once during a Dodgers game because she was excited about a grand slam. Sam had been in the office working; he immediately left work and went home to turn on the game. Since then, they have at least watched one game together over the phone. He really couldn't define their relationship as it stood now. Mackenzie seemed to be treating him like a friend.

Clarissa had cooled off on her pursuit. Sam made it a point to leave his office door open when he had meetings with her. He also declined any lunch that wasn't a work meeting. Every dinner idea was shot down. Privately, she seemed to have gotten the message; publicly, she still carried an air of possessiveness. Every time she did, Bianca would roll her eyes at him.

Sam didn't mind how things were between him and Mackenzie. He was just glad he didn't lose her completely. He wasn't going to kid himself, though. If he had heard Mackenzie was dating, it would have gutted him.

"You going to stop by Mackenzie's on the way home?" Clover asked.

"I was thinking about it since I will be going down PCH, but I don't know if popping in unannounced would be a good idea. Plus, there is this work charity thing that I should make an appearance at."

Clover tilted her head, looking at her son, shaking her head.

"You were always lousy at remembering dates," Clover sighed

His mother wasn't lying, and he was terrible at remembering what day it was. Sam often joked about it being impossible to remember any dates since the eight major and minor Jewish Holidays change with the Moon. The only two dates he remembered were his mother's and Mackenzie's birthdays.

Sam pulled out his phone, looked down, and saw the date. His eyes widened reading it.

"Mom, I got to go."

Not thirty minutes later Sam was knocking on Mackenzie's door. Mackenzie opened it holding an old wash cloth. He looked down at her arms and saw that there were orange and blue paint splattered all over them.

Sam sighed, taking a step into her house while taking off his shoes. He was secretly giddy that his Adidas slides, or as what Uncle Deano and Mac called them, *tsinelas* were still there. He slid them on and went onto her balcony seeing a metal bowl. He took a sniff and shook his head, carrying it to the sink and pouring out the contents. He walked back to the balcony refilling the bowl measuring out the glycerin and turpentine.

Mackenzie chuckled, walking out onto her balcony and sitting in one of the patio chairs. Sam took the other one, turning it to face her, and their knees almost touched. He held out a hand, cocking his brow up, motioning for Mackenzie to give him her arm. She complied with a small smile.

"You were going to burn your skin off," Sam muttered, taking the towel and dipping it in the solution. He gently wiped at the paint smears on her arm, watching it come off bit by bit, going to the next bit and doing the same.

"Not all of us took AP chemistry," Mackenzie quipped.

"I am glad I showed up," Sam said, still working on one arm. He looked up at her and smiled. "You're painting again."

Mackenzie nodded, biting her lip. He watched as her face turned red.

"That's really amazing."

They sat in silence as Sam continued to rub paint off her skin.

"I can't believe you still remember how to mix this up."

"I had to learn; you were scrubbing your skin raw."

They laughed, giving each other defiant looks.

"I guess you are here because of what day it is, right?" Mackenzie asked.

"To be honest, I didn't remember. My mom said something. As soon as I realized the day, I came down as fast as I could."

Mackenzie nodded again, looking out at the ocean.

"His birthdays are always harder than the anniversary of his death. I guess it is because it was the one day he would allow me to do things for him. I always felt like I was finally giving back. He sacrificed his whole life to raise me," Mac took a deep breath and exhaled.

"How are you holding up?" Sam asked, continuing to clean up her arms. He knew it had to be harder than normal since the passing of Hunter was so recent.

Mackenzie shook her head and then shrugged.

"I am actually allowing whatever I feel today to just happen. There was always a part of me that felt like I needed to be happy to celebrate his life and ignore the sadness. Now I am realizing I just need to feel what I feel. I haven't done that in a long time. I just keep holding things in," Mackenzie explained.

Sam stopped scrubbing and looked at Mackenzie. Something about what she just said triggered him. "Mackenzie, I'm sorry. I was a total asshole that day. You were right to break off the engagement."

Mackenzie smiled, shaking her head. "You didn't drive us to that point all on your own," she said.

"After Uncle Deano died, I was so afraid of anything else changing that I lost myself in everyone else's lives. Sam, you devoted your entire life to taking care of me. A part of me always felt guilty about that. So, I devoted myself to making sure you and our friends were always okay. I allowed myself to get lost in your world. This last year, I was trying to act like we were still from when we were kids. We weren't, I saw it; I knew you didn't or you weren't paying attention."

Sam took both her hands between his.

"Don't try to take blame," Sam said.

"Oh, I'm not. Trust me, you were a total dick that day."

Sam laughed hard, shaking his head. He could always count on Mac to call him out. At least she used to, he was glad she was doing it again.

"I was," Sam agreed. "I guess I got so caught up in climbing to the top of the pyramid that I didn't see you guys were being left behind. Man, looking at myself and having to deal with..."

"Your white privilege?" Mackenzie interrupted.

Sam sighed and nodded.

"It was idiotic of me to think somehow being Jewish made the world around me not see me as white. I am working on it, though. I had to do some brain reprogramming. I started by looking at some of the traits and factors. I realized I was more fixated on the things I wasn't doing or acting like. When I should have been diving into the things I was doing," Sam confessed.

Mackenzie squeezed his hand.

"It's weird. I didn't realize how much of a bubble we grew up in until getting the job downtown," Mackenzie said.

"I didn't notice it at all. I guess I walked right into it," Sam said, lowering his head in shame.

He started cleaning off her arm again. Both sat in silence for a long time.

"Did you get the Mocha Cake?" Sam asked.

Mackenzie playfully slapped him on the arm, "Of course."

Mackenzie gasped, suddenly remembering something.

"Don't you have the charity wine and cheese thing today?" Mac asked. "Bianca drew the short straw and had to go to represent her department. She invited me, but I turned her down for obvious reasons."

Sam nodded, twisting her arms around, finding paint splatters he hadn't seen the first time.

"I don't have to be there. There are other people from my team there," Sam said, shrugging his shoulders.

"But you never miss these things," Mackenzie argued.

Sam looked up at her; he swallowed hard, feeling his stomach turn.

"I probably would have gone today if we hadn't broken up. Completely forgot it was Uncle Deano's birthday. Accepted whatever excuse you would make as to why you couldn't go. Wouldn't I?" Sam said quietly.

He could tell Mackenzie was trying to not make things worse for him.

"Sam, I wouldn't have blamed you. Your trajectory was completely different from mine. All three of you jumped right into your careers. I was just a college dropout who was a grunt worker," She said, being self-deprecating.

"You have no idea how spectacular you are," Sam said. "You never have."

Mackenzie shrugged her shoulders the way she always did anytime she had trouble accepting a compliment.

"I remember we went to lunch one day, and I walked you back to your office," Sam stated, still wiping paint off her skin. "You introduced me to your new co-worker, Kai. They handed you an empty lunch tote, thanking you. You told them it was no problem, that you forgot we were going out for lunch that day, and that you hated wasting food. I thought it was weird since we had been steadily texting since the night before deciding where we were going to eat." Sam looked up, seeing Mac fidget. "I found out later that Kai had come out as non-binary to their very conservative family. They got kicked out of their home and had just started working there. Kai was struggling to even get to work because they were so broke. Other people would ignore them or maybe try to give them money. You knew it would feel too much like charity to them. So, you found ways to help them subtly. Bringing them lunch or making lame excuses about having extra Metro cards until a couple of paydays in. That awareness and caring isn't something a Masters or MBA program can teach."

He watched as Mackenzie turned her head away. Sam gently took her chin to face him. "You are extraordinary. Dropping out of college didn't mean you dropped out of life. If anything, it made you understand it better than the rest of us," Sam said.

Mackenzie bit her lip again.

"Thanks for saying that. I guess when I got the assistant job, I always felt like I suffered by comparison. Sometimes, when I went to your office, I would see you and Clarissa and think you would be the perfect couple if I wasn't around."

He watched as tears welled up in Mackenzie's eyes.

"Mackenzie," he whispered, his voice breaking. Seeing the pain in her eyes, he didn't have to tell her. He knew Mac could see the guilt on his face and sense that after she left town, the thought had crossed his mind a few times.

"It's not like I have room to play the victim. I did take off with a complete stranger for two weeks," Mackenzie said, shrugging her shoulders again.

"Mac, I..." suddenly, Sam's phone dinged. He looked and saw it was a text from Clarissa asking when and what time he was going to get to the Beverly Hotel.

He knew Mackenzie saw her name. She got up, dusting herself off.

"I am going to hop in the shower," she announced. "Just make sure you lock the door on the way out. Thanks for checking on me."

With that, Sam watched her scurry into her bathroom, hearing the shower turn on. He sat there, not getting up; he decided he wasn't going to leave. With that, he looked down at his phone again, shooting off a text.

After about five minutes, Mackenzie reappeared, surprised to see him standing there.

"I ordered spaghetti and fried chicken from that place Uncle Deano loved. It will be here in fifteen minutes." He walked over to the couch and plopped down, turning on the tv and scrolling to Netflix.

"What is the name of your current c-drama? You need to catch me up to speed."

Sam looked up, seeing Mackenzie standing there. Tears coming out of her eyes. He reached out, pulling her onto the couch handing her the remote. Mackenzie wiped away her tears scrolling to the right show.

"I get the frosting flower," Sam declared.

"Seriously?" Mackenzie said, laughing.

"This is the only time I get to eat it," he argued.

"You do realize they make it year-round, right?" she teased.

"They don't sell slices. I would have to figure out what to do with the rest of the cake. Unlike you who will eat it everyday for breakfast," Sam said ducking knowing a pillow was going to fly his way.

Chapter 41

MACKENZIE

"So how does it feel to be a multi-millionaire," Mackenzie asked Ollie.

Ollie groaned, shaking his head as he sat across from her at Beach Beans. She smiled looking over at the table remembering the two of them sitting there. Hunter announcing, they were going to Paris to tick something off her list.

Mackenzie had started working there at the coffee shop part time just to have some extra money. Also to get her out of the house and her painting studio.

She visited Ollie and Parker a few times. They also came down to visit her. They confessed they were on the beach when the fireworks happened and told her they debated calling and asking if she needed company but decided not to so she could be alone and think of Hunter.

"It's still bizarre," Ollie confessed. "My therapist says take it one day at a time."

Ollie had started seeing a therapist at Parker's urging. He was having a rough go at it between losing Hunter and finding out he was the sole beneficiary of his will.

Hunter had left the exact amount he had inherited for his parents and his sister to various childhood leukemia charities and organizations. The rest he had left to Ollie.

After making the adjustment and trying to work through suddenly becoming millionaires, Parker and Ollie decided to start a non-profit to help kids from China with leukemia. It would provide financial support for them and their families to come to the US and get treatment. They also decided to start a scholarship fund for childhood cancer survivors.

Mackenzie knew that Hunter felt Ollie and Parker would do good with his fortune.

"Mac if you need anything please let me know, okay? Hunter would want me to do it," Ollie said.

"I'm fine, I promise," Mac said, holding up her hand like she was being sworn in.

"Right now, I am trying to be the struggling artist I was meant to be," Mackenzie teased.

They sat there for another hour, and when they left Ollie insisted on walking her home. Mackenzie called out to Ollie as he walked passed her block, instead of turning down the corner of Mackenzie's street.

"Ollie, it's my street," she yelled.

"This is where your uncle's shop was right?" Ollie yelled back. Mackenzie jogged over, nodding her head. She always felt a pang of sorrow seeing it empty, knowing what the shop meant to her as well as the community.

She could almost see her uncle sitting on a chair right outside the door reading the Times, waiting for Mackenzie to come walking up after she got off from school.

"Yup, the legend itself," she said.

Ollie stopped in front of the vacant space that was once her uncle's record shop. Looking inside then turning back to Mackenzie.

Mackenzie saw the sold sign across the front.

"It sold," she smiled sadly. "At least I know they are not going to tear it down, it's a grandfathered in building. I wonder what it's going to be."

Ollie looked over at her and smiled.

"It's going to be a record shop."

Mackenzie looked at Ollie, confused, when suddenly it hit her.

"Ollie, no," she cried out, feeling like she was beginning to hyperventilate.

Ollie walked up to her and gave her a hug.

"Hunter couldn't change his will. He knew it would cause trouble if he did. He was sure this was your number eight."

He pointed at the shop, "This is your wildest dream. Don't deny it. You hated closing the shop. You have always wanted to reopen your uncle's record store. He asked me to make it happen."

Mackenzie shook her head, crying.

"I can't accept this, Ollie. Besides, even if I did, who knows if it's going to be successful," Mackenzie argued.

"If it makes you feel better when you are established, you can start making payments," Ollie teased.

Mackenzie shook her head, still trying to refuse.

"Ollie, I can't. I already feel like a complete leech when it comes to the things Hunter did for me. This is too big. I didn't do anything to deserve this."

Ollie leaned against the building, his head down. He sighed, closing his eyes.

"Did you know the night of the bonfire was supposed to be his last?" Ollie whispered.

Mackenzie gasped, her hand covering her mouth.

"Hunter had gotten everything in order. There was nothing left to settle. He was depressed, telling me he didn't want to wait around to die. That he had done everything he could possibly do, so it was time to go," Ollie said, gulping hard.

"He told me he didn't have the energy to go through the EOLA protocol. He could do it himself between his valium and sleeping pills."

Mackenzie walked up to him, her legs nearly giving out. She leaned against the wall, sliding down onto the pavement. Trying to let what Ollie was saying sink in.

Ollie crouched down, taking Mac's hands in his.

"He told us there was no way to finish his list, so he just wanted to let go. That's why we were at the Platform. It was Xiāng's last project before she died. I know you are aware that we heard what happened between you and Sam. Hunter kept looking at you when you walked away. He told me he was going to walk down the Venice boardwalk one more time. Check out of Hotel Erwin, build a bonfire, look at the stars for a while, then go home and end it," Ollie said tears were starting to flow from his eyes.

"You must have thought there was something seriously wrong when I agreed to go with him, " Mackenzie whispered.

Ollie chuckled, turning around to sit next to Mackenzie

"Mac, you have no idea how relieved I was when I saw you walking back to the car with him," Ollie said, his voice breaking.

Mackenzie put her arm around him, hugging him from the side. She closed her eyes, trying her best not to cry.

"That's why you weren't distrusting of me, right?" Mackenzie said.

Ollie shook his head.

"It was because whether or not you knew it, you had stopped him from leaving this world in sadness. When I saw you with him,

I knew he wasn't going to do it. Something told me inviting you made him decide to wait."

Ollie took a huge breath. Furiously wiping his tears.

"There was a part of me that thought he still might do it after we dropped you off. I was so afraid he was going to tell me he was checking out of the hotel. Instead, he told me I should tell Parker to meet me at the hotel to have breakfast the next day. He said he wanted to check out the coffee shop you were raving about."

"The coffee is awesome," Mackenzie said, trying to lighten the mood.

Ollie chuckled and nodded.

"It really is. I nearly fainted when I got the text from him saying that he had booked the three of us tickets to Paris. Parker cried. It wasn't because we didn't want him to have the right to choose. It was because so much of Hunter's life had been dealing with death. The only time I saw him somewhat happy was when he was working through his list."

"Really?" Mackenzie said in complete disbelief. "He always seemed to be happy. Was he faking it for my benefit?" Mackenzie asked.

Ollie looked at her and shook his head.

"Meeting you was like a light switch turning on. He was happy. He wasn't thinking about why he was still hanging around," Ollie explained.

"Mac, he never laughed, not really. Maybe a chuckle here and there. But the entire time I knew him, he never laughed. He was always so serious. You would make him laugh so hard his sides would hurt," Ollie said.

"He made me laugh that hard, too," Mackenzie said.

"That's what I am trying to explain. He never really joked around. He always had this dark cloud over his head."

Mackenzie leaned her head on Ollie's shoulder.

"You made him come alive. Made him feel like there was more to life than death. He's never cared about anything or anybody the way he cared about you," Ollie said, resting his head against hers too.

"At the end, I know he felt all he had to give us was his wealth. He didn't see his worth until he met you. So, Mackenzie, you must do this. If nothing else, do it for him. Finishing your list was the last thing he wanted to do," Ollie said.

"That's low, Ollie," she joked.

Ollie laughed.

"I learned how to gently strong-arm you from the best."

They sat there for a little while longer looking up at the stars thinking about the man that changed their lives.

Chapter 42

He wished he felt better than he did. The firm was throwing a party for him. Celebrating his new title and the closing of his biggest deal to date. The project had been the most lucrative deal for the company in a few years. So, they dished out a good amount of money for a space at Osteria on Melrose. When they asked him where he wanted the celebration to be he quickly said West Hollywood mostly so afterwards he could drive to Mac's with relative ease.

It was the biggest night of his career, and it would not have felt right if he hadn't seen her. He thought about inviting her. She had moved on from downtown LA and her old job. Unlike the way he acted before, he knew asking her to come would make her feel awkward. He didn't want her to feel obligated. He did invite Ezra. Bianca was coming as well. She was slowly forgiving him.

Besides all of that, he knew Mackenzie was in the middle of revamping the interior of the record shop. He couldn't help but feel a pang of jealousy when it came to Ollie buying the building for her. On top of that, he was funding the entire business until

Mackenzie could turn a profit. Sam knew what Hunter's net worth was. He could have opened up five or six more businesses and not made a dent in his fortune. Sam had to put Mackenzie before his own petty feelings. So, he encouraged her every time she would start to feel guilty.

He stood at the bar nursing his bourbon as people came up to him chatting, congratulating him. He was aware Clarissa was hovering, almost acting like she was his date for the evening. He had to set her straight. It had to stop. He knew Clarissa was not his future. He still wasn't sure what it was, but he was sure she wasn't it.

Just then, he heard Bianca's squeal as she ran up to Ezra, who had just arrived, giving him a hug. He could see Ezra's arm extended behind him, holding someone's hand. Ezra had asked if he could bring his new girlfriend, Miriam, with him. Sam told him it was no problem. His mother declined for reasons she did not have to explain. He knew she might mutter "Capitalist Pig" if someone said the wrong thing.

Ezra waved at him. Sam raised his glass to him, waving him over. Ezra stood there, not moving, with a smug expression on his face. Sam tilted his head in confusion.

His eyes widened in surprise as Ezra pulled his plus-one forward into Sam's view. It was Mackenzie.

"She's Got A Way" by Billy Joel, Uncle Deano said he would know he was in love if he heard a song and thought about that person every time. For him, it was "She's Got A Way," but Mackenzie didn't know that. He was planning on surprising her on their wedding day and switching out the song they agreed to do their first dance to. It was always his plan before he started to change.

As corny as it sounded in his head, the sight of Mackenzie took his breath away. Everyone had dressed up for the occasion. But as always, Mackenzie stood out. She was wearing a strapless satin handkerchief dress with a print that you would find on an Indian Lehenga. Her hair was down and untamed, and she had no jewelry except for the one silver chain that held her uncle's medallion and the silver ring she had been wearing constantly these days, which Hunter had given to her. He had gotten over the initial jealousy when it came to that as well. Sam straightened up as if he was going to make his way over to them. However, Ezra began to walk over to him with Bianca and Mackenzie in tow.

Ezra stood in front of him, giving him a huge hug. Sam looked over his shoulder at Mackenzie, who was doing her best not to fidget.

The four friends stood there, trying to act as normal as possible. Sam was pretty sure he was the cause of the tension. He kept looking at Mackenzie. Maybe he was gawking like some lovelorn idiot.

"Where's the booze, B?" Ezra asked, taking Bianca's hand and dragging her away. Mackenzie laughed.

"He's so subtle, right?" she said. He watched as she bit her lip. He knew between the lip bite and fidgeting that Mackenzie was debating something internally. He watched as she tried to hide the huge breath she took before she stepped forward, giving him a hug, pressing her cheek into his, and giving him an air kiss. He inhaled, closing his eyes, expecting to smell peaches; since they were kids, she always smelled like peaches. Instead, the fragrance surrounding her was perfume. The Tiffany's perfume he had gifted her. Sam opened his eyes, trying not to get visibly choked up by Mackenzie's subtle gesture.

Pulling back and looking at her, he watched as she looked up at him, eyes wide. Sam belatedly realized his hands were still gripping Mackenzie's waist lightly.

Sam let her go, not really wanting to remind himself this wasn't the past.

He could tell Mackenzie had a moment of struggle as well. He watched as her hand went up as if she was going to gently yank at his tie. It was how she used to flirt with him. She lowered her hands, placing them behind her back.

"You know I have always loved that tie," Mackenzie smiled.

He had purposely worn it intending to see her later. Sam smiled looking down at her then over at Ezra.

"I take it Ezra's got purse duty tonight?" he teased.

Mackenzie hated carrying a purse. Sam would always joke he was her purse because she would always hand him her phone and keys to put in his pocket. She never freshened up her make up or primped in any way when they were out. One of the many things he always loved about her.

Sam impulsively took her hand holding it. Not caring who was looking, wanting Mackenzie to feel his sincerity.

"I'm really glad you're here," he said, his voice breaking a little. "This didn't feel right without you."

Mac tilted her head, giving him a small smile. "Ezra said you wanted to invite me but didn't want to make me feel obligated to come so he made me his plus one," she explained.

"You should be really proud Sam. Congratulations," she added.

"Thank you," he responded, his eyes never leaving hers. "Seriously you don't know how much this means to me."

"Samson," he heard behind him. He turned to see Clarissa standing there next to Evelyn, a coworker of theirs. Bianca often called her one of Clarissa's minions. He could barely hide his irritation when Clarissa's eyes lowered, seeing Sam holding Mac's hand, feeling her pulling it away as if she was doing something she should feel guilty about.

"You wanted to know when Mr. Alexander arrived? He brought my father. They both just walked in. Dad has wanted to see you for a while now. He really enjoyed your conversation at our family dinner that night. Oh, hello, Mackenzie," she said a bit too sweetly, placing her hand on Sam's shoulder. He wanted to shake it off as soon as he saw the look on Mac's face but knew it would just cause a scene. Clarissa had fired off shots; Mackenzie knew it.

Sam looked over and saw his new boss and Clarissa's father standing together, shaking hands with a few people. He wanted to stay and talk to Mackenzie more. If he was honest, he wanted to spend the rest of the night with her tethered to his side. The debate ended as soon as Hayes looked his way and waved. He felt Clarissa gently nudge him. He resisted opening his mouth to say something to Mackenzie.

"Go, soak it all in," Mackenzie said, giving him a reassuring smile. He knew she was thinking it would be rude of him to not be available to everyone tonight. He opened his mouth trying again to invite her to come with him just as Bianca came up behind Mackenzie.

"Ezra's wondering where his plus one went," Bianca said, smiling a little too brightly.

He watched helplessly as Bianca pulled her towards Ezra and Clarissa pulled him toward Hayes. As if reminding him Mackenzie and him moved in two different worlds.

As the night progressed, he tried his best to keep himself in the moment and be present to anyone who came up to him. He knew he was failing miserably; his eyes kept drifting to wherever Mac was, watching her smile and chatting with people. He saw a group of guys standing at the bar and a few girls from work glancing over at Mackenzie from time to time. She never realized how much she drew other people's gaze. Part of her beauty was that she was so unassuming. Hunter falling in love with her was no shock to him.

Occasionally their eyes would meet then focus somewhere else. He would go over anytime she was talking to someone he hadn't greeted or thanked. Just to maybe say a few words to her.

Sam felt a hand brush against his bicep, looking down and seeing Clarissa.

"It's great that she was able to put things aside and be here for you," she said, her voice lacking any real sincerity. "That dress is very eclectic. Not everyone could pull off that look," she added. Sam looked down at Clarissa as she eyed Mackenzie. Clarissa was doing nothing to hide the air of judgment around her.

Sam turned toward Clarissa, his eyes boring into hers. "Yes, you're right, not everyone could. But that's what makes Mac extraordinary. Her ability to be herself in any situation no matter what or how other people may view her."

Sam took the last sip of his drink and then looked over at Mac. She was staring at him and Clarissa. The look on Mac's face let him know that she was misreading the intense look he was giving Clarissa. He watched as she turned away, giving Bianca and Ezra a hug before going toward the door. Sam saw her keys and phone in one hand, realizing she was leaving.

Sam let his feet carry him toward her. Feeling Clarissa momentarily grip his forearm before letting it go. One or two people tried to stop him, but Sam held a finger up, letting them know he would be right back.

"Mac!" he yelled, seeing her walk down the street slowly, looking at her phone.

Mac turned around.

"Hey there," she said, "I didn't want to distract you. You seemed busy. I was going to text you when I left."

"You're leaving?" he asked, trying not to sound pitiful. "Did you need me to call you an Uber or a Lyft?"

Mackenzie held up her phone, "Already handled. You should really get back to your party."

"Are you sure you can't stay longer? It's winding down. Maybe we could hang out for a bit?"

He saw Mackenzie look over his shoulder. Clarissa and Evelyn were standing outside talking pretending to fan themselves as if to imply they were getting a breath of fresh air.

"No, the first shipment of records arrives tomorrow. We open a week from next Friday so it is going to be insane until then. I just wanted to come and congratulate you," she explained.

He saw Mac's eyes drift toward Clarissa again. His heart dropped into his chest realizing Mac must have been replaying the scene at the Platform, that she was afraid he would give her the same horrible look of embarrassment and denial he'd given her that day.

"Thank you," he said softly. The irony was not lost on him. Unlike that day at the Platform when he was trying to get away, he would do anything to keep her there. He watched a car pull up and slow to a stop in front of her.

"Mac!" he yelled as she started to bend down to get in the car.

"I love you," Sam said, looking over at her. It was the first time he had said it since they broke up. "I just needed to say it. Let you know. You sacrificed a lot to help me get to this point. I just needed to tell you. I love you." He gulped hard, praying he didn't offend her or make her feel awkward.

He watched as Mac pulled her lips in and then gulped. He saw her eyes water as she looked at him.

"I love you too, Sam," she replied, ducking down and sliding into the car.

Chapter 43

MACKENZIE

Mackenzie got up the next day at dawn. The delivery trucks were due to arrive before eight to avoid traffic. The first batch of records arrived at around seven o'clock. She had been there since five-thirty, hardly slept the night before. She wasn't sure if it was because of the shipments or because of Sam's party.

She wasn't going to lie to herself. Seeing Clarissa act like she was Sam's partner and Clarissa letting her know they had spent time with her family stung hard. She kept telling herself she had no room to talk. She did take off with Hunter for two weeks. They formed a bond in that short time. She had loved him. So, Sam had every right to strengthen a bond with someone he was spending a lot of time with.

She knew without a doubt that Sam Madden would be a fixture in her life no matter what. She just wasn't sure in what way. She tried not to overthink it and concentrate on getting the shop together. Being there in the space she had grown up in grounded her. The more time she spent there, the more she was sure this was what she was supposed to be doing.

Bianca, Ollie, and Parker got there around 8:30. Ezra showed up an hour later.

Bianca had met Ollie and Parker a few weeks ago. As she predicted they clicked with each other instantly. So much so that they now had a group text where the four of them shared funny clips or memes.

Mackenzie had her laptop on the counter, trying to catalog everything that came in. Ezra was making the decision on where everything should go and in what order. Ezra worked in PR and brand marketing; far be it for her to tell him what would work the best.

"Punk needs to be on the corner to the left," Mackenzie said. It's the one thing she would not compromise on. She had spent most of her childhood in that corner listening to punk rock with Sam. She had intended to ask him if he wanted to pitch in today, but after seeing him with Clarissa, she decided against it.

Mackenzie looked at the time realizing it was 12:30. She pulled out her phone scrolling through a takeout app.

"I owe you guys something to eat. What does everyone want?" she asked.

"Actually, it's been taken care of," she heard, looking up and seeing Sam standing there with one of those huge grocery store insulated bags and a cooler in the other.

"Hey," she said, still in shock that Sam was there.

"Hey, I figured you guys might be hungry," Sam announced as he looked over at Ezra. Obviously, he'd known what Sam was up to, but surprisingly, the man had been able to keep his mouth shut. Sam walked over to the long counter, pulling out utensils and paper bowls. He looked over at Mackenzie and smirked. As he placed a huge Tupperware of white rice and another one filled with adobo. Mackenzie gasped, putting her hand over her mouth.

He opened the cooler and pulled a small mocha cake from the top of it, handing Mackenzie a ginger-ale. Sam knew Mackenzie carried stress in her stomach. Ginger ale was the one thing that always calmed it down.

Bianca and Ezra walked up first, fixing their plates. Mackenzie waved Ollie and Parker over.

"Ollie, Parker, this is Sam," Mackenzie said, smiling at them. Sam held out his hand as the boys shook it.

"Nice to meet you. I have heard a lot about the two of you," Sam said.

"Likewise," Parker said.

Mackenzie could not help but notice the slightly off looks they were giving each other. She wondered if there was going to be tension between the three of them. Maybe Sam felt threatened by their presence? Or did Ollie and Parker feel as if Sam was the love rival of their brother?

Sam scooped out some rice then poured adobo over it, handing a bowl to Ollie, then Parker. The strange moment drifting away.

Parker took a bite and moaned.

"This is so fucking good!" he said with his mouth partially full.

"Thanks," Sam said, handing Mackenzie a bowl with a smaller portion. Again, he had deduced correctly that Mackenzie's stomach was in knots.

"Mackenzie's Uncle Deano taught me how to make it," Sam said side eying Mackenzie. Mackenzie blinked a few times wondering if she had heard him correctly. So that explained how Sam made adobo better than her. Sam smiled over at her. She looked down for a moment in shock.

Overwhelmed by Sam's revelation and the fact that he made it a point to make it for her today, knowing how much it would mean to her. Mackenzie gulped hard, choking back her tears as she stared down at her plate.

"Eat up," she heard Sam say, his eyes never leaving hers as he handed her a plastic fork.

All six of them sat on the floor eating lunch, filling the air with small talk. Sam pulled out a trash bag for all their used dishware. Mackenzie laughed, shaking her head.

"The years of growing up with Uncle Deano are showing," Mackenzie said, giving Sam a wink. Sam laughed, nodding his head.

Uncle Deano always had a trash bag ready. It was his thing.

After they cleaned up, they got back to work as another delivery truck arrived. She watched Sam look around, putting his hands in his pockets.

"Do you need another set of hands?" Sam asked.

"You think I would ever turn down free labor?" Mackenzie teased.

Bianca was handling counting the boxes and checking the invoice, and then Ollie, Ezra, and Parker would take the audited boxes and start to unpack them.

Just as that truck unloaded, another one arrived.

"Mac, this is the studio stuff," Bianca called out.

"Oh awesome, you can put the boxes in the next room," Mackenzie instructed.

"Studio?" Sam asked.

Mackenzie nodded, cocking her head to the side, leading Sam down a small step and into the next room. Sam had noticed they had broken through the wall of the building. Because Ollie owned the entire building, they were able to expand into the extra space that once was a separate shop. The record shop was bigger than before, plus there was this side space they were now standing in.

She looked at Sam who was staring at the space in awe. There was a small kitchenette in the corner. With two rows of six easels side by side.

"When we started talking about breaking through the wall and expanding, I felt like the space would be way too big for just a record store. So, I brainstormed with Ollie and Parker. We came up with this.

She pointed toward the record shop. "Vinyl's In Venice naturally," she said. Then, she waved her hand in front of her. "And this is 'Brushstrokes By the Boardwalk'," Mackenzie said, smiling. "I am going to offer painting classes, rent it out for those paint parties businesses do for team building or just private paint parties. Also, I am going to try to start an afterschool program for kids who want to learn how to paint."

Mackenzie looked up, seeing Sam just staring at her.

"I was assured it was a good use of the space and a nice way to bring in more revenue," Mackenzie explained.

Sam shook his head, turning all the way around and doing a 360.

"Mackenzie, this couldn't be any more perfect. It's like you revived Uncle Deano's dream and then added on your own."

Mackenzie felt her face warm.

"Thanks, I feel really good about it. I just hope it isn't a money pit," Mackenzie said.

She heard Sam's phone ding then watched as he pulled out his phone reading the text. He shot off a reply, looking at his watch.

"If you need to take off, it's totally cool. I didn't ask you if you wanted to come and help today because I thought after the party, you might be too tired or have plans for the weekend," Mac said, looking down.

"Plans?" Sam asked.

Mackenzie shrugged her shoulders and swung one leg back and forth in front of her.

"Yeah, I wasn't sure," Mackenzie said.

"Sam, was the reason why you didn't invite me to your party because you were afraid I would feel awkward or hurt because of you and Clarissa?" she asked.

Sam walked up to her, quickly wrapping her in his arms. She felt his heart pounding hard.

"Jesus Christ Mac. No, not at all. I know that's how it looked, but honestly, it was because I didn't think you would want to be around people that made you unhappy. I had already planned to swing by your place when the party was done. I wasn't going to end the night without seeing you," Sam swore.

Mackenzie was stunned by his confession. Her arms hung to her sides as he held her, not because she did not want to hug him back but because Sam hugged her so tightly that she couldn't move. All she could do was lay her head on his chest, and he kept her wrapped in his arms. They heard someone clear their throats, immediately stepping away from each other.

"Everyone wants to eat cake," Ezra said, smiling at the two of them.

Sam cleared his throat and hopped up the step back into the record store space. Mackenzie told the others to go ahead and stayed behind counting the boxes as they came in.

A little while later Bianca came down the few steps, a plate of cake in each of her hands. Giving one to Mackenzie. Mackenzie thanked her best friend then looked over seeing Sam and Ezra joking around with Ollie and Parker. Whatever perceived tension was completely gone.

"You know I am Team Mac all the way, right?" Bianca said, taking a bite of her cake.

Mac nudged her, taking a bite as well, "Of course."

"Just wanted to tell you. Last night was all Clarissa. Things aren't how she made it seem. Not to say there wasn't a time when it looked like Sam might be heading that way, but not anymore. Not since they came back from Japan. Actually, not since you got back from Paris."

Mackenzie shrugged her shoulders, "I gave up my right to have an opinion. Besides, I can't fault him. There was Hunter."

Bianca looked at her, "No, that was completely different. Hunter was helping you heal and deal with shit. 'Thirsty Becky with the good hair' was out to conquer him."

Mackenzie laughed every time Bianca refused to call Clarissa by her name.

They walked up to the record shop part of the building just as Sam had finished wiring the sound for the record player.

"Okay, the first song played," Ezra said, "We should brainstorm this. It is completely significant."

Sam held up his hand.

"Actually, I have the perfect song."

Everyone watched as Sam rifled through a bit of Hunter's collection, pulling out an album and gently placed it on the record player.

Everyone cheered as Mackenzie hugged herself tightly, closing her eyes. The first chords of "Tiny Dancer" by Elton John filled the air.

Ezra walked up to Bianca, belting out the first lyrics, twirling her once, and dipping Bianca low. Mackenzie hopped up to sit on the counter, watching Ollie and Parker join Bianca and Ezra's antics.

Sam perched next to Mackenzie, watching everyone dance.

She could feel Uncle Deano singing to her.

Mac rested her head on Sam's shoulder, and Sam bent his head to rest against hers.

"You're right. This was the perfect song."

Chapter 44

SAM

Sam looked at the clock again. He needed to get out of work by four if he was going to make it on time. He had wanted to take the whole day off, but he had three meetings that could not be rescheduled. Also, as Mackenzie pointed out, it would look horrible if he took a day off right as he was starting his new position.

Sam started to gather up all his things and put his laptop in his messenger bag. He heard a knock on the door. He cringed knowing it wasn't Bianca, unlike him she managed to get the day off.

"Hey Sam, my family wanted to invite you to dinner," he heard Clarissa say.

Sam looked up and exhaled slowly.

"Sorry, Clarissa, I have plans tonight," Sam said.

"Well, that was my final attempt," Clarissa said, smiling.

Sam tried not to look relieved. He had been giving her hints for the last few weeks, trying to get her to stop.

"I know when to bow out of an investment," Clarissa laughed, leaning against his door frame.

Sam smiled, not able to muster a chuckle. The way she described it made him astonished that he had nearly gotten himself into something so shallow.

"To be honest, part of it was the challenge," Clarissa said.

"Challenge?" Sam asked.

"Oh, you know, you two were the golden couple. Childhood sweethearts destined for life. When you guys broke up, it looked like you might be interested. It was an ego boost to think I might have been able to change that," Clarissa's tone was catty enough to make Sam feel nauseous.

"I need to go," Sam said, putting his messenger bag on his shoulder. "See you Monday."

Sam began to walk past her. Clarissa held her hand out to his chest, stopping him.

"You do know she'll never be comfortable in your world, right?" Clarissa said.

Sam gently took Clarissa's hand off of him.

"That's where you are wrong," Sam said, looking Clarissa straight in the face. "Mackenzie is the most important part of my world. I stupidly forgot that. I won't do it again."

When Sam arrived at Vinyl's In Venice the place was already packed. There was a small area for dancing, food tables all around, and the side garage door was opened, allowing people to walk into Brushes By The Boardwalk. The doors to Vinyls In Venice were opened as well.

Sam laughed at seeing Ms. Eddy and Ms. Stella sitting at the check-in table, waiting for people to sign the guest book or leave their purchases to pick up after the party. Mackenzie had told them she just wanted them to come and enjoy themselves, obviously, to no avail. He waved over at Mr. Noah, who was on the other side of the door, greeting people as they walked in, letting them know they were going to leave their bags at the table.

He felt someone push him from behind, knowing it was Ezra.

"You made it on time," Ezra said.

"Don't remind me. I hate that I wasn't here until now," Sam said bitterly.

Ezra hugged Miriam close to him.

"Take it this way. You were the only one to actually listen to Mackenzie," Bianca said, walking up to them.

Sam chuckled, looking around.

"She's inside with Ollie and Parker being interviewed," Bianca said. "This is the hottest ticket in Venice right now."

Ezra fanned himself and sighed, "That's what happens when you hire the right PR person."

Sam and Bianca rolled their eyes. He kept looking inside, trying to find Mackenzie.

Suddenly a crowd dispersed. He could see her standing there. Next to Ollie and Parker. She looked nervous. Mackenzie hated being the center of attention. He stood there watching her. She was in a long flowy white dress with a pair of jeans and heels he knew she would regret wearing before the end of the night. She had a black headband with white beads across her forehead adding to her ethereal vibe. Sam couldn't help but smile.

"Need a napkin?" Ezra asked.

Sam glared at him and then made his way inside. He watched as Ollie, Parker, and Mac stepped away from the person interviewing them and made their way towards the back of the shop. They were whispering to each other, looking at something on the opposite wall from their corner. He watched as Ollie lowered his head, and Parker hugged him from behind. They were all looking at what seemed to be a painting. Someone called Ollie and Parker, wanting them to come over. They both gave Mackenzie a hug before they were dragged away, leaving her standing there by herself.

Mackenzie turned and gasped.

"Sam, you made it!" she said hugging him tight then letting go as if she did something wrong.

Sam chuckled. "As if I would have missed the grand reopening," he said.

"How long have you been here?"

Sam took a step to her, putting his hands behind his back. He bent down and whispered as best as he could over all the noise, "Since I was ten."

Mackenzie laughed playfully, nudging him. Sam looked at the painting, and they all admired it.

It was done in black ink. It was a side profile of who he knew had to be Hunter, his hand and forehead pressed against a mountain. In the background there was another mountain in the distance with one silhouette standing on the top of it with their arms up in the air while three other silhouettes stood behind him. Sam just kept looking at it stunned.

"Mackenzie, this is amazing," Sam said, still in awe of it. He knew it had been years since Mackenzie had painted, yet her work did not reflect it. He could see all the thought and detail she had put into it.

"I think this is your best work," Sam said, turning to her and smiling.

Mackenzie looked up at him, then back at the painting. "You think so?" she asked.

"You don't?" Sam argued.

Mackenzie shook her head. He felt Mac grab him by the wrist, pulling him behind her. He veered through the crowd of people, trying not to lose Mac's grip. She stopped in front of the counter and directed his gaze up to the painting that hung behind it.

"I feel like this is my best work," she said, looking at him.

Sam felt a lump in his throat. The canvas was large, taking up the entire back wall, and the painting on it was abstract and painterly with a touch of surrealism. Patting himself on the back for being able to describe the style. It was an image of Mackenzie's front room. The sofa and the open door to her balcony, the curtain blowing out, revealing a bit of the ocean. Her record player with a record on it lines around it to indicate it was playing as musical notes floating through the air. The bulk of the painting was of Mackenzie's light blue kitchen. There were two silhouettes in the center of it. Sam found himself chuckling at the image. It was of a green silhouette holding a mug, hunched over as an orange silhouette clung on behind it, riding piggyback. It was a scene he was familiar with. One that he had lived throughout his life. Sam found himself tearing up, taking a deep breath as he cleared his throat.

"I know I haven't been acting like it, Sam," Mackenzie said softly, looking up at him. "But you still sit in the center of who I am. I don't think that will ever change."

Sam looked at her speechless, wanting to say something, but all his words were stuck in his throat.

Ezra walked up to them, pulling at Mackenzie.

"Sorry, it's almost speech time," Ezra said.

Mackenzie let out an eep, letting him drag her off.

He watched as Mackenzie did her best to hold it together. She thanked everyone for supporting the reopening of her uncle's shop. He made sure he was standing somewhere that she had a clear view of him. Mackenzie often looked his way when she had to do any sort of public speaking. He heard everyone clap.

"I would like to open the dancing portion of the evening by dedicating this first song to my Uncle Deano," she looked up and smiled.

"Mahal Kita Taytay," she said into the mic as everyone clapped. Sam heard the first few strings of the song being played; it was Uncle Deano's favorite Filipino song "Silayan" , the Florante Aguilar and Lori Abucayan version. It had a ballroom feel to it. Mackenzie handed the microphone to the dj.

She walked halfway across the dance floor, stopping and looking over at Sam. Sam chuckled softly making his way to her. He reached out taking her into his arms as they started to dance a tango.

He cleared his throat again, losing count of how many times he nearly lost his cool tonight. He led her as they danced. Thinking about all the nights he spent at their house as Uncle Deano taught them all the ballroom dances, he knew. Sam had been reluctant at first. Then Uncle Deano said he could just ask one of the kids, his Filipino friends, to help teach Mackenzie.

Sam spun Mackenzie as everyone clapped. Mac buried her head in Sam's chest in embarrassment. Other people started dancing, taking focus away from the two of them.

Sam heard a jingle and looked down and saw the silver charm bracelet he had given her for her fourteenth birthday. He gave her a charm every birthday and holiday until there was no more room left. It was always the little things Mackenzie did that made his heart soar. Like her wearing the bracelet tonight. Despite everything he knew he was still important to her. Sam lowered his head and whispered in her ear.

"Congratulations Zie-Zie. Uncle Deano would be so proud. So would Hunter."

Mackenzie looked up at him, tears falling from her eyes, "I didn't know how much I needed to hear that. Thank you."

A little while later, Sam sat in one of the white plastic chairs, watching Mackenzie dance with Bianca's cousin Marlon. Laughing at the way Marlon was trying to teach Mac a dance move while she purposely and comically messed up.

Parker took a seat next to him, with Ollie at the other side.

"You know I am not going to lie if she ever asks," Ollie said.

"I know, but you also said you wouldn't say anything unless she asked," Sam said, watching Mackenzie.

"I don't understand why you just don't just tell her. You did so much, from getting the deal closed to getting the building sold to standing in front of the city council. Without that, we wouldn't be here," Parker said.

He looked at the two men, shaking his head. He knew hiding the fact that he had met Ollie and Parker way before the day they were setting up the shop might backfire on him but he was willing to take that risk. Ollie had come to Sam to try to figure out the best way to get approval from the Venice Beach City Council and close the sale of the building. Sam had spoken at the city council meeting. He persuaded them to approve the sale of the building. He brought old photos of the shop and talked about the history of the neighborhood and the Almazan presence felt throughout the community. Sam had stayed at the office late at night working on the deal after hours, closing the deal faster than anyone would have thought possible.

Sam shook his head, his eyes never leaving Mackenzie's dancing form.

"I want her to come back to me because I earned her trust again. Not because she's grateful," Sam said. "I screwed up so bad. I don't want any favors or gimmes. I need to work for it..."

Ollie looked over at Mackenzie.

"Would you hate me if I told you I am grateful for your fuck up?" Ollie asked. "We wouldn't have known her if you didn't. Hunter would have left this world, never experiencing how it felt to truly laugh."

Sam shook his head, "I hate that I understand that."

The three men held out their water bottles, tapping them together.

Mackenzie waved at them. Sam waved back. He had finally figured out who he was. Where he wanted to go. He vowed he would do everything in his power to make sure Mackenzie Almazan was standing right there with him.

Sam heard a rustling behind him. He turned to see Bianca standing there, looking down at him in shock.

"Bianca. I..." Sam said, clearing his throat, the look she was giving him conveyed she heard their entire conversation.

Bianca took a step forward so she was standing next to Sam. She looked out at Mackenzie who was playfully dancing with her father, Mr. Noah. Sam watched as a small smile spread across Bianca's face as she continued to look at the scene in front of her.

"It's B. You can call me B."

Chapter 45

MACKENZIE

Later that evening, Mackenzie sat at her vanity, staring at her reflection in the mirror. She hadn't done it in a very long time. Most of the time, she avoided mirrors. Maybe it was because she was afraid of what she might see. She would see the person hiding in everyone else's world with no desire to make one of her own. Just grateful to not be alone. Now she realized that wasn't the way to live.

Her feet were still killing her even with Sam showing up in front of her with a pair of vans he bought from the skate store next door.

"Watching you try to walk on those things is making my feet hurt," Sam muttered as he helped her put the pair of vans on. Later, Sam and Clover, who had shown up after the crowd dispersed, insisted on walking her back to her house. Sam took it one step further, forcing her to take a piggyback from him after he saw her struggling to walk because her feet were so sore.

Mackenzie smiled, still looking at her reflection. So many things were different now, but some things would never change. Like the love she and Sam shared for each other. Some things needed to change. Like the way she saw herself and how she wanted to live her life.

Mackenzie unclipped her charm bracelet putting it in the ballerina jewelry box that Sam gifted her when they were kids. She looked down at Hunter's ring, slipping it off and placing it in the box. She took a deep breath as she took off her uncle's necklace. Putting it in the box as well. She knew she would wear all of the items again but she did not have to wear Hunter's ring or Uncle Deano's necklace all the time.

She felt vulnerable, naked as she looked in the mirror again. She knew Uncle Deano and Hunter wouldn't want her to always be reminded they were not there anymore; she didn't have to wear their pieces of jewelry constantly as if she had to be a walking memorial to them. She was slowly accepting just living was the best way to remember them.

"Look out, not down," she said to herself in the mirror.

Mackenzie got up walking onto her balcony watching the waves crash against the shore. She heard a car door open below. Looking to see a person get out of the car. She didn't need to see the face of the person with their hands in their pockets to know who it was.

It was the person that spent most of her life standing there. It was something Sam did when they were growing up. He would stand there sometimes on the nights when Uncle Deano worked or went out to play mahjong. They used to yell out to each other while having whole conversations. Sometimes, she would just watch him do tricks on his skateboard. Every once in a while, he would yell for her to lock the sliding glass door if she didn't appear on the balcony.

It was later when they were older and dating that Sam confessed, he did that because he didn't want to say goodbye. He just wanted to spend as much time as he could with her. He ducked into his car turning the music up a bit louder. Mackenzie could make out it was a song by Benson Boone, "Beautiful Things."

She watched as Sam emerged holding a skateboard. Mackenzie felt her heart pound against her chest as Sam skated on it, getting the feel for it. She gasped as he nearly hit the pavement attempting to do a hospital flip. Failing miserably, much like she had the day they met. Finally, she watched the skateboard flip and Sam accomplished the trick that guided them into each other's lives.

She laughed, shaking her head as he waved, putting the skateboard back in his car. Laughing even harder when he pretended to slide into his car in pain.

She watched him leave, thinking that it's been a long time since she had seen him. Really seen him. She wondered if he felt the same way when he looked at her.

Chapter 46

Sam

S am saw Ezra's name appear across the screen.

"Dude, if you are wasted call an Uber I am on my way somewhere," Sam said driving his car down the 10 freeway.

"What? It's 10 p.m. on a work night. How are you anywhere but your bed or at your desk?" Ezra asked.

"Okay, dad, what did you need," Sam said.

"I was just calling to ask you how things were going with Mac. Have you asked her how she feels now? Have you told her how you feel?" Ezra asked.

Sam sighed, shaking his head even though he knew Ezra could not see him.

"No, not yet. I think we are both taking our time. Getting to know each other again," Sam explained.

"You spend every weekend at the shop with her. How much more time do you need," he heard Bianca yell in the background, knowing now he was on speakerphone.

It was true, Sam did spend most of his time at the shop with Mackenzie. He worked long hours because of his new position so he couldn't get down there during the week. He would always call her at 9:50 p.m. and stay on the phone talking to her as she shut things down for the night before walking home.

Clarissa found a new victim who was all too willing for the position. He could tell it irritated Clarissa to no end that he didn't care or pay attention to them. Sam had lobbied hard for Bianca to take over his old position. Ready to spit nails when they promoted someone else instead. Bianca did not seem bothered. She had her plan and was sticking to it. Sam didn't work with the same passion he had in the past. Everyone assumed it was because he and Mac had worked things out. In reality, there was another reason.

"Why are you asking?" Sam questioned.

Ezra cleared his throat.

"Well, so it's like this. We are in Santa Monica. We texted asking if we could come over and say hi," Ezra explained.

"Okay?" Sam asked.

"She told us she wouldn't be home and that she had plans," Bianca said. "We know it's not with you. She would have said something."

"What? B is actually asking me how to hunt someone down? You have her location," Sam pointed out.

"I know she's at the Loft. What the fuck is she doing at the Loft?!" Bianca screamed.

Sam sighed, shaking his head.

"Would it help mom and dad to know I am actually on the way there now?" Sam laughed trying to concentrate on driving which was difficult because his friends were bickering back and forth.

"Wait, are you guys going out on a date?" Ezra asked.

"It can't be a date Mac would have told me!" he heard Bianca say.

He could almost see the two of them fighting for the phone. Sam loved his friends, but sometimes they were entirely too nosy.

"Something like that," Sam responded, dropping the call. Chuckling, thinking about how much Bianca and Ezra not knowing would drive them crazy.

Sam stood on the elevator of the Loft Hotel, watching the numbers of each floor light up until it stopped on the rooftop. He stepped off the elevator and then looked around. There were beach recliners set up in rows in front of a large screen. Sam scanned the area and found Mackenzie in the second row, sitting there looking at her phone. He moved quietly, trying not to be seen. He sat down in the recliner right next to hers. He sat sideways, facing her, waiting for her to take notice.

Mackenzie looked up and literally screamed. Sam laughed, holding his hands up. Then looking at the people around them.

"It's okay, I just spooked her," Sam yelled.

Mackenzie waved her hand up, holding a thumb in the air, laughing. She tilted her head in confusion.

"What are you doing here? More importantly, how did you know I was here?" she asked.

Sam smirked, taking the blanket off his recliner and laying it over the one that was already covering her legs. Mackenzie started freezing anytime the temperature fell below 75 degrees.

Mackenzie stared at him as he cocked his brow up.

Mackenzie laughed, shaking her head.

"Of course," she said quietly.

Sam thought back to the last part of Hunter's letter.

Finally, "Rebecca" will be playing on the rooftop of the Loft Hotel seven months from now. I don't have to tell you it's her favorite movie, but I am anyway just because I want to say it. If I could, I would take her and see her face as the movie played with the view of the stars above. If you are the guy I think you are, you'll use the ticket inside and start making things up to her. If you're not, well, then don't go. Leave that seat open. Who knows, maybe the guy who is supposed to be next to her for the rest of her life will show up and take the open seat. Remember, Sam, there are all kinds of ways to make money and be rich, but there's only one Mackenzie Almazan in this world. And you're the lucky bastard that she loves. Take care of her, Sam. I understand if you do not believe me, but I truly wish you the best of luck.

Hunter.

"It's a work night, and you are going to be exhausted tomorrow," Mackenzie commented.

"I'll just go in late," Sam said, shrugging. Sam took her hand in between rubbing it knowing it was ice cold before touching it. Mackenzie gave him an incredulous look and held her other hand to his forehead.

"You all right? Are you sure you are Sam?" Mackenzie teased.

Sam chuckled. "It's hard to be dedicated to the place now," Sam admitted. "Besides, I have a new plan."

Mackenzie gave him an inquisitive look, "Oh?"

Sam nodded, smirking at her.

"Yeah, it's a two year plan, then I am going to start a small business investment firm with the smartest person we know," Sam said.

Mackenzie blinked. "Really?" she asked "Sorry it's just you are the fast track to being in the millionaire club. You've worked hard for it."

Sam nodded. "I know I won't make as much money. Hell, I may end up living with my mom but it's a risk I am willing to take. I want to like myself again," Sam said.

Mackenzie nodded, "I know the feeling."

Mackenzie looked up at the stars in the sky and then back at Sam. Sam felt his heart begin to beat rapidly.

"Mac, I love you," he said. "I mean, I'm in love with you. I know I hurt you, and you might not be in love with me. I get it. I just wanted you to know."

He watched as Mackenzie took a deep breath.

"Sam I…"

"Hunter's letter," Sam interrupted. "I read it again today. In his letter, he reminded me of what makes you so incredible. But there were some things he left out."

Mackenzie bit her lip, her breath becoming quicker, letting him know she was nervous.

"You smile with your eyes. Every time you smile, I always look into your eyes to see which smile I am getting."

"If cake is an option, it will likely happen, and when you take your first bite, you always close your eyes like it's the best thing you ever tasted," Sam said, making Mackenzie laugh.

"You think looking up at the stars from the beach at night is the closest thing to heaven anyone can feel."

Sam took her hands in his and continued.

"He also said he thought I just lost my way. That part isn't true; I knew exactly where I was going and felt very little guilt about it. At first, I told myself I was doing it for you. Using my promise to Uncle Deano to take care of you as an excuse. Somehow, it morphed into it being all about me. I told myself losing a few things I had for something more profitable would just be a sacrifice I made. It wasn't until I saw that look on your face at the restaurant that I realized the thing I was giving up was you. God, when I walked into my apartment and saw the keys, the ring, the box of my stuff. It was like a wound that just kept getting worse," Sam said.

"Bianca showed me the clip of you dancing atop the Eiffel Tower. You looked so happy. Dancing with French strangers. That's where you wanted to go on our honeymoon. I coaxed you into Manhattan, knowing you would hate every minute of it. But if it made me happy, you would find a way not to let it sting your heart. I looked in the mirror; I didn't want to be the person staring back at me. It was a guy that took for granted that he held Mackenzie Almazan's heart," Sam said, reaching over and wiping the lone tear running down Mac's cheek.

"I know I am no longer the guy that would read Bukowski to you either. But still, I wanted nothing more than to be the guy spinning you as you laughed."

"I wanted you to be him," Mac said in a whispered voice, giving him a small smile. He looked into her eyes. Vulnerability—that was what her eyes spoke of right then. He would have commented that when Mac was vulnerable was when her strength shined through, except he didn't want to lose focus. It had taken him a long time to figure out everything he wanted to say to her and find the courage to do it.

"I know. I want to be that guy again if you're, maybe, still willing to accept me. Maybe learn to fall in love with the guy I am now. I'm willing to start from the beginning."

"Are you sure? Do you think you are in love with me, with who I am now, or with the girl who always needed you to take care of her?" Mackenzie whispered.

Sam blinked a few times, shaking his head in disbelief.

"Is that what you think? That I felt obligated to take care of you?" Sam asked, completely floored by her question.

Mackenzie lowered her head, picking at her nails, silently confirming his question was on point.

"You have never needed anyone to take care of you, Mackenzie. I have just always wanted to."

"Why?' she asked.

Sam took one of her hands in his. He raised it to his mouth blowing on it. The action made Mackenzie laugh.

"Because you chose me. You decided I got to be the guy to hold your heart. The guy that saw parts of you, no one ever would. You made me the one who got to see the way you love, how you view the world before anyone else had. You showed me how to stay true to myself because you always did. You have no idea how many people I had to almost beat off you with a baseball bat when we were growing up. Every time you looked at me, I could see how you saw me. The way you always believed in me. It made me believe in myself. So, you see, the only thing I had to offer was the ability to take care of you when you needed it."

Sam took a deep breath, hating to bring up what he was about to do.

"I haven't been true to myself for a while now. I think a part of me was ashamed. You said I thought you were not good enough for me, in my world when, in truth, it was me. I wasn't good enough to be in yours anymore."

He heard Mackenzie gulp hard, and her legs bounced. He knew she was trying not to cry.

"I just want the chance for you to have faith in me again," Sam pleaded, his voice betraying him.

Mackenzie shook her head as if she was trying to clear her thoughts. She looked down at Hunter's ring on her finger. It didn't surprise him. He knew she would be wearing it since he obviously sent her a ticket as well.

"What do you think?" he asked.

Mackenzie looked down for a few seconds to Sam. It felt like an eternity.

She rested her head on her knees then scooted down the beach lounger, making room for him. Sam smiled, feeling a lump in his throat. He slid in behind her then pulled her toward him letting her back rest against his chest.

The lights dimmed as the movie started.

The gates of Manderley opened on the black and white screen. Sam leaned over and whispered in unison with the movie, "Last night I dreamt of marmalade."

He always said that when Mac put on this movie. Mac laughed then quickly covered her mouth trying to muffle the sound. Sam pulled her hand away and laughed as loud as she did. Making a vow right there that he would never again let Mac censor who she was.

Mackenzie turned toward Sam. She smiled. This smile made his heart stop, it was the smile he hadn't seen since that horrible day at the restaurant. The smile that she gave only to him, her eyes shining as if she was looking at her future.

"Hey, Sam," she whispered.

Sam nodded, trying to keep his composure.

She looked up at him and softly said, "Best of luck."

Sam chuckled as he slid his hand over the cheek on the far side of her face. Watching Mackenzie close her eyes, a tear falling from them. He pulled her closer to him, feeling his own eyes water. He closed his eyes, pressing his lips to her temple as he gave her a soft kiss.

Hunter

C haoxiang "Hunter" Zhou had never believed in fate. Although it would stand to reason, if anyone could make a strong argument for the idea that things are beyond a person's control and predestined by some omniscient power, it would be him. His parents acquired a fortune and were killed not long after. His sister, Xiāng, became a world-renowned designer and then died from a form of leukemia that was extremely rare for someone her age to get. Then, of course, his own diagnosis. Still, he had never believed in fate.

That was until he met Mackenzie Almazan. The girl was currently spinning around the dance floor at Greystone Mansion. They say your life flashes before your eyes when you are dying. While he wasn't taking his last breath just yet, he found himself drifting off into memories of his life.

Xiāng standing outside of his school, waiting for him to get out when he was just a kid.

His parents announcing they were moving to the US to get treatment for his sister.

Sitting on the plane with his father looking out the window. Being sent back to China and living with his family friends so he had a better chance of getting into Tsinghua University. A small part of him wondered if his parents were really doing it for him or if they were just too busy to take care of him.

Late nights staying at the library to study, determined to get into Tsinghua University. If for no other reason than to show his parents that he was more than a late-life child that they didn't seem to want around.

How arrogant he became because he was deemed a prodigy. Vowing he would be more successful than anyone he knew.

Sitting in the noodle shop with his sister during one of her many visits after she went into remission.

He was standing inside his dorm room at Oxford when Xiāng called to let him know their parents were gone. Listening to her cry while he was already so closed off that the only thing he thought about was how quickly he could sell his family business so he could get back to his goals.

Ollie stormed into his office telling him that he needed to man up and go see Xiàng be there for her during her treatments.

Crying at his sister's bedside so many nights as quietly as he could, knowing he was going to lose the only person he truly felt cared about him. Then, getting his own diagnosis.

It was funny to him that fulfilling his wildest dreams did not make him feel the joy he did watching Mackenzie live out hers.

Hunter jumped when a part of the song crescendoed, breaking him free of his memories. Focusing back on Mackenzie, her eyes were dancing as she looked around a room she never thought she would step into. He thought back to the day they met, mystified when he saw her sitting there amidst the thousands of people on the boardwalk. He was so stunned he didn't even remember walking up to her. Suddenly, he was there in front of her, asking if he could sit next to her.

The conversation itself was what people would feel is typical of such a bizarre coincidence. There was just something about Mackenzie Almazan. People in his previous circle would call it a certain "je ne sais quoi." He had known Mackenzie all of five minutes yet knew she would hate it if he used the pretentious description to describe her. Instead, he thought of her as beautifully candid. There was an honesty about her that he didn't see in a whole lot of people. He found himself inviting her to his pre-arranged bonfire, just wanting to talk to her more, especially after the crass comment about how American men sat. It wasn't just the comment but the look on her face after she said it that incited him to laugh harder than he had in his entire life. He hadn't found himself wanting to invite anyone to anything in a long time, and he almost couldn't believe his luck that she accepted.

He was weirdly eager to see her list, wanting to see what she considered her "Wildest Dreams." Excited that her number six was completely doable. He initially thought he could just help her get the ball rolling. Leave knowing he gave her something she could do to help heal her heartbreak.

Helping anyone vulnerable was not something Hunter had ever thought to do. He was ruthless before Xiāng was diagnosed with AML. Looking back at who he was before made him shudder. The arrogance and the entitlement he felt he had.

Hunter took stock of himself. One does that when staring death in the eye. He appreciated Ollie and Parker's care and presence in his life. He slowly felt himself changing as he started to figure out how to make things easier for them after he was gone. He allowed himself to feel their love. Admired the love between them. Thinking he would leave this place without ever feeling that for himself.

Hunter knew the exact moment he fell in love with Mackenzie Almazan. He knew he felt something as they danced on the Eiffel Tower. The way he could feel her joy, watching her skip around, was like feeling a light shining on his dark heart. He knew for sure he was in love with her when the gondola driver asked, "*Innamorato?*" While he shook his head no, he knew he was lying. Oddly, falling deeper in love with her, watching how she looked when she talked about Sam.

He knew she irrevocably owned his heart when she came running up to him, Parker, and Ollie, jumping up and down, telling them there was a way to fulfill Hunter's number three. How she battled her vertigo with the four-wheel of a hill that even the bravest of souls would be fearful of. He made a vow as he spun her around on the top of Mount Olympus that he would do whatever he could when they got back to make sure she would find happiness again.

Agreeing to let her stay was the most selfish thing he had ever done. Which spoke volumes because Hunter was proudly shallow for a good portion of his life. Still, he wanted more time with her. He even debated staying around completely noncoherent just to be able to be with her for a few more stolen moments. Hunter knew she had gone through that once. He would not do that to her again.

He quietly made plans with Ollie to make sure she was taken care of.

Hunter knew Ollie would make sure it happened. He didn't want Ollie to know that he left everything he had to him. It wasn't that he owed Ollie. It was because Ollie was the most authentic relationship he had ever had outside of the one he had with his sister. He started out as an employee, then slowly became a family. He and Parker were the only family he had left in this world. It was only right that he left him everything, much like his family did for him. The knowledge that Parker and Ollie would want for nothing, knowing they would do good things with his fortune because that was the kind of people they were.

He felt more emotions than he had ever felt in a single sitting as he wrote his letter to Sam. God, he was so jealous, but he understood the man—how one could get tunnel vision in chasing his fortune, how his priorities could change. Still, he thought he was an imbecile for overlooking Mackenzie. He knew Mackenzie was in love with him, though, so he had to try to make him see what he was giving up. Hunter knew if he wasn't dying, he was ruthless enough and persistent enough to at least make her look his way. Then again, if he wasn't dying, there was no way he would have ever met Mackenzie. Fate must have gotten a good laugh at the irony.

He had purposely waited until the very last minute to give her the Saint Laurent white slip dress Ollie had picked out for her and Christian Louboutin heels. Mackenzie would break out in hives if she knew she was wearing a solid twelve thousand dollars worth of designer clothing on her body. Secretly, he was a little sad he wouldn't be around to see her outrage when she undoubtedly Googled it and found out. He knew it was a matter of days before it became unbearable between having no strength and the pain. He had already caught himself asking questions or talking to Mackenzie in Mandarin. Losing time and not knowing how many times Mac had to hold him through panic attacks. He knew it was time.

He had so much he wanted to tell Mackenzie to try to express how he felt about leaving her. He decided that "Run" by Snow Patrol was the best way. Music was the language Mackenzie spoke best. She would understand.

This was the final thing he could gift Mackenzie while he was still here. He wanted Mac to be able to look out and see her favorite view. He decided they would walk out and look at the city afterward. Mackenzie looked like an angel as she spun around. He mustered whatever strength he had to walk up to her and dance with her one last time. He noticed the pain in her eyes as she tried to remain in the moment, trying not to feel guilty.

Instead, he closed his eyes and thought about the other moments when she didn't look so torn apart. The times when her eyes would light up anytime, she saw something that got her excited. That pensive, far-off look she gets when she gazes up at the stars or out in the water. Wanting desperately to go wherever her mind went just to be in that space with her. All the moments where he listened to her stories or choice of odd topics of conversation. Seeing how carefree and uncaring she is when she decides it's time to do something goofy.

He held her as tight as he could, savoring the last few moments where it was just the two of them living one of her wildest dreams.

Hunter swayed on his feet knowing he was shaking as he looked out and saw the scene in front of him. It looked like a winter wonderland, everything covered in artificial white snow. There were two Christmas trees with white lights, huge ornaments on the ground along with a few snowmen and large plastic candy canes . White lights all around the walls. It truly looked like the first time he saw Christmas in the States.

The fact that the three of them had done this for him made him feel like his legs would give out. He smiled and thought, "So this is what being loved feels like."

He saw Mackenzie walking toward him on Parker's arm, holding a small bouquet of white orchids. "Secret Garden" by Bruce Springsteen played in his head as she approached. He had purposely played the soundtrack to Jerry Macguire earlier that week under the guise of telling Mackenzie that it was the first American movie he had watched that he didn't need subtitles to fully understand. In truth, he wanted to listen to "Secret Garden" and steal looks at her as she closed her eyes, listening to the vinyl. It was the song he knew was hers.

"Number five and six, Hunter," She whispered. He looked at the three of them, understanding they were trying to help him finish his list. He felt like she had a vice grip on his heart. He could not express how much this meant to him.

He'd emptied out his heart to her. He was truly relieved she wasn't in love with him. If she had fallen in love with him, another piece of her brilliantly beautiful heart would have died with him. He couldn't bear that to happen. He looked down at his hand and then gave her the most important possession he owned. Of all the things money could buy, he was leaving her this, knowing it would mean the most to her. He pressed his forehead to hers as he thought.

"Please be happy."
"Please don't use my ring-like armor to not allow yourself to live beyond grief."
"I hope Sam comes back to you."
"Please spend your life making people laugh just being in your presence."
"Enjoy the fireworks."
"Don't feel guilty about the record store."
"Live Mackenzie. Just live."
"God, I love you. I love you more than I thought I could."

Hunter swallowed down six valium trying to quell the panic. He wasn't scared, he was just worried about the three people he loved most in the world and how they would deal with the aftermath. He gave Mackenzie one last out, not knowing if he wanted her to take it or stay with him. Again, selfishly glad she would be there at the end.

As he laid down, he felt Mackenzie slip behind him holding her to him. He was already struggling to stay conscious; he wanted to thank her for being with him. But he knew he needed to say the few things he needed her to truly feel. He reached for her weakly, feeling his arm slowly sinking down because he was losing strength. Mac must have known what he was trying to do. He held his hand pressing it to her cheek.

"Remember number one on your list. Don't forget to look out, not down," he whispered.

He didn't know how much time had passed before she thanked Mackenzie for being his *bái yuèguāng.*

"Xièxiè, Da Ge," Hunter said *"Xièxiè"* He was being sincere yet at the same time teasing the man that looked out for him the last six years of his life. Ollie was who he worried about most.

He looked back at Mackenzie. She was trying to be brave. He hoped with all his might that his death would be the thing that helped her let go of all her pain. He reached for the bottle that he had laid beside him, still looking at Mackenzie.

"Close your eyes Zie Zie," he whispered, not wanting her to watch him take what was left of his life. He didn't want her to have that image in her head.

He tried his best to raise his hand to his lips feeling Mackenzie whimper. Trying his best to drink it down and not keep them in this torturous moment. He nearly started to cry himself not being able to reach up. Then he felt a hand wrap around his wrist. He opened his eyes and saw it was Parker.

Hunter looked up at him. He wanted to say something to him. Tell Parker how much he meant to him. That he knew Parker was always the one to make sure everyone was taken care of. He wanted to tell him thank you that he, too, was his brother. Hunter opened his mouth to attempt to say something. Parker smiled, shaking his head as if letting Hunter know he didn't need to.

He saw Parker mouth what he thought was, "Don't worry, I will take care of them." Almost as if he knew what Hunter was thinking right at that moment. Hunter reached out weakly, pushing Parker's hand away once the medicine touched his bottom lip. He needed to do this part on his own. He drank down the liquid, hearing Parker cry out, taking hold of his wrist again and sliding the bottle out of his hands. Parker closed his eyes and kissed Hunter's hand.

He wasn't sure how much time had passed. Trying to find the coherency to tell Mackenzie one last thing.

"Number eight, in my next life. In my next life..." He muttered, trying to finish his thought.

Mackenzie smiled down at him and said, "In our next life, come find me so I can be there for your number eight."

The urgency to voice what he thought drifted away as Mackenzie held him a bit tighter and whispered, "Number seven, Hunter."

Hunter felt a slam of consciousness knowing what she was about to do. She lowered her head, their lips a breath away from touching and whispered, "Chaoxiang. *Wǒ ài nǐ*. Chaoxiang. *Wǒ ài nǐ.*"

He felt tears come down his face. The bit of consciousness drifted away, knowing this was the last time he would be this close to still being in this world.

Hunter watched as she pulled away slightly. He tried to give her a smile. Tears freely fell from his face as she gently wiped them away. She kissed him, then kissed him again. On the third kiss, she deepened it, breathing her air into his mouth. Feeling it filled him with warmth and peace. It was the most beautiful thing he ever felt. It was better than any dream he had. He was trying hard to look at her as long as he could, feeling his body quake and his lips quiver. He kept his eyes open, seeing she was doing the same.

Hunter shuddered, feeling both heartbroken and euphoric. Smiling as best as he could through their kiss. Mackenzie kept her lips pressed to his. He exhaled, feeling Mackenzie take his breath into her lungs. He knew he was giving her his last breath, hoping it would give her the strength to keep her promise and let go of all the pain she had been holding onto for most of her life. Hunter felt his eyes slowly closing; he looked into Mackenzie's eyes one last time, his final thought fixated on his wildest dream as he drifted away.

"Number eight, in my next life. I get to meet her first..."

Author's Notes

At the beginning of most books there is usually a disclaimer that reads "Any resemblance to actual persons, living or dead, or actual events is purely coincidental."
The truth of the matter is that I could not place it there because every character is inspired by people who influenced in shaping the person I am today.
Whether it be in support, love or inspiration, the heart and soul of each of these characters embodied someone that has impacted my life.
If the characters seem real, it's because they are melds of actual people that championed me through the years.
Writing has always been my passion. It's only right that I use it to celebrate and show my gratitude to all of them.

About the author

Meridith Claire is an award-winning Author and Screenplay Writer that was born and raised in Los Angeles, CA. Most of her childhood years consisted of roaming the streets of Hollywood, going to The Culver Theater or catching waves and walking the boardwalk of Venice Beach.

She spends her days staring at a blank page and rearranging the 26 letters in the alphabet to bring her pen people to life.

Her downtime consists of having her head down in books, dreaming of new fantastic realities and finding the next best cup of coffee she has ever had.